THE SECRET OF
ZOOM

LYNNE JONELL

THE SECRET OF ZOOM

SQUARE
FISH

Henry Holt and Company
New York

SQUARE
FISH

An Imprint of Macmillan

THE SECRET OF ZOOM. Copyright © 2009 by Lynne Jonell. All rights reserved.
Printed in the United States of America by R. R. Donnelley & Sons Company,
Harrisonburg, Virginia. For information, address Square Fish, 175 Fifth Avenue,
New York, NY 10010.

Square Fish and the Square Fish logo are trademarks of Macmillan and are used by
Henry Holt and Company under license from Macmillan.

Library of Congress Cataloging-in-Publication Data
Jonell, Lynne.
The secret of zoom / Lynne Jonell.
p.   cm.
Summary: Ten-year-old Christina lives a sheltered life until she discovers a secret tunnel,
a plot to enslave orphans, and a mysterious source of energy known as zoom.
ISBN 978-0-312-65933-2
[1. Adventure and adventurers—Fiction.]   I. Title.
PZ7.J675Se 2009   [Fic]—dc22   2008050276

Originally published in the United States by Henry Holt and Company
First Square Fish Edition: July 2011
Square Fish logo designed by Filomena Tuosto
Book designed by April Ward
www.squarefishbooks.com

10 9 8 7 6

AR: 5.1 / F&P: U / LEXILE: 770L

To my dear father,
for whom ninety-nine
was never enough

THE SECRET OF
ZOOM

CHAPTER 1
SECRETS

CHRISTINA had fallen asleep while reading under the dining room table and awakened to the clink of silverware and the sound of grown-up voices telling secrets. And that was how she found out, long after it had happened, that her mother had been blown up.

"Blown to smithereens," said a lady's voice cheerfully. "Right in her own laboratory, poor dear. And her daughter was just a little thing, too."

"Those scientific experiments can be tricky," said a man's voice. "Pass the salt, please."

Christina sat up attentively. All around her were legs—black- and gray-trousered legs for the men, nylon-stockinged legs for the women, except for one woman with hairy knees who wore white socks and sandals. The crimson tablecloth hung down to their grown-up laps, giving the light beneath the table a reddish hue. As usual, someone had dropped a roll. Christina poked at it with her finger, dimpling the crust.

She didn't remember her mother. Or, rather, she remembered only bits of her mother. A comfortable lap. A hand, patting. A rocking motion and a voice, singing low.

Christina pressed her finger into the roll again, and a third time. The three holes looked like two eyes and a nose. She was considering the mouth—should the face be happy or sad?—when heavy footsteps crossed the floor.

"I'm sorry I was called away," said the deep voice of Christina's father, and the chair at the head of the table was pulled out. "There was a problem at the lab—you know how it is."

Adult voices murmured agreement as Christina broke little pieces off the roll. Her father, Dr. Adnoid, was the top scientist at Loompski Laboratories. His friends were all scientists. And all her life, people had told Christina that she would grow up to be a scientist, too. But now, after hearing what had happened to her mother, she wasn't sure she liked the idea.

It occurred to her as well that her father might get blown up someday in *his* laboratory. And while Christina didn't see Dr. Adnoid that often—and when she did, he only seemed interested in her math grades—still, he *was* her father, and if he died, then she would be an orphan. And orphans, as she well knew, went to the Loompski Orphan Home just down the road and were taught useful trades like shoe shining and floor mopping and garbage collecting.

Of course that all sounded like fun to Christina. She had often envied the orphans, watching from her window as they came down the street in their orange and red vests, dumping garbage cans into the rear of a big truck painted with happy faces and banging the lids back on in a businesslike manner. And every so often, if she was lucky, she would see the big rear panel come down with a bang and press all the garbage back with an interesting grinding noise.

She wasn't allowed out when the orphans came by, though. In fact, she wasn't allowed out at all, except for an hour a day, when she stood at the tall iron rails that fenced in her yard and stared longingly through the bars at the world going past.

Christina's house was big, old, and set on a hill. It had been built years ago when Dr. Leo Loompski, one of the famed scientific Loompskis, had come from the city to visit his brother and find a place for his laboratories.

He had stepped off the riverboat at the sleepy little town of Dorf and looked up. Above him were foothills and a spreading forest, and beyond that was nothing but the bare gray rock of the Starkian Mountain Ridge and the nests of some large and high-flying birds.

He had been a small man—almost the size of a child, some said—but all the same, he put on big heavy boots, grabbed a walking stick, and hiked straight up.

When he came back, smiling as if at some great and wonderful secret, he bought the land. Then he promptly fenced off a hundred acres of forest, built his laboratories at the very center, and put up a stone house for himself at the edge of the woods. And ever since Leo Loompski's time, the head scientist of Loompski Labs had lived in the very same house.

The house was full of portraits of the Loompski family

members and their awards. Although Leo's parents had been rather ordinary, four of their five sons were anything but. Between Leo, Lester, Lars, and Ludwig, they had won all the major mathematical and scientific prizes; they had married unusual and talented women; and even their dog, Lucky, had her portrait on the wall. (Lucky had won Best of Show nine years running for being able to tap out the first seven numbers in the Fibonacci sequence.)

But in pride of place was Leo Loompski's portrait, hanging next to the Karsnicky Medal. The medal was a golden disc on a silver ribbon, and the highest honor a scientist could achieve, but Christina liked the portrait best. Leo Loompski's eyes were bright blue, his ears stuck out from beneath his white hair, and the smile on his face looked happy and kind. Christina knew he *must* have been kind, for hadn't he even set up an orphanage to care for homeless children?

Still, he had built the sort of laboratory where mothers could get blown up. And he had put up a fence in the forest that was twenty feet high, made of crisscrossed barbed wire and humming with electricity. The signs posted on it said things like DANGER! and TRESPASSERS WILL BE BOILED and THIS MEANS YOU!

Christina didn't really like to look at the fence, or the forest beyond that hid Loompski Labs. So on the afternoons when she was let out, she mostly stood in her front yard. If she pressed her face between the gate's iron palings, she couldn't see any fence at all between herself and the town of Dorf below, with its river that curled through the valley like a long blue snake. On cloudy days, it looked more like a gray snake, but it didn't much matter what color it was—Christina knew, no matter how she begged, that she would never be allowed to play on its banks.

"But *why* do I have to stay in the yard?" she asked at breakfast, the morning after her father's dinner party. She had asked many times before, of course, but Christina hoped that if she kept asking, someone might one day give in.

"The world is a dangerous place," said Nanny, squeezing Christina in her plump arms. "Your father wants to keep you safe. Eat up, now."

Nanny's hugs were a little on the smothering side. Christina squirmed away. What was so great about being safe all the time? She could think of much more important things—like meeting kids her own age and having a little *fun* now and then.

"Your father already lost his wife," said Cook darkly, coming in with a tray of muffins. "He doesn't want to lose you, too."

Christina crumbled a muffin into bits. She had heard this before. When she was younger, she used to wonder if her mother had been lost in the Loompski forest and might find her way back someday. It hadn't been until recently that Christina had understood: When people said her mother had been *lost*, they meant she had *died*.

"I could at least go to school," Christina said rebelliously. "Kids are *supposed* to go to school, aren't they?"

"But your computer classes are far superior to any ordinary school," said her father, wandering past with a cup of coffee in one hand and a calculator in the other. "You have the finest instructors from all over the world, and you never have to leave your room. Speaking of which, how are you doing in math these days?"

"Fine," muttered Christina, making a face.

"You know, math is so much more fun than you realize. Here, I'll show you."

"No—really, I'm *fine*—"

Dr. Adnoid pulled a notebook and pen from his pocket. "You're going to enjoy this problem—just listen for a minute, now. Say you had seven integers, three of which were divisible by two . . ."

Christina ate her oatmeal in gloomy silence. When her father finally put his pen away to leave for work, she was so relieved that she followed him out to wave good-bye.

Dr. Adnoid's dark green car pulled out of the carriage house, passed the front gate, and disappeared down the gravel road that led into the forest. The gate shut with a metallic clang. Christina winced—she hated that noise—and stood a moment in the bright morning air, facing the house.

The house that Leo Loompski had built was a little like a castle, with brass-studded doors, stone lions at the steps, and grinning gargoyles on the roof. If Christina hadn't been so lonely, she would have loved living there. The inside was filled with surprising little closets and cupboards big enough to crawl into and window seats in the oddest places.

"Christina! Time to come in!" Nanny stood at the door, hands on her sizable hips.

Christina dragged her feet, looking wistfully at the stone facade. If only she were allowed to climb on the roof! There were unusual-looking places behind the stone gargoyles that she would love to explore.

There was nothing new left to discover indoors—she had already located everything that was interesting. Rumor had it that Dr. Loompski had built a secret tunnel, but rumor was wrong. Christina had never found it, and she had searched for years.

CHAPTER 2

TAFT

CHRISTINA stared grumpily at her computer. She had already done spelling, history, and Spanish verbs. She had passed a health screening (apparently she wasn't colorblind) and finished three workbook pages, and it wasn't even time for lunch.

Dancing numbers filled the screen, each with its own happy face. "Here comes Math!" intoned a falsely cheerful voice from the speakers. "It's fun, *fun*, FUN, and YOU get to solve the problems *YOUR* way—"

Christina snapped it off, irritated, and went to her telescope on its tripod by the window.

She turned the focusing knobs carefully, first one and then the other, until the schoolyard of Dorf Elementary came into view. She flipped her straw-colored braids back over her shoulders, looked through the eyepiece, and sighed with longing. Recess again.

Of course it was fun to watch the kids arrive and leave school, too. Christina loved the bright orange flags that the big kids held out over the street so the little ones could cross safely.

But recess was both the best and the worst to watch. It was the best because the kids were having the most fun, running and swinging and climbing up and sliding down. And it was the worst because she wanted so much to join them, and couldn't.

What were they playing today? Christina squinted at the mass of kids running about and recognized one of her favorite games—Chase and Tap. Or at least that was the name she gave it in her mind.

But today they had added something new: Kids froze in place when the chaser tapped them and ran off when someone else tapped them again. Christina pulled a small notebook out of her back pocket and penciled in "Chase, Tap, and Freeze" at the bottom of her list. If she ever *did* get a chance to play with other kids, at least she would know something about their games.

She looked through the telescope again. Some of the kids were climbing trees. Was it hard? she wondered. Maybe she could try it herself, in her yard.

She knocked at Nanny's door. "Please, can I go out early? I've done my morning work."

The door, unlatched, drifted open. Nanny was lying down with an afghan over her legs, snoring.

Christina moved closer. Flat on her back and rather thick about the middle, Nanny sounded exactly like a lawn mower that someone kept trying—and failing—to start.

"Nanny?" Christina said softly. "Can I go outside?" She

tried not to stare at the thin line of drool that slid from the corner of Nanny's open mouth across her double chin—and then a flash of orange from the window caught Christina's eye.

She looked out. The orphans were collecting trash across the street.

"I'll stay in the yard," Christina said in a whisper, and shut Nanny's door behind her.

"Where are you going, young lady?" Cook wagged a finger at her from the kitchen. "It's not time for your afternoon outing yet, is it?"

"I've done my morning work," said Christina, "and I asked Nanny if I could go outside."

"Well, what did she say?"

"She didn't say no," Christina said cheerfully, and skipped out the door.

"*Psst!*"

Christina jumped away from the tree she had been attempting to climb. A hand beckoned from the bushes on the other side of the iron railing.

Christina peered in between the leaves to see a lean boy's face, with dark straight hair and worried gray eyes, thickly lashed. She stared, fascinated. She had never seen someone her own age up close before, at least not that she could remember.

"Don't *look* at me!"

Christina was startled. Was this what kids usually said when they met someone?

"Act like you're doing something else. I'm not supposed to be talking to you." The boy glanced over his shoulder.

"Oh." Christina looked down at her knee and pretended to pick a scab. She understood about trying to get around grown-up rules. "I'm not supposed to be talking to you, either. Who are you, anyway?" She slanted a look upward and caught a glimpse of an orange and red vest. "Oh, wait, I know—you're one of the orphans."

"That's right," said the boy, sounding annoyed, "just one of the orphans. We have *names*, you know."

Christina sat back on her heels. She had always wanted to talk to another child, but this one seemed kind of rude. "You haven't *told* me your name," she pointed out. "I'm Christina."

"Yes, I know. And your father's the head of Loompski Labs." The boy's voice was eager. "What's it like to have a dad who's a scientist?"

"Boring," said Christina.

"But—what about when his scientist friends come over, and talk—"

"Double boring," said Christina.

"—about their experiments? That *can't* be boring."

"Want to bet?" Christina pretended to find a rock in her shoe. "How come you're so interested in science, anyway? Do they teach it at the orphanage?"

The boy snorted. "Are you kidding? They teach us all about mop cleaning—and trash compacting—and the proper way to scrub plastic—"

"No Spanish verbs?" said Christina dreamily. "No math?"

"Just the boring kind of math," said the boy. "All we get to learn is adding and subtracting and multiplying, enough so we can count the plastic toys that we find in the garbage and keep an inventory. No algebra. No *x* times *y* squared. Nothing *fun*—"

"You should meet my father," said Christina gloomily. "You'd be his dream come true."

"I wish I *could*," said the boy fervently.

"Taft!" a loud voice called from the street. "Keep moving!"

Christina heard a loud clang and then the grinding motorized whine of the garbage truck as it crushed the trash. Through the bars of her front gate she could see a small girl dragging an empty can back to the curb.

The boy pressed his face to the iron bars. "Look, I've got to go. But listen—" He looked over his shoulder.

"What?"

"Have you found the tunnel yet?"

Christina stared at him. "That's just a rumor."

"It's *not* just a rumor." The boy gripped her arm through the bars. "I heard it from a guy who heard it from his cousin's best friend who got it from the nephew of somebody who actually swept floors for old Leo himself."

"I've looked in the cellar," said Christina hurriedly, "and I've looked for trapdoors on the ground floor—"

"But those are the *obvious* places," Taft insisted. "Leo Loompski was brilliant, he was a genius, he won the Karsnicky *Medal*. He wouldn't have hidden a tunnel in the first place anyone would *look*. You've got to keep trying—think bigger—look higher—"

"TAFT!"

"Coming!" Taft backed out of the bushes and onto the sidewalk. "Some litter blew into the bushes," Christina heard him say. "I thought I should get it out."

"You're not paid to *think*," roared the voice. "Get a move on, boy, or I'll put you on the next truck up the mountain!"

Think bigger—look higher—

What had Taft meant?

Christina understood about looking higher. Up until now, she had only searched the cellar and first floor. It wasn't likely that a tunnel would be on the upper floors, but at least they were *higher*.

But think bigger? It didn't make sense. For one thing, everyone said Leo Loompski had been a very small man— probably not much larger than Christina herself. If anything, she should think *smaller*.

Maybe the entrance to the tunnel was just Leo's size?

Christina nodded decidedly. That would be easy. She had long ago searched out all kinds of small places in Leo Loompski's big old house.

There was the window seat in the music room, with its velvet curtain that could be pulled shut, hiding her from everyone.

There was a narrow space behind the couch on the landing and a dusty but private spot in back of the overstuffed chair in the corner.

The dining room had a long wooden bench with a carved seat that was hollow beneath and very convenient for playing fort. Under the table was good, too, if there was a tablecloth, and the built-in cupboard in the hall had space to squeeze in, if she was careful not to bump the dishes.

And of course there were the closets. Christina went to every one, carefully tapping the walls and floors for signs of a door or hidden panel. She carried a tape measure and wrote numbers down in a notebook so that she would seem to be doing homework—and no one stopped her or even asked what she was doing.

But it was all for nothing. Christina slumped up the steps to the third floor. The only rooms up here were a bathroom and the large, long space that was her bedroom, schoolroom, and playroom combined.

She flopped disgustedly on her bed. She could search this level, but what would be the use? The third floor was her domain, and she had long ago examined every inch of it.

Christina let her head hang back over the edge of the bed and stared at the ceiling. It was stupid to look for a tunnel on the third floor. The only thing more stupid would be to look in the . . .

She sat up suddenly. She had never been in the attic, not once, although there was a trapdoor in the ceiling of her closet. Nanny had always forbidden her to open it, and Christina had never been able to reach the handle anyway.

But it was a long time since she had tried.

Christina bounced off the bed and dragged a chair into the closet. She pushed aside her winter coats that had been hung up for storage, stepped on the chair, and reached on tiptoe toward the polished square of wood with its brass handle that had both fascinated and frightened her since she was little.

Well, she was bigger now, and if there *was* anything in the attic—the very same attic that creaked at night and made her think of burglars and ghosts and mice—then it could just get out of her way. It was daylight now, and she was ten years old, and she wasn't afraid of anything.

CHAPTER 3
THE ATTIC

CHRISTINA got a good grip on the brass handle and pulled. The trapdoor swung silently downward, and a ladder slid into place with a click.

She stood still, her heart beating in her fingertips.

No one was coming up the stairs. No one was calling her name.

Christina grasped the smooth wooden rail and stepped onto the rungs. Hand over hand she climbed until her head cleared the square hole and she could look around.

The attic was huge, and nearly bare. Dim light filtered in through air vents, and dust swirled through the strips of sunlight and lay thick upon the floor.

There wasn't a sign of mice or burglars. But the furniture that stood against the walls, covered with sheets, made the attic look as if it were haunted by a number of large and lumpy ghosts. Christina hauled herself up and padded across the floor in her socks.

The air vent was too high. She dragged over a chair with a

broken back, stood on it, and peered through the narrow slats. She could see more than through her window one level below. There was a tan brick building at the edge of the forest that she had never noticed before. The trees had hidden it, she supposed. There was a clearing around it, with tiny moving patches of orange, and something that looked like a garbage truck . . .

Christina started. She knew what the tan building was now.

She jumped off the chair and scrambled down the ladder, sneezing in the dust she kicked up, and grabbed her telescope from its place by her bedroom window. Then she was back in the attic, with the tripod balanced on the chair arms and herself standing on the seat.

She turned the focusing knobs, intent on the moving orange patches. There. She'd found the orphanage, and one of those moving children might be Taft.

But why were the orphans all lined up?

She flipped a knob for greater magnification and zeroed in on the faces. There was a big, burly man walking slowly down the line of orphans. Every so often, he would put out a hand, and one of the orphans would step forward.

Christina noticed that he was picking the biggest orphans, the ones who looked the strongest . . . but they slumped when they stepped forward, and none of them looked happy. And then, next to a tall boy with a large head and heavy shoulders, she saw Taft.

Of course the man would choose the bigger boy and leave Taft alone . . .

Christina tensed as the man ignored the tall boy and paused in front of Taft. The man lifted his hand halfway, hesitated, and pulled back.

Taft's big eyes and frightened face showed up plainly in her scope. He had almost been picked. Next time, maybe he *would* be chosen—but for what? And why did he look so scared?

"Christina!"

Nanny's voice was faint but insistent. Christina slid across the attic floor and down the ladder, yanked the coats back into place, and skidded out of the closet.

"Time for your afternoon outing." Nanny's voice floated up as Christina appeared at the top of the stairs, grinning a little. Nanny would never climb the stairs if she could help it—she was too fat.

"Good gracious, child! Whatever have you been doing to get so dirty?" Nanny demanded.

Christina looked down through the open stairwell, past the second-floor landing, to Nanny's round face staring up from the first floor's polished hall.

"Oh—measuring closets and things," Christina said vaguely, looking at her hands. They were certainly far from clean.

"Well, don't do it again. You'll have to take a bath this instant, and now you won't have time to go out before dinner."

Christina looked down at Nanny's perspiring face. "Then could I go out earlier tomorrow? To make up for missing today?"

"I suppose," Nanny grumbled, "though you get plenty of vitamin D from one hour in the sun. If it wasn't for that, you wouldn't need to go outside at all, what with the stack of games and toys and computer programs you have. You could stay in your room for years and never lack for anything to do."

Christina splashed in the tub, already thinking about tomorrow. She had gotten permission to go out early so she might see Taft again—and she had to clean up the attic somehow. She couldn't keep getting dusty; Nanny would get suspicious. Could she haul the vacuum up that ladder? Or would a broom be better?

"Dad?" Christina buttered her dinner roll and set down her knife. "How come the orphans have to work so hard?"

Her father, who was sipping his drink, coughed suddenly. Liquid spurted from his nose, and he had to leave the table, hacking into his napkin.

When he returned, Christina promptly asked him again. His face grew red.

"They work an appropriate amount for their condition," he said shortly. "Speaking of work, how did you do on math today?"

Christina ignored the question. "But other kids go to school," she said. "Aren't kids supposed to be learning?"

"There is a school at the orphanage," said her father. "They learn quite as much as is good for them. Eat your peas."

"But—"

"Eat your peas, I said!" Her father banged his fork on the table. "And I don't want to hear another word about those orphans! Life is dangerous enough without unhealthy interests! You haven't been *talking* to one of them, have you?"

Christina paled. "You told me not to," she whispered, shocked at the sight of her father in a temper.

"That's right, my girl." Dr. Adnoid attempted a smile. "I am doing everything in my power to keep you safe and well. Take no interest in the orphans, and you will come to no harm." He pushed back his chair, ran his hand through his hair until it was standing on end, and walked out, his neck stiff.

Christina looked questioningly at Cook, who had paused with a bowl of potatoes.

"Don't mind him, child." Cook shook her head. "He's just grieving the loss of your mother."

Christina frowned. "But what does that have to do with the orphans?"

"Why, your mother, God rest her soul, took an interest in the orphans herself. Just before she died, that is."

CHAPTER 4
THE ROOF

THE next morning Christina had a music lesson.

This was usually the highlight of her week. It was the one time she had a real live teacher; even Dr. Adnoid had to admit that the computer couldn't teach piano, and had hired the school's music teacher to give her private instruction. But today, anxious to go out and see Taft, Christina could hardly keep still.

"My dear, what *is* the matter?" Mrs. Lisowsky, a tiny old woman with a fuzz of light red hair, peered at Christina like an inquisitive bird. "You're absolutely murdering that poor piano sonata."

Christina lifted her fingers guiltily from the keys. "Sorry," she murmured.

"Is something distracting you, dear?"

Christina had been sneaking quick glances out the window, but she shifted her gaze to the framed portrait on one side. "Um, I was just wondering about"—she looked at the nameplate—"Glenda Loompski. Funny, her name doesn't begin with an *L*."

"Well, she wasn't born a Loompski, you know—she only married one of the Loompski boys. Lars, was it? Or Larry?"

Christina didn't think there *had* been a Larry Loompski, but she couldn't imagine caring either way.

"Glenda was just as talented as the Loompski brothers," went on Mrs. Lisowsky. "Well, as four of them, anyway. When I was just a girl, I heard her play Rachmaninoff's entire Concerto in D Minor on a series of test tubes filled with water—a truly striking combination of art and science!"

Christina tried to maintain an expression of deep interest, but it was hard going. She smothered a yawn and sneaked another look through the window.

"Well, let's try something different. How about singing? You have a nice, clear voice. Let's work on scales. Stand up, dear, and give me a C."

Mrs. Lisowsky slipped onto the piano bench and poised her finger above the keys. But Christina, in a hurry to get the lesson over with, sang the note before it was played.

The music teacher looked up quickly. "That sounds right," she said to herself, and quietly played a note. She looked up again. "Go up a third from C, will you? And then a fifth?"

Christina sang the third note and then the fifth in the scale.

"Now can you sing an E-flat?"

"High or low?" asked Christina.

"Whichever you like, dear," said Mrs. Lisowsky absently.

Christina sang it.

"And a B-flat, followed by an F, and then a G-sharp?"

Christina sang the notes in order, checking the window again. Was that a bit of orange-red vest she had seen through the bushes?

"My child," announced Mrs. Lisowsky triumphantly, "you have perfect pitch. I shall let your father know; I'm sure he will be pleased."

"Okay," mumbled Christina, still concentrating on the window. No, it was just a cardinal, half hidden in the leaves. But the moment Mrs. Lisowsky trotted from the house, Christina slipped out before anyone noticed and waited by the fence for Taft.

She amused herself by making dandelion necklaces and hunting for four-leaf clovers and whistling with a blade of grass stretched tight between her thumbs. But the orphans didn't seem to be about, and no one came near, unless you counted two men who arrived in a battered pickup truck.

"Grab the extension cord, Gus!" bawled a stocky man in blue overalls, wrestling a ladder out of the truckbed and staggering with it to the side of Christina's house.

Gus, heavier than his partner, with a brown mustache that drooped at the corners of his mouth, clanked past with a belt full of tools.

"Why are we using a ladder, Jake?" Gus scratched his head, looking upward. "Isn't there a service door from the attic?"

"Won't do us any good." Jake grinned. "I'm too fat, and you're even fatter. What we need is a skinny helper."

"I'm just well built," Gus mumbled, hitching up his pants.

"Folks must've been underfed back in the day when this house was built." He gave Christina a shy smile. "You've got yourself a real nice day for daisy chains, little missy."

"Christina!" Nanny's voice trumpeted from the front door. "Lunchtime!"

Christina edged closer to Gus. "What are you going to do, mister? Climb up to the roof?"

"Fix the gutters," said Gus, pointing upward. "And anything else that needs patching."

"CHRISTINA!"

"Coming!" called Christina, casting a last glance toward the fence. Still no Taft. Maybe the orphans were on a different street today.

Well, there was always tomorrow. And in the meantime, she had the attic. But first she had to get it clean.

Christina dawdled over lunch, chewing each bite until there was nothing left to chew. She swirled her spoon in her pudding, watching as Nanny took a last swallow, set down her napkin, and climbed ponderously up the stairs.

As soon as the bedsprings squeaked in Nanny's room above, Christina slid quietly out of her chair and disappeared into the broom closet.

She would need the vacuum and an extension cord. Maybe a bucket and some rags, too. Oh, and the broom and a dustpan, just in case . . . and what about some bags to hold all the dust?

Heavily loaded, Christina staggered up the steps. She was beginning to think she should have made two trips, when the bucket caught on the banister and everything slipped out of her grasp in a long, racketing clatter.

"Christina!" Nanny appeared in the doorway, frowning.

Christina picked up the broom, trying to look virtuous. "I'm just going to clean my room."

Nanny's frown deepened. "I was planning to clean it," she said defensively, "only my knees have been bothering me—and my sciatica is acting up—"

"I *know*," said Christina swiftly, "that's why I want to do it myself. Besides, you don't want me to be spoiled, do you?"

Nanny looked suspicious.

"Most kids have to clean their own rooms, right?"

"Uh—"

"Why should I be any different?"

"Well, when you put it that way—"

"And it's good exercise. I'm doing a unit in health on the computer and it's all about getting plenty of activity—"

"All right, for goodness' sake, go ahead! Only don't make too much noise over my room. I'm going to take my afternoon nap."

The problem, thought Christina as she lugged the vacuum up the ladder to the attic, was that now she actually *would* have to clean her room. But first, while Nanny was safely napping, she would get the attic floor clear. She couldn't keep coming down from there, dusty to her eyeballs. Sooner or later, someone would figure out what she was doing—and then, of course, they would tell her she couldn't do it anymore.

No, Christina thought as she vacuumed, poking the hose into corners and around boxes, she had to keep the attic a secret. Besides, she liked being able to see the orphanage, and Taft, through her telescope.

The vacuum's dust bag was full. Christina switched off the machine and unhooked the bag, and heard men's voices.

"We'll have to get some roof tiles and come back. See those missing ones?"

Christina stepped onto the broken-backed chair and looked out the ventilation slats.

"See here? And here?"

Heavy feet crunched on the roof.

"I still say it'd be easier to bring everything through the attic. Where's that service door, anyway, Jake?"

The attic wall rattled as someone banged on it from outside. "Here it is. It's locked, though, or stuck. You want to crawl through *that*?"

Christina watched in fascination as a crack of light appeared—disappeared—and appeared again, outlining a short rectangle, almost a square, in the attic wall.

"Not much of a service door," grumbled Gus, as the men's footsteps receded. "Who did old Loompski think was going to work on his roof? Midgets?"

Christina held her breath as the men's heavy boots sounded on the ladder rungs. Then she tiptoed across the floor to the attic wall, holding her breath.

It was true! It was a real door!

She hadn't seen it at first; the cracks outlining the rough door looked like any other cracks in the attic paneling. There was no doorknob, but there was a little latch to turn, half hidden behind a wooden crossbeam.

Christina hugged herself in silent delight. In her boring, boring life, suddenly everything was happening at once!

She had met a real live orphan. She had been tall enough to finally get into the attic. And although she hadn't found the legendary Loompski tunnel, she *had* discovered a door that opened onto the rooftop—and the minute Gus and his boss were gone for the day, she intended to go through it. She had always wanted to see one of those gargoyles up close.

It was nearly sunset. Supper was safely over. Christina's father, working late at the laboratory, had not been home to ask any uncomfortable questions about her math assignments.

It was a good thing, too, Christina thought guiltily as she mounted the stairs to her room. She hadn't gotten around to math in the morning, and then after seeing the door to the roof, she had been too excited to concentrate.

Besides, Gus and Jake had been making a lot of noise. They had clumped around the roof all afternoon, hammering and clanking and grumbling. But just before dinner they had roared off in their battered brown pickup; Christina had watched with deep satisfaction as their taillights disappeared.

Now she put on dark jeans and a jacket, shoved her feet into rubber-soled shoes, and dug out a flashlight from beneath her bed. She arranged two pillows underneath her blankets in a realistic-looking lump, just in case anyone looked in. And then she pulled down the attic ladder and, with a light, excited feeling in her stomach, began to climb.

Christina shut the trapdoor behind her with a soft *snick*. A rosy glow seeped into the attic through the ventilation slats, and even the faint crack around the child-sized door had a pinkish cast. The catch was stiff, but Christina managed to turn it after a few taps with her flashlight, and the door opened at last with a protesting screech.

The rooftop was edged in light. The sun was setting in a blaze of pink and gold, and the battlements and towers of Leo Loompski's house seemed lifted from a fairy-tale castle. Grinning gargoyles, their wings uplifted, looked almost angelic in the sun's amber rays.

Christina stepped carefully out onto the roof's sloping tiles. Little pieces of grit rolled beneath her shoes, and she held on to the nearest gargoyle to keep from sliding. The stone was rough and weather-pitted and still warm from the day's heat. Christina ran her fingers over the carved face.

If only Taft were here! There were so many great places for hide-and-seek. And what a perfect spot for playing spy!

She wandered over the whole roof, climbing chimneys and balancing on battlements in the sun's waning light. There was something about being up so high that she loved. Even without her telescope, she could see the orphanage, and the sunset blazing off its windows in rows of golden rectangles was so bright that it hurt her eyes.

Christina blinked as light flashed again from an orphanage window. But the color was fading, the sun slipping behind the trees, and the windows turning to gray. Still—there was another flash.

Was someone signaling? But why? And to whom?

Maybe she should get her telescope. Christina turned back quickly, holding on to another gargoyle's wing for balance. But the wing twisted under her hand and then the whole gargoyle moved with it, grating over its base with a sound like a cement mixer.

Christina gaped. There, where the gargoyle had been, was an opening, set in the chimney next to the attic wall, just the size and shape of a door.

It *was* a door, in fact. And although the light was dying, she could still make out the first few steps of a staircase leading down.

CHAPTER 5
THE TUNNEL

CHRISTINA switched on her flashlight.

The top few steps showed up clearly in the beam. Crafted of dark, polished wood, they curved to the left, spiraling down into darkness. Along the rounding wall ran a handrail.

Beating back anxious thoughts of what might be waiting below, Christina took a step forward, shining the flashlight on the stairs, the wall, the cobweb about to touch her face—

Ugh. Christina batted at the cobweb with her free hand and shook off the clinging fibers. Maybe it would be better to explore the stairs during the day.

But a stairway with no windows would be just as dark in the daytime as at night.

And anyway, she was too curious to wait.

She went cautiously, feeling her way, checking the strength of the flashlight's beam. She didn't want the battery to go out while she was in the tower stair. Feeling her way back up in pitch-dark would be a little *too* exciting.

Fifteen steps down, Christina grinned. Through the wall she could hear Nanny's steady snores and the drone of a radio that was still on.

Fifteen more steps, and the rattle of pans and a sloshing sound told her that Cook was doing the dishes.

And fifteen steps beyond that, she could hear a subdued *whoosh* as the oil furnace lit down in the cellar. It must be getting chilly outside, but deep in the tower, Christina couldn't feel it.

And still the stairs went down. Slowly, slowly, Christina descended—twenty steps—thirty steps—

She was at the bottom. She played her flashlight over the floor, the wall—and there, above the rail, was a light switch.

She could hardly expect it to still work. But she flipped the switch all the same. And with rising excitement, Christina watched as a row of lights flickered on overhead, a bulb every few yards, stretching on down a hallway so long that she couldn't see the end.

It wasn't really a hallway, after all. It was Leo Loompski's tunnel, and she had found it at last!

But where did it lead? Consumed with curiosity, Christina kept going.

She walked and walked. When she saw her first burned-out bulb, she remembered to switch off her flashlight. After more walking still, she came to a door on the left.

Unlike the other doors she had seen in her life so far, this one was huge, and as wide as it was tall. She rattled the big brass handle with its large, old-fashioned keyhole set beneath . . . but it was locked.

Christina stood on one leg in indecision. The tunnel went on, past the locked door, but she was getting tired. She still had to walk all the way back and climb all those stairs, too.

She would go just a little farther. If she didn't come to the end of the tunnel, she could always explore it another day.

But the tunnel began to slope upward, and the air suddenly felt different. Cooler and fresher, as if there were an opening to the outside.

All at once there were leaves in front of her, hanging from thick vines. Christina pushed her way through the greenery and blinked.

Above her were stars. Around her was the forest. A little farther away was a high, electrified fence. And through the trees, perhaps fifty yards away, stood a massive building of pale brick, lit up like a jail. There was a confused sound of voices and an idling engine. Christina squinted against the harsh yard lights. In front of the square building was a garbage truck painted with happy faces, and a line of children in orange and red vests.

Christina crept closer, through the ferns and twigs on the forest floor. The knees of her jeans grew damp, and once she put her palm down on a sharp rock, but she kept on until she was nearly to the fence. A faint odor of soured milk and rotting produce wafted past, and she could hear the voice of a man barking orders.

"You, and you," he said. "And you. Line up at the side of the truck. Come on, now, no shirking—Happy Orphans *want* to help Lenny Loompski!"

Christina brushed back a leaf that was tickling her nose.

Who was *Lenny* Loompski? She hadn't seen *his* portrait on the walls of her house.

"No sniveling!" cried the man. "That means no tears, no sniffles, no whimpers, no crying for mama—"

"None of us *has* a mama," piped a shrill voice.

"No crying for the mama you wish you had, whining, moaning, or fuss of any kind. Any of the above will get you two weeks' hard labor."

"We already *do* hard labor," said a surly boy's voice.

"Two weeks' VERY hard labor," the voice went on, "after which you'll go back to plain hard labor—if you're lucky. Any more smart comments?"

There was silence. Christina, who had crawled close enough to see the children's faces, saw that most of them looked as if they either had been crying or were just about to burst into tears.

And then she saw Taft. He was first in line, next to the truck, and he was bending down to tie the shoes of another orphan—the tall, large-headed boy Christina had seen once before.

The big boy stood patiently, his thick arms hanging. A push broom lay at his feet.

"Hey! Get back to work, you big lug!" The man's sharp voice carried across the yard.

The tall boy blinked. He rubbed his large head as if it hurt. "But I want to go with you," he said slowly, looking down at Taft.

"No, Danny." Taft gave the boy's shoelace a final tug and handed him the push broom. "You stay here. It's safer."

"But when will you come back?"

"Go *on*," Taft said urgently, giving Danny a shove. "You'll get us both in trouble if you don't start sweeping."

The big boy shambled obediently off, pushing his broom across the dirty asphalt. "But who will tie my *shoes?*" he said aloud.

Taft turned away. He pressed his palms against the side of the truck and stood with his head down.

Christina watched him for a moment. So Taft wasn't always rude, then . . .

She pulled her flashlight carefully out of her jacket pocket and aimed it at Taft's feet. On—off. On—off. The tops of his shoes shone briefly with reflected light.

Taft blinked, peering straight at her, through the fence and into the darkened forest.

Christina waited until the man's back was turned and then she shone the flashlight up to illuminate her own face while she counted one thousand one, one thousand two.

Taft stiffened, glanced over his shoulder, and seemed to hesitate. Then, all at once, he dropped to the ground and wriggled under the truck.

The second child in line opened her eyes wide and studiously looked away. Taft, hidden in the shadow beneath the truck, was motionless. Christina began to chew her fingernails.

What was Taft planning? Even if he managed to avoid being run over, once the truck pulled away, his hiding place would be gone. And he couldn't escape—the electrified fence prevented that.

"All right, you know the drill. Deep breath and SING!" The man pulled something that looked like a large, two-pronged fork from his back pocket, and hit it against a rod.

A high, clear tone filled the air.

Christina stretched her neck forward, straining to hear. The stocky man with the short, bristly hair stood in front of each child in turn.

"Match your voices to the tuning fork," the man bellowed. "Come on, now—you can do better than that!"

But the children were terribly off-key.

"All right, the rest of you go back inside." The man picked up a cardboard box at his feet. "What are you waiting for, orphans? Into the hopper!"

The children in line shuffled to the rear of the garbage truck. The heavy hinged panel that packed the garbage was open, and one by one the children were boosted into the large metal cavity where the garbage was dumped.

Christina was shocked. That couldn't possibly be safe. And the smell must be terrible.

The stocky man loaded the cardboard box into the passenger side of the cab and slammed the door, whistling tunelessly between his teeth. "Hey! Driver! Wake up!"

Someone sat up straight in the driver's seat, thrashing his way clear of the blanket that had been over his head. "Any singers?" the driver called through the window.

"Not this trip," said the yard boss carelessly. "Shut that ram panel, will you? I don't want kids jumping out on the road."

The driver shook his head. "That would be dangerous, all right. They might get hurt."

The stubbly-haired boss chuckled. "Or they might escape, which would be worse."

The driver leaned out the window, raking back the thick blond hair that hung in his face. "But they're *Happy* Orphans, boss. They wouldn't want to escape."

Christina glanced under the truck at Taft's feet, just barely visible, and then at the row of thin, frightened faces peering over the edge of the rusting metal hopper. Was the driver *serious*?

"You're new, aren't you, son?" The yard boss grinned.

The driver's hair fell back over his eyes, giving him the look of a large, not overly bright sheepdog. "I just started last week. I did real good on the test!"

The test for what? Christina thought. Dumbness?

"Here at Loompski Enterprises," the driver went on, sounding as if he were quoting from a manual, "we're all One Big Happy Family. I'm Barney Boolay, and I'm proud to be on the Loompski Team!"

"Yeah, aren't we all," said the yard boss. He scratched himself under his shirt. "You're kind of a smart one, aren't you, Boolay?"

The driver beamed. "I only had to take the employee test four times before I passed. The lady at the desk said she'd never seen *anybody* do that before."

The stocky man's grin widened. "Well, *that* ought to make your momma proud."

"She died last year," said Barney earnestly, "so I can't tell if she's proud or not. But look here!" Barney stretched out his left hand and twisted a ring on his pinky finger until it caught the light. "See? It's only my first week, and already I found this in the garbage! It's got a real emerald!"

The yard boss peered at the ring. "Looks more like a fake ruby to me, but hey, whatever turns your crank. Now, go ahead and lower that ram panel, will you? No, no, NOT the red button—the green one!"

"Sorry, boss. Gee, I always get that wrong."

"FINGERS IN!" yelled the yard boss, and the orphans snatched their hands away from the edge of the hopper as the ram panel clanged down.

Christina flinched as the anxious little faces disappeared behind a moving wall of solid steel. If any of the orphans cried out, she couldn't hear them over the revving of the engine.

With a lurch, the truck was put into gear—and in that instant, a slim figure rolled out from beneath the truck to the side that was hidden from the orphanage, leapt up to grab a handhold, and hung on, legs dangling.

The garbage truck rumbled toward the electrified fence. With a screech of metal, a buzzer sounded, a high gate swung open, and the big truck with the happy faces painted on the side rolled through into the forest.

Taft clung to the truck until just past the first bushes and then let go. The truck engine was making so much noise that the crash of a body into the underbrush was hardly noticeable.

The gate swung shut and locked with a clank. The garbage truck dwindled in the distance, belching exhaust as it labored up the dirt road through the forest. And Christina, keeping her flashlight prudently off, crawled on hands and knees to the place where Taft had landed.

CHAPTER 6

A SECRET GUEST

"I *knew* there was a tunnel," said Taft. His narrow face, lit from below by Christina's flashlight, was smudged but elated.

Christina leaned back against the tunnel's interior wall, proud of herself. She had not only found Taft but (to her great relief) had actually managed to locate the tunnel's entrance again in the dark. "You're coming back with me, right?"

"Back where?"

"My house, of course." She looked at him worriedly. Now that she finally had a friend—sort of—it would be nice to keep him. And he had to stay somewhere.

Taft shook his head. "All I want is to stay here long enough for them to forget about me, and then I'm going to run away. I've got to find a good place for me and—"

"But what about food?" Christina interrupted.

Taft shrugged. "I don't eat much. Anyway, maybe I can find something to eat in the woods. Berries and things. You know."

"But you could stay in my attic. No one's been up there for

years. And"—Christina leaned forward, struck with inspiration—"you can learn math on my computer."

Taft turned his head alertly. "Math?"

Christina clapped in glee. "You can do all my assignments! You'll love it, I won't have to do them, and my father will be happy. It's the *perfect* plan."

Taft looked thoughtful. "But if I stay in your house, they'll catch me for sure."

"Who will?"

"Your father, or whoever takes care of you . . . no one is going to want a dirty orphan around," he added bitterly. "They'll send me straight back to the orphanage, and then I'll be in *real* trouble."

"I told you, no one ever goes in the attic. Hardly anyone even comes up to the third floor, where my room is. Nanny is too fat to climb the stairs, and my father is too busy, and Cook just stays in the kitchen. Come on, I'll show you."

Christina tugged Taft to his feet and pulled him along Leo Loompski's dimly lit tunnel, still talking. "I'll bring blankets and a pillow, and I'll make you a bed behind some boxes. If anyone does come up, they'll never see you, if you don't move."

"A pillow?" said Taft, trotting after her. "A real pillow?"

The attic was dark, but the flashlight, set on end, made a circle of brightness on the ceiling and illumined a corner of the vast room.

"So where does the garbage truck go?" Christina folded over an old quilt to make a sleeping pad and laid two extra blankets on top.

"Nobody knows." Taft took another bite of the pie Christina had sneaked from the kitchen and a drink of milk from a thermos. "They say it's up the mountain to break rocks in a mine, but that can't be true. Who needs broken rocks?"

"But what happens to the kids?" Christina plumped a spare pillow.

"No one knows that, either." Taft's mouth, blueberry-rimmed, turned down at the corners. "They go on the garbage truck, and they never come back."

Christina's hands stilled. "Never?"

Taft shook his head.

"And you almost had to go!" Christina was horrified.

"I would have gotten picked before that, if I hadn't sung off-key," said Taft, calmly licking his fingers.

Christina sat back. "What does singing have to do with getting picked?"

Taft shrugged. "I'm not exactly sure. But I figured out that if you sang on pitch, you got picked to go on the truck first of all. So now everybody sings like a hyena, unless they're new and don't know."

He scooped the last of the blueberry pie into his mouth. "This place is way better than the orphanage already," he said through a mouthful of crust. "Do you have any more pie?"

Christina looked at him thoughtfully. If Taft was going to have a big appetite, it might be hard to sneak enough food without raising suspicion. "I thought you said you didn't eat much."

Taft hunched one shoulder. "I don't eat much orphanage food. Burnt potatoes and dried peas and oatmeal without sugar . . . no thanks. But this," he said, gazing with reverence at the blue stains left on his plate, "is worth eating." He licked the plate and wiped his mouth with his sleeve. "So when can I do some math?"

Christina made a face. "Right now, if you want. Come on down to my room. Nobody will come up tonight—it's too late."

"Go-Go, Chickie-Chickie, Chickie-Go Math!" squeaked the computer, showing a horde of dancing chickens, each dangling a mathematical symbol from its beak. Taft watched with a rapt expression on his face, hardly blinking.

"This is *great*," he said. "I can't *believe* this."

Christina gazed at the chickens as they goose-stepped their way across the screen. She couldn't believe it, either. With any luck, she would never have to deal with mathematical poultry again.

She showed him how the program worked. "For starters, you can do my last three assignments. I skipped them."

She ran the vacuum while he began the first problem, cleaning her room to keep Nanny from getting suspicious. Now and then she helped Taft navigate the computer screen; he picked it up very quickly. But when she bent to change the vacuum bag, she heard footsteps on the stairs.

"Shh!" she hissed. "Quick! Under the bed!" She lifted the scalloped edge of her quilt to let Taft scoot beneath. No one ever came upstairs—well, hardly ever. Why did someone have to come tonight?

She smelled her father's pipe in the hall. There was a

knock at her door. Christina scrambled into her computer chair. "Come in!"

"Well!" Her father, sounding pleased, put a hand on her shoulder. "Doing math, are you?"

Christina faced the screen, feeling her eyes glaze over as she looked at the numbers. "Just a little," she said, pushing a button at random.

Dr. Adnoid bent over. "But surely you're farther along than this?"

"I just thought I'd do some review," Christina said in a hurry, turning the monitor off. She swiveled to face her father, hoping fervently that he hadn't come to help her with math or, worse yet, question her about an escaped orphan. "How was work today?" she asked, in an attempt to head him off.

Her father's eyebrows drew down slightly. "Work was fine." He set a large green scrapbook on Christina's desk and pulled out a tape measure. "Here, let's see how tall you are this year."

Christina stood up, eyeing the bulky album as her father stretched the tape measure from her toes to the top of her head. She had seen that book before. Once a year, her father opened it and wrote down her weight and height and anything else he could measure. It all struck her as remarkably pointless, but since it didn't happen often, she tried not to complain.

"Four feet, eight inches—very good. You've grown two inches since last year."

Christina made an effort to be interested in this information. "Two inches doesn't seem like much."

"You're in the sixty-fifth percentile for height for girls your age. That's about half a standard deviation above average—perfectly normal. Now, your weight . . . let's see." He walked Christina to the bathroom scale and noted the figure. "Hmmm. Only fifty-second percentile for weight. You need to take in more calories. I'll tell Cook to add oil to your broccoli."

Christina resisted this suggestion. "How about if I just eat more ice cream?"

Dr. Adnoid shook his head. "Trans fats. Too many. Now, what about your shoe size?"

Christina sat kicking one foot while her father measured the other with calipers. "Is it really important to write all this down?"

"Well . . ." Her father straightened. "Perhaps not. But your mother"—he paused to clear his throat—"she began this book when you were a baby, and I know she would have wanted me to keep it up. So I have done my best."

Dr. Adnoid fished a large handkerchief out of his pocket, rubbed at his eyes, blew his nose with a protracted honk, and tucked it away. "Now, then. What else can we write about you that's interesting?" He picked up the book and sat down heavily on Christina's bed. "Dental work, perhaps? Did you have any cavities this year?"

The springs creaked under Dr. Adnoid's weight, and a small surprised grunt came from beneath the bed. Christina coughed loudly to cover it and slid her foot under the bed frame, nudging a thin brown hand back into the shadows.

"Or how about math grades? Those might be exciting!"

Christina suppressed a shudder and cast around in her mind for something her father could write that wouldn't lead back to the dreaded subject of numbers. Suddenly she knew.

"I have perfect pitch," Christina announced with relief.

Dr. Adnoid sprang up, his face pale. "Who told you that?"

"Mrs. Lisowsky," Christina said, surprised. "My music teacher. I was singing for her today, and that's when she found out."

Dr. Adnoid gripped the edge of the desk. "I'll call Mrs. Lisowsky at once," he muttered. "She can't be allowed to spread such rumors. I only hope she hasn't mentioned it outside these walls."

He whirled to face Christina. "You mustn't tell anyone. Do you hear me?"

Christina nodded. She heard him, all right. She just didn't understand.

"And don't sing anymore," Dr. Adnoid said as he hurried out of her room. "Not one note. It's *dangerous*."

CHAPTER 7

A MUFFLED BOOM

THE door clicked shut. "All clear," Christina said in a low voice.

Taft rolled out from beneath the bed in a wreath of dust, rubbing one shoulder. "I wish your dad hadn't sat down so hard." He looked at her accusingly. "I thought you said no one ever came up here."

"Sorry. Hardly anyone ever does." Christina looked at the green scrapbook her father had forgotten. "Why do you suppose he was so worried about me having perfect pitch?"

Taft shrugged. "It's obvious, isn't it? He doesn't want you going to the mines with the other orphans."

"But I'm not an orphan!"

"That wouldn't matter to Lenny Loompski. If he knew you could sing, he'd find a way to get you."

Christina grabbed the sides of her head in frustration. "And who is this *Lenny* Loompski? I thought it was Leo!"

Taft glanced around the room. "I'll tell you, but let's go to the attic. Your father might come back."

"All right." Christina lumped a blanket under her bedspread in what she hoped was a lifelike manner and turned out the light. Then, sock-footed, flashlight bobbing, they slipped into the closet and up the ladder.

The attic wasn't quite as dark as before. The moon had risen and was shining in flat trapezoidal stripes through the vent in the wall. Its pale light glanced off the curved cylinder of the telescope, still on its tripod on the broken chair, and spread along the wooden floor.

"Hey!" Taft reached out to touch the telescope's smooth barrel. "I've never seen one up close. Let's look through it!"

"Later." Christina lifted the tripod down from the chair and set it aside.

Taft's eyes were shadowed. He hunched one shoulder. "I suppose you don't want a dirty orphan touching your things."

Christina stared at him in dismay. "I didn't mean that at all. I just wanted you to tell me about Lenny Loompski first."

"Oh." Taft's shoulder relaxed. "All right, then." He sat down on his pallet and curled his knees to his chest. "Leo Loompski was one of the famous Loompski brothers, and the founder of Loompski Labs. And he built the orphanage, too, for a public charity."

"Everyone knows *that*," said Christina, still grumpy at being misunderstood.

"And he was a great scientist, and he had all these ideas, and so he set up his laboratories here so he could try to see if any of his ideas worked. I guess he liked it here by the Starkian Mountain Ridge, or something. And I think one of his brothers lived here."

"I *know* all that. What about Lenny?"

"Hang on, I'm getting there. So anyway, Leo wanted to work on his theories and inventions, but it was taking more and more time to manage Loompski Labs and the orphanage, too, so he asked his nephew Lenny—"

"I *knew* it had to be a relative!"

"—his nephew Lenny," repeated Taft, glaring at her, "to run the orphanage. Listen, if you want to tell this, just go ahead."

Christina sighed. If all kids were this touchy, she wasn't sure she wanted to meet any more. "Go on."

Taft tucked his chin on his arms. "So Lenny ran the orphanage, and later he started to help manage Loompski Labs, too. Leo was busy in his private lab somewhere, doing experiments of his own, and he was happy to let Lenny give the orders. Then after a while people just never heard anything about Leo anymore. Nobody knew where he'd gone. And now Lenny runs the lab and the orphanage and probably the mines, too, if they really exist."

Christina leaned against the wall, watching him. "How do you know all this?"

Taft lifted both shoulders. "I hear things. They talk, over at the orphanage."

Christina was silent for a moment. "Have you ever seen Lenny Loompski?"

"Oh, sure, all the time. He drives up to the orphanage in this long black car, and we have to say how happy we are to see him. And how *he's* going to win the Karsnicky Medal some-day." Taft's foot tapped against the floor. "So can we look through the telescope *now?*"

Christina nodded. "Let's take it out onto the roof."

Taft gazed at the face of the moon and the town of Dorf, and after that he wanted to look at the orphanage. Christina helped him patiently with the focusing knobs, and then sat down on a low balustrade, looking up at the looming rock of the Starkian Mountain Ridge.

It rose above the tops of the trees, sharply etched in the moonlight, and Christina wondered if the truckload of orphans had really gone right up to the top. Maybe she could look through the telescope and find out.

"I want a turn, Taft," she said.

"In a minute."

Christina waited a minute, then two. "Come *on.*"

Taft stepped away from the telescope, his face unhappy. "I found some lighted windows, but the shades were all pulled. I couldn't see anything, really."

"What were you hoping to see?" Christina put one eye to the telescope, still aimed at the orphanage, and closed the other. A dimly lit rectangle sprang into view, crisscrossed with mullions and brighter at the bottom. As she watched, a shadow passed behind the window and was gone.

Taft gave a half shrug. "I thought I'd check on Danny. You know, see how he's doing."

"Danny? Is that the guy with the big head? The slow one?"

"He's not that slow," said Taft quickly. "You just have to tell him things more often, is all. And he understands more than people think he does."

Christina glanced at him.

"He understands that I've gone away, for one," said Taft, very low. "I hope he doesn't try to follow the truck. He'll only get in trouble."

Christina swiveled the telescope to face the Starkian Ridge. Was it possible to see where the garbage truck had gone? No—not when she couldn't even see the road.

Still, it was interesting to look at the ridge in the moonlight. The high edge of rock was like a black paper cutout against the lighter sky. There were large, high-flying birds that lived up there—harriers, they were called—and sometimes during the day she had heard their distant cries. It was a lonesome sound that fit with the bleak, windswept peaks, and she had always wished that someday she could climb the Starkian Mountain Ridge and see the harriers for herself.

Christina lifted her head with sudden realization. Now she could! Now she had a tunnel that led straight into the forest. She could go tomorrow, during Nanny's nap. If she returned before supper, no one would miss her at all.

Taft tapped her on the back and she gave up the telescope, shivering a little in the cooling air. Off in the distance, a car engine growled as it changed gears, and headlights cast faint twin beams that showed in gaps through the trees. Christina looked up at the ridge and rubbed her arms for warmth.

Were the orphans really breaking rocks up there? And why didn't any of them ever come back?

Christina frowned. Something else was bothering her. Did her father know what happened to the orphans? He certainly seemed worried enough about her ability to sing on pitch. And the man in front of the orphanage had been just as interested in the orphans' ability to sing, though Christina couldn't imagine why. To help Lenny Loompski, was all the man had said.

But if Lenny Loompski was the manager of Loompski Labs, then he was her father's boss—wasn't he?

Christina brushed her bangs out of her eyes with an impatient hand. It was all too confusing, and she didn't want to think about it anymore. She was getting the feeling she always got when she looked at those dancing chickens with the numbers in their beaks—as if her brain had frozen solid.

She tapped Taft on the shoulder, and he gave up the telescope at once. Christina was just thinking that his manners were improving, when he tapped her again.

"What?" Christina was annoyed. "Can't you let me look one minute?"

"Shhh!" Taft put up a hand in warning. "Listen."

Christina straightened. A car's headlights glowed, closer now, and the smooth grumble of a well-tuned engine reached their ears.

She shrugged. "That's just some scientist driving home late from the laborator—"

The ridge above them bloomed with sudden orange light, as if a firework had gone off behind the highest rocks.

Two seconds later, there came a muffled *boom*. The house beneath them trembled slightly. Above the Starkian Ridge, a clot of harriers lifted, scattered, and came flying over the treetops in a flurry of beating wings. One, slender and dark against the moonlit sky, wheeled over Christina's house with a cry like that of a frightened child.

And on the forest road a long, black shadow flicked off its headlights, took the turning to Christina's house, rolled smoothly past the iron fence, and stopped at the front gate.

CHAPTER 8

A QUESTION OF LOYALTY

THE ridged wing of a stone gargoyle was cool and rough under Christina's hand. She stood on the rooftop without moving, looking down on her father as he emerged from the house into the night. Beside her, Taft took a soundless step back into the shadow of the roof's peak.

The moon shone silver on Dr. Adnoid's hair and the tops of his shoulders. He walked slowly down the brick path to the gate, where a long black car waited.

"Yes, Mr. Loompski?"

An elbow pushed out of the driver's window, followed by a forearm encased in a pinstriped sleeve. A meaty hand splayed on the car's door. "Wilfer, my man. Good of you to meet me." Lenny Loompski's jovial voice carried clearly in the still night air.

Taft looked at Christina. "Wilfer?" he mouthed, his eyebrows expressive.

Christina frowned at him. Her father's first name might be odd, but it was no weirder than Taft.

"But what's this I hear about you requesting an inspector?" Lenny Loompski's voice was suddenly less friendly.

Dr. Adnoid cleared his throat. "I was thinking it was time we had someone look in on the orphans—you know, to make sure we're in compliance with the child labor laws."

The silence from the car had an incredulous quality.

"I just want to make sure they're safe. Working with zoomstones can be tricky, you know."

Zoomstones? Christina glanced at Taft, but he looked as confused as she felt.

"Wilfer, Wilfer, Wilfer." The shadowy figure in the car shook his head. "You amaze me, you really do. I would have expected more loyalty from you."

"It's not a matter of loyalty, sir."

"Who promoted you to head scientist? Who got you into this house after Uncle Leo disappeared on one of his wild-goose chases? Who *pays* you, Wilfer?"

"You, sir, but—"

"Are you saying you don't *trust* me?"

"Of course not, Mr. Loompski, but—"

"You keep saying 'but,' Wilfer. Those orphans are getting the very best of care. They receive the finest schooling, with the most advanced teaching methods—"

Taft expelled a small breath in a sound of disgust.

"—they are given pleasant and healthful outdoor tasks—"

"Collecting *garbage!*" whispered Taft, his voice outraged.

"—and up on the mountain, all they do is sing. The acoustics are quite fine up there, you know, with those rocks all around. You might almost say that we have an orphan choir. It's an extracurricular activity, so to speak."

Dr. Adnoid's feet scraped on the walk as he shifted his weight. "If all that's true, then why would you have any objection to an inspector?"

Lenny Loompski's thick fingers began to tap the car door, one at a time.

"And as long as we're speaking frankly," said Dr. Adnoid, his voice growing stronger, "I'd like to do research on Leo Loompski's theories again. He brought me here to help him unlock the secrets of the Starkian Ridge—to explore the far edges of quantum mechanics, to do the noble work of adding to the world's scientific knowledge—"

Lenny Loompski chuckled. "Not much money in *that* racket."

"—but you! All you want is to turn Loompski Labs into a factory for cheap fuel! We scientists aren't even allowed up on the ridge anymore—there are electric fences and warning signs everywhere—"

"For the protection of the orphans, of course," Lenny said smoothly.

"Zoom is highly unstable—you know that—and I'm not convinced that you have every safety measure in place for the children. I think it's about time an inspector came to check things out!"

Up on the rooftop, Christina barely avoided cheering aloud, and Taft gave a vigorous nod. But on the ground, the silence was ominous.

Christina's father fumbled in a pocket for his pipe. There was a sound of a match striking and a little glow of flame. For a moment, in the brief flickering light, Christina caught a glimpse of Lenny Loompski's flat, pale face, his cheeks like two slabs of ham.

"You seem upset, Wilfer." The voice from the car had a soothing tone. "Maybe you need a little vacation. I hear there are some truly exciting spots in the . . . Middle East, perhaps?"

Dr. Adnoid's shoulders stiffened. A scent of tobacco rose in the air as he took his pipe from his mouth. "I don't need a vacation, Mr. Loompski. I'm just asking for an inspec—"

"You wouldn't have to bring your daughter along, you know. I'd be happy to take care of her while you're gone." Lenny Loompski leaned his head out the window and stared up at his employee. "By the way, I hear she has perfect pitch."

Christina stopped breathing. Somewhere a cricket chirped loudly in the sudden stillness.

"My spies are everywhere, you see." Lenny smiled, his flat cheeks bunching.

Dr. Adnoid made a strangled sort of sound. "She *doesn't* have perfect pitch."

"You think not? We could use her in the children's choir."

"She has nothing to do with you." Dr. Adnoid leaned forward. "Keep away from her, do you hear?"

"I'd *like* to, Wilfer, really I would. But if you're going to call in an inspector, I think he would be impressed to see that the daughter of our head scientist was singing right along with the orphans . . . Don't you agree?" He pulled in his arm. The car engine started up.

"Wait! I've changed my mind about the inspector!" cried Christina's father, banging on the car door.

Lenny Loompski put the car into gear. "I had a feeling you might, Wilfer."

Silently, Christina folded up the tripod and tucked her telescope under one arm. She followed Taft through the service door and back into the attic. He was talking—she heard words like "zoomstones" and "your father" and "Lenny"—but she wasn't listening. She said good night and stepped down the ladder.

She put on her pajamas in a sort of daze. She had the same numb, stupefied feeling she always got when staring at a math problem. There were too many pieces of information, and she couldn't seem to put any of them together. She half expected to see a dancing chicken come into the room with a sign in its beak that said PRETTY GOOD WORK! or EXTRA CREDIT FOR TRYING!, leaving her unsure if she'd gotten the problem right or wrong.

She brushed her teeth mechanically and got into bed. There was a lump under the covers—the blankets she had rolled up to imitate the bulk of a sleeping person. There was another lump, too, with hard, square edges. Christina flicked on her bedside lamp and looked at the green scrapbook in her hands.

She had seen it many times before and had felt absolutely no interest at all. She knew the kind of thing her father wrote in it.

But tonight he'd said that her mother had made the first

few entries. Christina turned to the first pages and saw her mother's handwriting.

It was elegant and flowing, unlike Dr. Adnoid's squared printing, and for a moment Christina laid her cheek against the page. Then she lifted her head and began to read.

"Today Christina took her first steps. Such chubby little legs!" There was a picture with that one of a laughing baby in a white bonnet.

"Today she brought me her first flower—the head of a dandelion, crumpled and flat in her moist fist. A dozen roses couldn't be more beautiful!" A brownish bit of fluff was taped next to this entry. It might have been a dandelion, once. And next to that was another picture, this time of a smiling woman with honey-colored hair holding a squirming toddler on a green hill studded with small yellow flowers.

Christina studied it as if it were a photo of a strange new species. There was no house in the picture and no iron palings. The mother and child were outside, on a hill somewhere in the world, and there were no fences at all.

Christina felt an odd, deep pull within her, as if she wanted something very much but didn't know quite what it was. She wasn't sure that she missed her mother, exactly—could you miss someone you barely remembered?—but she did wish that her mother hadn't been blown up.

Christina turned the page with a careful hand. Another photo showed her parents and a group of friends picnicking on the same hill, with children playing together in the foreground. One of the children—somewhat blurry, she was in motion—had wispy pale hair. The caption below read

"Christina with Peter, Celia, and Tommy." She couldn't remember any of them, but it was nice to think that she might have had friends, once.

Christina read every entry, but when she came to the fall after her fourth birthday, the elegant script stopped. One year later, there was her father's dry, careful printing, scratching in statistics: weight, height, eye exam results, shoe size. One time he had apparently tried to record clothing sizes but had given up in confusion. There were no more entries about chubby legs or crumpled flowers.

Christina looked at the page for her sixth year. She had learned to roller-skate that spring, going back and forth on the driveway inside the gate, and she had fallen and scraped her knee. That night, her knee had throbbed and bled through the bandage Nanny had put on, and in the morning it had been stuck to the sheets.

Her father, appalled that she had hurt herself, had taken the skates away, but Christina thought it was the kind of thing her mother would have wanted in the book, so she put it in. She drew a picture of herself on the skates, and another of herself falling down, and used a red marker for the drops of blood.

She looked at her work with satisfaction. Her father had tried, but he didn't know what was important to put in a scrapbook. She would remember everything, and she would finish it the way her mother would have wanted it done.

Christina was deep into a drawing of the time she had made snow ice cream when she heard a muffled sound from the floor beneath. She padded softly down the steps and paused by her father's study door. She pushed it open slightly.

Dr. Adnoid was sitting at his desk with his head in his hands. Before him was a picture of his wife.

"Oh, Bethie," he said, and Christina could hear that he had been crying. "What now?"

Christina stepped back. She did not like seeing her father this way. Grown-ups were always supposed to know what to do.

But what if they didn't? Were the kids just supposed to wait around until the adults figured things out? Christina frowned. Taft and the orphans had waited a long time already.

She tiptoed back up the stairs. There must be *something* she could do. For starters, she could refuse to sing even one note for Lenny Loompski. That would show him.

And tomorrow she would go down the tunnel again and begin to find things out.

CHAPTER 9

A SMALL GOLD BAND

AT breakfast Christina's father made a pronouncement.

"No going out in the yard today," he said. "Or tomorrow. Or the next day."

"What?" Nanny was shocked. "Christina needs sunshine for vitamin D!"

All eyes turned toward Nanny. Christina took advantage of the moment and slid a piece of buttered toast into the pocket of her sweatshirt, which she had worn especially for this purpose.

"It's for her own protection," said Dr. Adnoid, gazing down at his plate of scrambled eggs. He put a hand over his forehead and sighed.

Cook and Nanny exchanged glances. Christina spooned scrambled eggs on another piece of toast, topped it with a third, and jammed the whole thing into her sweatshirt's front pouch while everyone was busy looking at one another. There, that ought to be enough for Taft. He could get water from the bathroom faucet if he was thirsty. She wasn't about to bring orange juice or milk upstairs in her pocket.

"I'm sorry, Christina." Dr. Adnoid blinked miserably at his daughter. "But it's safest this way."

Christina was just thinking that it was a very good thing she had discovered the tunnel, otherwise she didn't know how she could have stood it. Being kept safe was too much like being in jail.

She was relieved, too, that he had said no going out in the *yard*; she could obey him perfectly and still have a wonderful time in the forest, once Nanny went down for her afternoon nap. But she had better change the subject before he said "no going out at all."

"You forgot the scrapbook in my room last night," she said. "I read it."

Dr. Adnoid tried to smile. "Did you find it interesting? I can't say I'm very clever at thinking what to write."

Christina considered this. "You write facts," she said, "because that's what you're good at. But I was mostly reading what Mom— Mother—wrote." She hesitated over what to call her mother. Christina couldn't remember calling her anything at all.

"Do you miss your mother very much?" Her father toyed with his fork.

Christina knew she *should* miss her mother. But when the only things she could recall were a soft lap, a rocking motion, and a fragment of a song, it was hard to express exactly what it was that she longed for.

She tried to shrug. "I can barely remember her, Dad. I don't even have anything to remember her *by*." She frowned. "Last night was the first time I saw any pictures of her besides the one on your desk."

Her father pushed back his chair. "Wait here. I have something I've been saving for you."

He disappeared into his bedroom. There was a scuffing sound, and then a tumbling noise of boxes falling, and a muffled oath. At last Dr. Adnoid reappeared, carrying a polished wooden box. He blew the dust off the top. "I think you're old enough to have this now."

Christina lifted the lid. Three tiers swung up, lined with green velvet. There was a shimmer of gold chains, silver earrings, and an assortment of brooches set with semiprecious stones. There was a locket with a green stone and a slender wristwatch, and in the bottom compartment was a jumble of things—ribbon, spools of thread, old keys, a nail clipper, and even a pocketknife.

"She didn't keep just jewelry in there, I guess," said Dr. Adnoid. "A few odds and ends of nothing."

"It's nice." Christina opened up the locket to see a picture on either side—one of a smiling baby, and the other of a much younger Dr. Adnoid. She set it down and picked up a ring, turning it in the light.

It looked like an ordinary wedding ring—a plain gold band—but set within it was a small oblong of gray rock. As Christina looked closely, she could see streaks of pink and green. "What's this?"

Dr. Adnoid straightened. "I forgot that was there. That was her wedding band. Give it to me, please."

The ring felt strangely warm in Christina's hand. She passed it over with reluctance. "But, Dad—"

"How did math go yesterday?" Dr. Adnoid asked abruptly,

shuffling through the sections of the morning paper. "Did you finish your review?"

"Uh . . . sort of . . ."

"I'll look in tonight and see if you need any extra help. Do today's assignment and have it ready for me to check."

Christina swallowed hard. She couldn't remember what she was supposed to be working on, though it probably involved chickens. Taft could do her assignment, of course— but if she had to answer her father's questions, she'd be lost.

Dr. Adnoid folded the paper. "Now, remember what I told you. No going out—"

"In the *yard*," Christina finished, and hurriedly changed the subject before he could say anything more. "Dad, would you tell me—what *is* perfect pitch?"

Dr. Adnoid looked down at Christina, his face worried. "It's rather complex. First, you have to understand that pitch is the ear's response to sound frequencies. A frequency is a vibration in the air. But pitch also includes overtones and harmonics—see, a frequency is harmonic if it's an integer multiple of the fundamental frequency, and a harmonic series is a mathematical definition, so to speak. Would you like me to describe the arithmetic series for you?" He laid down the paper and dug in his briefcase for a pencil. "Or perhaps the octave series? It's a geometric progression, and might be more interesting."

Christina shook her head, appalled. If perfect pitch had anything to do with math, she wanted no part of it.

Her father reached for his car keys. "Well, another time perhaps. But remember—whatever you do, *don't sing*."

Christina listened for the sound of the front door closing. She shut her mother's jewelry box with care and looked up at Nanny. Something had occurred to her, but she didn't know quite how to say it.

"That ring," she said at last. "Don't they usually bury wedding rings with the—" She stopped, unable to say the word. She fiddled nervously with the edge of the newspaper her father had left on the table. There was a slight scraping sound, as if something hard beneath it slid against the tabletop.

"But there was no body, dear." Nanny laid a plump hand on Christina's shoulder. "There was nothing left to bury. Your mother's lab was completely blown to bits; later, in the rubble, the ring was found."

"Oh." Christina lifted a corner of the paper and peeked beneath. Her heart gave a sudden flip; her free hand darted under the sports section and closed on the small round object her father had forgotten.

Nanny plucked the newspaper from the table. "Oh, good—no one's done the crossword puzzle yet!"

Christina slid her hand carefully off the table and into her pocket. She poked a forefinger through the circle of her mother's ring, feeling its strange warmth. "Who found it?"

Nanny picked up a pencil. "The ring? Everyone was searching, of course. But I believe—yes, I'm almost sure that it was Lenny Loompski."

CHAPTER 10

STUPID MATH

"IT'S stupid!" said Taft. He was staring at Christina's computer, with its screen full of line-dancing poultry. "Stupid, stupid, stupid!"

The back of his thin neck was turning red. Christina set down her mother's jewelry box and dug into her sweatshirt pocket for the egg-and-toast sandwich. "Math *is* pretty stupid," she agreed.

"Not the *math*." Taft scowled. "What's stupid is the way they *teach* it."

"What? The dancing chickens?" Christina laid his breakfast on the desk.

Taft picked lint off the toast, looking moody. "More than that. See, instead of teaching you one way to solve a problem, this program shows you about *ten*. Pretty soon all the methods are mixed up in your head, and you use a bit of one and a piece of another and get everything wrong, and then those chickens come beaking around with signs that say 'almost right!' and 'points for trying!'"

"It's supposed to build up your self-esteem," said Christina, trying not to laugh. She cleared a space on one of her bookshelves for the jewelry box and stood back to admire. It would have looked better if it wasn't surrounded by math books—her father supervised the book-buying in the house and kept hoping to get her interested in numbers—but still it was wonderful to have something of her mother's.

Taft made an exasperated noise and swallowed a mouthful of scrambled egg. "What would build up my self-esteem," he said through his teeth, "is to *know* how to do a problem and then get it *right*. I figured it out after a while—this level isn't that hard, I'm still doing review—but it's going to be tough to learn anything new. No wonder you hate it so much. They've taken all the *true* fun out of math."

"Yeah, right," said Christina, "and it was *so* much fun to begin with." She slumped to the floor, her back against the desk, and pulled at the frayed edge of her sweatshirt sleeve.

"Well, it *is* fun," said Taft stubbornly, finishing off the toast.

"You can do my assignment for today, then." Christina curled up her knees and laid her head on her arms. "I just wish you could talk to my dad for me, too. He's going to check my work and ask how I got my answers, and of course I won't know. And then he's going to explain and *explain*, and I won't understand a word."

"It's not that hard," said Taft earnestly. "Really, math *is* fun, if you—"

"Listen!" said Christina fiercely. "Math is *not* fun. It's horrible. You can talk all you want, but I'm never going to get it. There's no right answer, and the rules always keep changing, and I'm sick of it."

"But don't you see?" Taft leaned over the back of his chair. "That's the beauty of math—there *is* a right answer, the rules *never* change, and you always know exactly where you are. You do the problem step by step, and it comes out the same every time. And if you make a mistake, you just go back step by step, and you can find out exactly where you went wrong."

"It doesn't work that way for me," said Christina. "I'm stupid at math." She put a hand in her pocket and rubbed the edge of her mother's ring. Her mother was a scientist. Her mother must have loved math. Would her mother be ashamed of her? she wondered.

Taft snapped off the monitor. "I always thought the orphanage school was bad," he said, walking over to her wall of bookshelves, "because we only had one computer for the whole place, and the math books were old and beat-up. But maybe it wasn't as bad as I thought."

He ran his finger over a series of dusty books under a label that said *Mathematics*. "Aha!" He pounced on a book with battered corners, covered in a dull, water-stained maroon. He scanned several pages and nodded with satisfaction. "*This* is what you need."

Christina backed away. "Oh, no."

Taft blew off the dust and banged the book on her desk. "Sit down," he said. "You can do math if you take it one step at a time."

Christina frowned. She *couldn't* do math. She had proven that over and over again; even the happy dancing chickens never told her she'd done it right. "I'm stupid with numbers," she insisted. "Don't even bother, because I can't—"

"You are *not* stupid." Taft looked at her, his dark eyes serious.

"Some people are, you know. They can't get things no matter how hard they try. That's not *your* problem."

"But we've got to make plans," said Christina. "We're going through the tunnel after lunch, right? What do you want to do first? Climb trees? Run?"

Taft opened the book to the first page. "You're stalling. Sharpen your pencil."

Christina looked at the computer keyboard. "Pencil?"

"Yes. We're going to do this the old-fashioned way."

Taft was right, Christina had to admit an hour later. He had made her repeat her multiplication tables until she had them down cold, he had shown her a trick for remembering the nine-times table, and he had shown her one—and only one—way to multiply on paper. Now she was doing a whole page of multiplication problems, one after the other, and finding that what Taft had said was true—it wasn't that hard.

In fact, she hated to admit it, but it *was* actually fun to get the right answer time after time. She had a feeling of accomplishment that had nothing to do with overly enthusiastic chickens.

"Done!" Christina checked her last problem, smiled broadly—she'd gotten it right again!—and slammed the book shut. "Now we can make plans for this afternoon."

Taft shook his head. "I'm not waiting until then. I'm going"—he glanced at the clock and pushed back his chair—"right now."

"But we can't leave until Nanny takes her nap. They'll come looking for me if I don't go downstairs for lunch."

Taft headed for the closet. "They won't come looking for *me*. I'm taking off."

"By yourself?" Christina's voice rose. "That's no fair. I rescued you, remember? I found the tunnel, and I brought you here, and I even fed you *pie*—"

Taft pulled down the trapdoor ladder and grinned. "It was good, too. Got any more?"

Christina glared at him. "If you're going to go off by yourself and have all kinds of fun without me, then you can forget about any more pie. You're going to miss lunch, too, and supper if you're not back in time—"

"I'm used to it." Taft shrugged. "I had to miss meals at the orphanage if I talked back."

"I bet you missed them all the time, then," Christina countered, but suddenly she noticed the thinness of Taft's neck and the way his shoulder bones showed through his shirt. What had they done at that orphanage—starved him?

"Listen," Taft said. "I can come back for you if you want. But I want to go check on Danny."

"Oh." Christina looked up, her irritation fading.

"I can't stay here forever, anyway—I've got to figure out a place where he can live with me." Taft disappeared up through the trapdoor.

"Wait!" Christina hopped up the ladder and poked her head into the attic. "I've got an idea! Just give me ten minutes, okay?"

Taft turned with his hand on the service door's latch, his head cocked to one side. "Okay. But I'm leaving then, whether you're coming or not."

"You can watch the orphanage through the telescope

while you wait," said Christina, pointing past the sheet-draped furniture to the broken chair beneath the air vent. "Stay inside, though. Someone might see you on the roof."

Christina skidded down the stairs and into the kitchen, where Nanny and Cook were having a final cup of coffee. "I need to pack a lunch. A big one. I'm going on an adventure."

"Eh?" said Cook, staring.

"To a desert island," said Christina, inventing on the spot. "I'm going to sail away."

Nanny and Cook did not seem able to comprehend this.

Christina tried again. "If I can't go outside," she explained patiently, "I'm just going to have to pretend, aren't I?"

"Ah!" said Nanny.

"Oh!" said Cook.

"I'll go up to my room," Christina said, "and set sail. I'll be gone all day, and if I take a lunch, you won't even see me until suppertime."

"I'll make you one this minute," said Cook, getting up.

"Make enough for two," said Christina with sudden inspiration. "I'm taking a friend with me."

"An imaginary friend," Nanny explained to Cook in an elaborate whisper.

"Poor little tyke," mumbled Cook in return. "Trying to make the best of it. I'll make her a lunch big enough for three, so I will."

Christina heaved the lunch sack through the trapdoor, climbed into the attic, and pulled the ladder up behind her with a *click*.

The morning light shone in hazy stripes through the slats of the air vent and outlined the cracks in the small door to the roof. Taft was still there, hunched over the telescope, but he had discarded the broken-backed chair and was standing on a child's dresser instead. Skid marks showed where he had dragged it across the floor, and a pile of sheets lay crumpled where he had tossed them in search of a sturdy piece of furniture.

Christina hadn't bothered to look under the dust covers before. She had assumed it was just old furniture under the sheets—and it was. But it was *her* old furniture. The child's dresser that Taft stood on was painted with a row of yellow ducks that she had seen before. Over against the wall was a crib, and next to the crib was a rocking chair.

Christina trailed her fingers across its carved wooden back and down curved spindles to the sturdy arms of the rocker. This must have been in her nursery once. Her mother had sat in this chair, rocking—

"Hey!" Taft jumped down from the dresser and crossed to the service door in three leaping strides. "The kids are out in the orphanage yard. Come *on!*"

CHAPTER 11

HAPPY HAPPY ORPHANS

TAFT clambered across the slanted roof to the gargoyle that stood twisted open, the door behind it a dark rectangle in the morning light. He plunged down the gloomy stair and was lost to view.

Christina followed more carefully, annoyed that he had forgotten to duck as he crossed the rooftop. What if someone on the ground had been looking up? He could have ruined everything.

She wasn't any happier when she reached the bottom and heard his footsteps echoing far ahead in the dimly lit tunnel. She took off at her fastest pace, the lunch sack banging her leg at every step, but she couldn't catch up. She didn't even have time to rattle the latch of the big square wooden door as she passed. Of course it must still be locked, but she would have liked to have made *sure*. And why was Taft in such a hurry, anyway? The orphans weren't going anywhere.

But maybe they were. Christina emerged from the tunnel into leafy green light, blinked, and crawled up behind Taft, who was crouching in the bushes. Ahead, past the barbed and electrified fence, five columns of ragged children stood waiting in the circular driveway that looped past the orphanage. The yard boss, the man with the short bristly hair, paced in front of the columns, looking at his watch.

"I hope they're not waiting for the garbage truck," said Taft worriedly. "Danny likes to sing, and I always had to remind him to sing the wrong notes. I hope he remembers, that's all."

"Where *is* Danny?" whispered Christina.

Taft's eyes scanned the ranks of orphans, back and forth. "There. Fourth column, back row."

Christina could see him now, one of the taller boys, his head noticeably large even from this distance. She glanced at Taft, and hesitated. "What's wrong with him?"

Taft frowned and muttered something that she could not hear.

"Was he born like that?" Christina persisted. She didn't want to be rude, but she really wanted to find out.

Taft squinted narrowly at her through his dense lashes. "I don't know," he said, looking annoyed. "He was like that when they brought him on the truck from the city. Why should *you* care? Nobody else does."

Christina blinked. Sometimes she thought Taft was getting nicer, and then all of a sudden, he was mad again for no reason.

"Once I heard somebody say it was 'water on the brain.' But I don't know what that *means*. Nobody explains things in there." Taft jerked his chin in the direction of the pale brick building that squatted in the clearing like a large square mushroom.

"You're lucky to live with a scientist. I bet all you have to do is ask your father anything you want to know, and you'll get an answer."

"Sometimes a very *long* answer," Christina said cautiously.

"At least you've got a father," said Taft, a flush rising in his neck. "Anyway, so what if Danny's a little slow? He's *good*. And he tries harder than anybody."

"Listen, I didn't mean—" Christina began, but the whine of a powerful engine cut her off.

The yard boss blew his whistle. The slumping shoulders of the orphans straightened to attention. And as a long black car pulled up with a crunch of gravel and its tinted window rolled down, their wavering voices rose in what sounded— improbably—like a cheer.

Give me an *L*! (*clap, clap*)
Give me an *L-E*! (*clap*)
Give me an *L-E-N-N-Y*, and then a Loompski!
  (*stomp, stomp*)
He's the Happy Orphans' daddy
(He's a goody, not a baddy),
When we see him we're so gladdy—
Lenny Loompski! (*clap, stomp*)

The car door opened. A gray-trousered leg (the trousers were a little tight) kicked out, followed by the sausagelike body of Lenny Loompski. He straightened, his mirrored sunglasses glinting, and moved his head slowly back and forth, scanning the ranks of orphans.

"Who," he rasped, "composed that poem?"

The yard boss tapped his hands nervously together. "Didn't you like it? I picked the one I thought was best, but if you'd rather hear another"—he snapped his fingers at the nearest orphan. "You, there! Recite the poem you composed in Mr. Loompski's honor!"

A small boy stepped forward, twisted the end of his ragged shirt between his hands, and piped, "Loompski, Loompski, he's our man, if he can't crush you, no one can—"

Lenny put up a hand. "No, I liked the first one. That was a real Happy Orphan welcome, Crumley!"

Crumley bobbed his bristly head some ten or twelve times. "*All* our orphans are happy orphans, Mr. Loompski."

In the bushes, Taft glanced bitterly at Christina. "They wouldn't dare be anything else."

Lenny put his hands on his hips and stood with his legs apart. "But *which* happy orphan composed this splendid poem in my honor, I wonder?"

"Here, you!" the yard boss shouted, and a slight girl with tangled brown curls stepped forward to stand at the front of the line, her eyes dark in her pale face.

"But what's this? She's not *smiling*!" roared Lenny Loompski, with a jolly laugh that echoed against the bricks.

The girl swayed as his voice blasted. She stretched her lips over her teeth and turned up the corners with her fingers.

"What's your name, little orphan?"

The girl looked up. "Dorset," she said, her voice high and unsteady.

Lenny patted her on the head with several blunt thumps.

"And you wrote that poem all by yourself? Just for Lenny Loompski?"

Dorset staggered slightly and nodded, her smile still frozen in place.

"Because?" urged Lenny Loompski, bending over her until his sunglasses almost touched her face.

Dorset shut her eyes. "Because you're a wonderful wonderful person," she recited, "and . . ." She faltered and appeared to swallow hard. "And we *love* you, Mr. Loompski."

"Good, good! And . . . anything else?"

Dorset glanced at the orphan behind her, who leaned forward to whisper in her ear. "Oh! And when you win the Karsnicky Medal, everyone else will know how wonderful you are, too."

Lenny Loompski chuckled and turned to the yard boss, his fat cheeks bunched. "See that Dorset gets a special treat today. Here at the Happy Orphan Home, we *reward* creative writing!"

"Yes, sir!" Crumley stood up straighter. The girl's smile became real. The ranks of children moved restlessly.

Hidden in the bushes, Christina turned to Taft. "She can't *really* love him?"

"Of course not," whispered Taft. "But she knows she'll get extra food if she pretends." He shrugged. "I've written a few poems for Lenny Loompski, too. Only I could never bring myself to say he's going to win the Karsnicky Medal. He's not even a *scientist*."

"So Dorset's special treat is—"

"Tonight, at least, she won't go to bed hungry."

Outraged, Christina glared at Lenny, at the yard boss, at the shabby starveling children. No wonder Taft was mad all the time. She was starting to feel furious herself.

Lenny, though, seemed terribly pleased. He flung out his arms, his flat face pink. "Is that how you really feel?" he cried. "Do you *all* think I'm wonderful?"

"You're wuuuuuuunderful, Mr. Loompski!" bellowed all the orphans together.

"Then here's another special treat for *everyone*—an extra hour of school, right now, *before* you collect trash!"

The orphans raised a ragged cheer, waving their thin arms in the air.

"You can type in *all* your poems on the computer," Lenny said, raising his voice, "and print them out for me. I'll be able to see just how much you admire your Happy Orphan Daddy!"

He started his car and drove slowly toward the electrified gate, waving out the window like a president on parade. The gate clanged behind him, the horn blasted a last farewell, and the snarling black car disappeared up the mountain road.

The yard boss barked an order. The orphans turned, line by line, and filed up the front steps. Danny followed, looking eager, but Crumley pulled him out of the line.

"Not you."

Danny lifted his heavy head. "But I don't push in line . . . and I can sharpen my own pencil . . . and I know A . . . B . . . C."

"Well, sometime you might learn D, too, but not today. Today I want you to scrub plastic toys. There's a whole pile out back in the wheelbarrow. Get your bucket, boy." The bristle-headed man slapped him on the back and disappeared through the large double doors, whistling between his teeth.

Christina glanced at Taft. His face was pale, and his fists were clenched.

"He wants to learn just as much as anybody," Taft said, very low. "More. It's not *fair*."

Christina watched as Danny lumbered around the corner of the large brick building, bucket in hand. She didn't really understand why the orphans were so eager to have lessons—she wouldn't mind if she had fewer, herself—but she supposed that if she had to work instead of learn, she might prefer to learn.

Taft elbowed her in the ribs. "Come on. He's going around to the back. There's a place near the stream where the fence comes up close."

Christina wriggled after Taft through the weeds. "But what if he tells someone he's seen us? Can he keep a secret?"

Taft shook his head. "We won't show ourselves. I just want to see if he's okay. You know, see if he's got any bruises."

CHAPTER 12

WHAT DANNY FOUND

CHRISTINA lay flat on her stomach among some weeds on a little rise of ground and looked between the humming strands of the electric fence to the swirling water just beyond.

The stream, coming from some source higher up the mountain, twisted and turned behind them with a rush of foam. But as it approached the flatter land near the orphanage, it calmed, spreading out into a small, irregular pool fringed with reeds and tall stalks with purple flowers. The water still moved and eddied, but sluggishly, and in one spot a flat, jutting boulder had created a backwash, a place where leaves and half-submerged branches and other detritus piled and stuck fast, leaving the stream free to take up its course again on the other side. Farther on, the land sloped and the stream became noisy once more as it ran down the mountain, joined with other rivulets, and became at last the river that flowed like a blue and gray snake winding through the valley town of Dorf.

Danny climbed out onto the boulder, his bucket banging at his hip.

"There's a good place to dip his bucket on the other side of the rock," Taft whispered in Christina's ear. "I only had to show him that once, and he never forgot it. If it's anything he can do with his hands, Danny remembers."

Christina could see that the jutting boulder, which set up a logjam for trash on the near side, was balanced by a swirl of deeper water on the far side. But Danny sat down, pulled something white and purple out of his pocket, and began to dance it up and down his arm.

"Is that a . . . *bath* toy?" Christina glanced at Taft, who looked embarrassed.

"It's a rubber cow," he mumbled. "I saved it from the trash for him once. He sleeps with it every night."

The cow was back in Danny's pocket. Now he lay on the boulder with his feet hanging over the deep water and reached his hand down into the piled river trash.

"What's he doing?" Taft popped his head up. "No, Danny! Put that down—that's glass. You'll cut yourself!"

Danny opened his hand with a guilty start, his mouth falling open. "Taff!" He scrambled to his feet and stood on the boulder, irresolute, his arms hanging. "Why are you over there, Taff? You went away on the truck!"

"I got free, Danny. Get down! Pretend you're getting water. Somebody might be watching from the windows!"

Danny sat down obediently and picked up his bucket. "You went on the truck and then you got free?" He blinked twice, looking at his friend.

"Yes, that's right. Now dip the bucket, Danny. Get some water and don't look over here. What were you doing, picking up glass? You know I've told you never to do that!"

Danny, his tongue between his teeth, lowered the bucket carefully into the deep water and let it fill.

"I thought you weren't going to show yourself," murmured Christina.

Taft turned, exasperated. "What, you want to let him bleed to death?"

"He wasn't bleeding at all. He was just picking up a—" Christina peered through the weeds. The narrow cylinder Danny had found lay on top of the pile, glinting in the sun.

"It's a test tube," Taft said disgustedly. "Somebody at the lab farther upstream must have dumped a bunch long ago, because they all ended up buried in that pile. Danny fished around in it once and found a broken one, and he almost *did* bleed to death before I found him."

"Oh." Christina squinted at the test tube. She could see the crack in it from where she was, and the jagged top edge. Taft had been right to stop Danny, but—would Danny know enough to keep the secret? Or would he tell that he had seen Taft?

Danny pulled up the sloshing bucket and turned his head carefully sideways. "Are you coming back, Taff?"

"I will sometime, Danny. When I can find a place for us. Then we'll both be free. But until then, no more glass, you understand?"

Danny's eyes clouded. "Not even in my pocket?"

"*Especially* not in your pocket," said Taft.

"But it says A . . . B . . . C," Danny said. "I can *read* it, Taff."

Taft narrowed his eyes until his lashes looked like a fringe. "*Danny*," he warned.

Danny's hand went guiltily to his jacket pocket. "You said I could hide things, Taff."

"I said you could hide the rubber *cow*. Show me what else you have."

Slowly, reluctantly, Danny pulled out his hand. On his palm lay a test tube, unbroken, with a black stopper at one end.

"Throw it here," said Taft in a terrible voice. "Danny, Danny, what if you'd cut yourself again and I wasn't there to help you?"

"I'm sorry, Taff," said Danny, and his eyes welled up with tears. "I just wanted to practice my A—"

Christina yanked at Taft's elbow. "Someone's coming!" she hissed.

Taft ducked back into the weeds. "Don't tell anyone I was here, Danny!" he said urgently. "Just wait for me and I'll get you free!"

Danny nodded, mumbling something that sounded to Christina like "truck" and "free," and then lifted his bucket as the girl named Dorset approached.

"What's the matter, Danny?" She held out her hand to help him clamber down from the boulder. "The boss wants to know why you aren't working. We can never play with the toys, you know."

"I know," said Danny. He smiled at her. "I'll start now. But first I got to throw something."

He wiped his eyes and turned. "I sure hope somebody finds this who knows their A . . . B . . . C . . . ," he said loudly, and threw the test tube across the water in a high, turning arc.

Christina went hunting for the test tube as soon as Dorset had gone back inside.

"What's the point?" asked Taft, watching Danny in the distance as he scrubbed a heap of small plastic toys and laid them in a cardboard box. "It's just an old test tube. I can't believe those scientists dumped them in the stream. You'd think they'd know better."

"But Danny said it had an ABC on it. What's that about? I wonder." Christina, who had followed the test tube's flight with her eyes, reached under a clump of bushes and felt around.

"Don't scientists label their test tubes on the outside, so they know what chemicals are on the inside? There were probably other letters on it, too, but those are the only ones Danny knows." Taft rummaged in the lunch sack.

"Save some for Danny," said Christina over her shoulder. "We can toss him a couple of sandwiches when he comes to get his next bucket of water."

"Okay," said Taft, his mouth already full. "Hey, maybe that tunnel of Leo Loompski's would be a good place for Danny and me. If I could get work with somebody in town, I could earn enough for food."

Christina's hand closed on something smooth and narrow. "There were some workmen who fixed our roof," she said. "Gus and Jake. Maybe they could use a helper. They kept saying they were too fat to get into the narrow places."

"Well, I'm skinny enough," said Taft, who had finished one sandwich and was digging in the sack again. "Isn't there *any* pie in this lunch?"

Christina did not answer.

Taft crawled through the undergrowth to where she was. "Here. Have a sandwich."

Christina sat motionless, looking at something in her hand.

"Did you find Danny's ABC?"

Christina turned. She let the test tube and its black rubber stopper fall into her lap, and released the edges of a piece of paper. It curled up, as if it had been tightly rolled for a very long time.

Taft took the paper and flattened it on the ground. He saw at once Danny's capital A-B-C, written in a slanting, clear script. But there were other letters, too. The *A* was followed by *dnoid*, the *B* by *eth*, the *C* by *hristina*. And in between those words were other words, words like *trapped* and *cave-in* and *help*, that made Taft stare and swallow hard.

"It's a message from my mother," said Christina, in a voice that cracked.

CHAPTER 13

A HIGH, PIERCING CRY

"HEY! Wait up, will you?" Taft, panting, followed in Christina's wake, the lunch sack bumping at his side.

But Christina continued running up the mountain. She kept the stream on her left as she leapt over rocks and springy tussocks of moss and up slopes dappled with sun and thick with the scent of pine. She had to run, she couldn't slow down; she was so full of emotion that she felt if she didn't move, she would scream.

The creek passed under a bridge on the mountain road, doubled on itself in a long, curving loop, and narrowed. Christina took a shortcut through the water, hopping from stone to stone, and landed on the other side with a satisfying thud. Behind her, muttering under his breath, Taft jumped onto the first stone and slipped.

There was a splash and a muffled cry. Christina looked back as Taft struggled out of the stream, soaking wet.

She was out of breath, anyway—and she had a stitch in her side. Christina sank down, scattering pinecones, her hand to her middle. Taft threw himself damply to the ground and lay there, catching his breath.

"Listen," he said at last, wringing water from his shirt-sleeves. "That note from your mom. It had to be written a long time ago. You can't help her now."

Christina curled up her knees and pressed her chin on her arms.

"She probably wrote a bunch of those messages when she was first trapped in the mountain," Taft went on. "But most of the test tubes broke, and the paper inside was ruined. And they all ended up in the same place—buried in the crud from the stream. That doesn't mean she's alive *now*."

Of course her mother was dead. Christina knew that. But what she hadn't known was *how* Beth Adnoid had died. Not in a laboratory explosion, as she had been told. But trapped in a cave on the mountain somewhere. And Lenny Loompski had lied about it.

"But how did the test tubes get in the stream?" Christina looked at the rushing water. If she followed it long enough, would she come to the blocked cave?

"Here." Taft handed her a sandwich wrapped in plastic. "It's only a little soggy."

Christina shook her head. She couldn't eat. "Let's just go."

They went, but at a slower pace. And when at last they came to the first great boulders at the base of the Starkian Ridge, they saw where the stream came from. Out of a wall of solid rock, much higher than their heads, water poured through a narrow crack. Above it, the crags reared up, gray and steep, and beyond was nothing but blue sky and a high, soaring bird.

Christina felt a great tiredness as she gazed up at the dark wet stone of the cliff, oddly streaked with pink and green. She slipped her hand inside her pocket and felt for the test tube with its rubber stopper, and the small, hard circle of her mother's ring.

Taft pointed to the water where it rushed from the crack. "A little tube could make it out of there," he said. "Not a person, though."

There was an ache in Christina's throat, as if it had been wrapped with a too-tight bandage. She thought of her mother trapped inside the mountain, hopefully floating message after message in carefully sealed test tubes until at last her food ran out. She would have had water from the stream, of course . . . how long did it take to starve to death? Christina wondered dully.

She had run too far, too fast; her legs were trembling beneath her. She sank to the ground, leaned back against the trunk of a large tree, and closed her eyes.

The bark was rough and scaly through her sweatshirt, and the sharp smell of pine filled her nose. Nearby an insect buzzed, and in the distance she could hear the faint cry of a harrier. It was a thin, lonesome sound.

Taft shaded his eyes against the sun. "If the garbage truck really takes the kids up the mountain to break rocks, then they're up there right now. If we could just get to them—"

"There's no point trying to climb the cliff. It's way too steep." Christina picked up one of the smaller gray rocks that littered the ground and traced its pink and green streaks with her finger. Was this the same kind of stone that was in her mother's ring? It looked like it.

"The road goes to the top, probably. We could find it and follow it."

"Sure, but where *is* the road? It's a long time since we passed the bridge." Christina tucked the streaked rock into her sweatshirt pocket, for a souvenir. Her fingers touched her mother's ring and she pulled it out, trying it on, but it was too big even for her thumb.

Well, it could go into the test tube for safekeeping. She didn't want to lose it.

Taft squinted upward at the tallest pine, its sturdy limbs well spaced around the main trunk. "I could climb that tree and get high enough to see the road, I bet."

"I'm coming, too," said Christina. She had always wanted to climb a tree, but the ones in her yard had no low branches.

Climbing a pine was easy, though. Christina reached and grasped and pulled herself up after Taft, setting her feet on branches one after another—it was just like the ladder to the attic. The breeze pulled fine, pale wisps of hair from her braids that tickled her nose and got into her mouth. She blew them off her face and went on climbing, her hands sticky with sap.

When she was even with the waterfall's source, she paused. Yes, the crack was far too narrow for a person. It was barely big enough for a small fish. But now that she was in the tree, she could see a shimmer of moving water farther away, in a deeper cleft. Was there more to the stream, then, higher up?

The pine swayed under the combined weight of two children as Christina resumed her climb and the wind picked up. There was more sun now, and they were above the tops of some surrounding trees. Christina wedged herself near Taft, twisted in her perch, and searched the landscape below. There was the town of Dorf—easy to identify, with its patchwork of colored roofs set in the bend of the river. Halfway up the mountain, she could see the square yellow brick of the orphanage and an occasional glint where the light reflected off the electrified fence.

"There's the road." Taft pointed to a thinning line of birches. "And those buildings way over there must be Loompski Labs."

Christina wished she had brought her binoculars. She could see the rooftop of her own house, but it was surprisingly distant. They had come a long way. It was good the trip back would be all downhill—

Crieeee—eeee!

Taft jerked, startled, and Christina almost lost her grip on the tree. A Starkian harrier, soaring silently on an updraft of warm air, had flown close without their noticing. Suddenly it screamed, plunged, and disappeared below.

Christina wrapped her arms tightly around the trunk and pressed against the warm bark. Too warm, especially next to her stomach, it was almost *hot*—

She yanked the gray rock from her sweatshirt pocket. It was as hot as a just-boiled egg, and in the instant before she dropped it, she saw that the pink and green streaks had intensified in color—the streaks were shimmering, they were *liquid* with color—

They *were* liquid. The rock slipped from Christina's hand. She looked, incredulous, at her palm, glistening now with drops of pink and green.

The rock hissed downward and hit the ground a second and a half later with a flare of orange and a small sharp explosion that shook the tree.

Taft's eyes met hers in disbelief. "How did *that* happen?"

Christina stared at the wisp of smoke rising from the ground. "I don't know! It was hot—you saw it, the streaks were *melted*—"

"That doesn't even make sense!"

"I know, I know! And look, my skin isn't burned at all—"

She looked at her hand. The drops weren't liquid anymore, either. They had cooled and solidified into a sort of gel—no, more like soft plastic—and the colors were dimming, too. She looked at the thin viscous streaks on her palm, utterly mystified.

A harrier screamed, farther away than the first, giving its long, drawn-out cry. Christina, still looking at her hand, gasped aloud. The streaks grew warmer, brighter; they quivered and turned gel-like. Then, as she watched, they cooled again, turning dull and solid once more.

The harrier's cry had melted the rock.

"Unbelievable . . . ," Taft breathed. "Let's get another one and see if it will do it again! You go on down first—you're below me—"

Christina shifted her foot and then stopped. Could she imitate the cry? She thought back, remembering the pitch. It sounded like—yes, a high G-sharp, falling to an F-natural. Maybe *that* was perfect pitch—just knowing what the notes were, without an instrument playing along?

"Go *on*," said Taft impatiently.

"Wait, I want to try something." Christina opened her mouth and gave a high, shrill cry, G-sharp, trailing off to an F. She looked at the pink and green streaks. They seemed a little brighter, but otherwise there was no change.

She frowned. Then her expression lightened as a harrier, seemingly attracted by her call, approached with deep, long wing beats.

Slightly above her, Taft grinned, his eyes alert.

Christina put her hand up so she could watch the streaks and the bird at the same time, and repeated the harrier's call. Her hand tingled slightly but did not grow warm.

Crieeee—eeee! The slender dark bird opened its yellow beak, fixed her with a fierce black eye, and screeched.

Christina ducked as it flew overhead. Her palm was suddenly warm and trembling with liquid color. She held it flat to cool and tried to think.

"Wow." Taft reached down a finger to touch the green streak, yelped, and pulled it back. "It's hot!"

"I *told* you," said Christina absently, staring at her hand. Her pitch had been correct. But there was something more to the harrier's cry, something she couldn't identify. What were the words her father had used—harmonics? Overtones?

Harmony she had studied before. That was when two or more different notes sounded good together. She couldn't remember ever learning about overtones.

But there *had* been something different about the harrier's call. Something more than just the pure notes, a quality that shaded the pitch into something sharp and piercing and forlorn.

"Crieeee—eeee!" Christina tried the sound again, looking at her palm to see if the streaks softened. They didn't.

"Let's climb down," said Taft. "I know where the road is now."

Christina nodded, and as she began her descent, she practiced the call of the harriers, experimenting. But nothing worked.

Then suddenly, as she began another attempt, a branch snapped and she lost her balance.

Her harrier cry was loud with sudden panic. She flung out her hands, but the branches slid by, slipping through her grasp while pine needles lashed her cheek. She banged an elbow, a knee—she hooked her legs over anything they touched—felt branches give, break, then finally hold. She grabbed with both arms for the solid wood of the trunk and clung there, dizzy and trembling.

It was a long way down. Christina shut her eyes, feeling sick, unable to answer Taft's worried calls from above. She tried to calm her breathing, slow the frightened patter of her heart.

Her palm was warm where she had scraped it. No, it was hot, it was *burning*—

Christina looked at her right hand, glowing again with melted rock, dripping now onto the ground beneath, drops popping when they landed, like a string of firecrackers. And suddenly she knew what quality her harrier's cry had been lacking when she'd practiced in the tree, what had been missing until the moment that she fell.

It was the overtone of fear.

CHAPTER 14

PICK ME!

"**S**O *that's* why Lenny Loompski wants orphans who can sing." Taft pushed through the undergrowth and ducked under a low-hanging branch. "He wants kids who can make the streaky stuff melt out of the rock."

"But why? What's it good for?" Christina followed, hoping that he hadn't gotten turned around. They had left the stream far behind, and if they didn't come upon the forest road soon, they'd be lost. And hungry, too—the sack with what was left of their lunch had been forgotten under the pine trees.

Taft shrugged. "It's good for explosions, at least."

"I bet that's what they call zoom. My dad said zoomstones were dangerous to work with." Christina snagged her sleeve on a sharp twig and yanked it away. "But I still don't see what good it is, unless Lenny Loompski wants to make *bombs*—" She stopped, aghast.

"It wouldn't have to be bombs. Stuff that explodes like that—they can turn it into energy. Fuel. And that's worth a lot." Taft surged ahead. "Look, there's the road!"

Christina caught up with him on the forest track and swung into step, her feet scuffing up a fine tan dust. "Hey, that's it! Remember what my father said last night? He said Lenny wanted to turn Loompski Labs into a factory for cheap fuel."

"So singing like a hyena kept me out of the fuel factory— and Danny, too." Taft grinned. "Danny would copy me so well, he'd sound like *two* hyenas."

Christina cocked her head, listening. "Hide!" she urged, tugging at Taft's elbow as the rumbling sound of an engine grew louder.

They ducked down into the undergrowth at the side of the road and waited as the garbage truck with the happy faces chugged past on its way down from the ridge, belching black smoke and leaving a fog of dust in its wake.

Christina looked up as Taft leapt to his feet. Where was he going? The ridge was in the other direction.

She ran to catch up to Taft, who was following the garbage truck down the mountain at a fast trot. He turned, his features blurred by the dust that still hung in the air. "I forgot—to remind Danny—to sing off-key," he jerked out as he ran. "And that truck—is going to the orphanage—I'll bet you anything."

"You can't beat a *truck*," Christina protested, but Taft only increased his speed. Resignedly, she followed on weary legs. At least they were going downhill.

By the time they arrived at the orphanage, exhausted, the selection was almost complete. Christina crept through a stand of ferns to crouch beside Taft, and saw to her relief that Danny was *not* standing in the line of kids waiting to scramble in the hopper.

She stretched out flat, breathing in the rich, musty odors of earth and decomposing leaves. She didn't care if Taft wanted to go back up to the ridge after this—she wasn't going. She was tired, and she wanted her supper. At the thought, her stomach growled. She looked around; the afternoon shadows were growing long. What time was it? She had to get back before she was called for dinner, or someone would go to her room and discover she was missing.

"Can *I* go on the truck?"

Christina stiffened. Was that *Danny's* voice?

Taft's face was horrified. "*No!*" he breathed.

The large-headed boy lumbered closer to the yard boss. "Pick me!" he said, patting his chest. "Pick me, boss!"

The driver smiled broadly, pointing out the window, and the cheap ring on his hand gleamed red in the slanted light of late afternoon. "That's a *real* Happy Orphan, boss. Let him come, why don't you?"

The yard boss shook his bristled head. "Nah. He's only good for scrubbing and sweeping."

"But I want to get free!" Danny protested. "Go on the truck and get free! Like Taff!"

Taft put his face in his hands and moaned softly.

"You can't even *sing*, boy," said the yard boss. "I've heard you. What good would you be up on the mountain?" He loaded a cardboard box into the truck and waved at the driver. "That's all this trip, take 'em away."

The truck driver lifted the children into the hopper. The yard boss turned aside. And suddenly a clear, sweet voice sang one pure note, high and lingering in the still air.

Every head turned. Danny, swaying where he stood, was singing.

The yard boss froze, his mouth open. Slowly he reached in his back pocket and took out the tuning fork Christina had seen once before. He tapped it against a rod and it rang out, silvery and piercing; the exact note Danny had just sung.

"Well, boy, I guess you get your wish!" The yard boss grinned widely, slapped Danny on the shoulder, and propelled him up over the high edge of the hopper.

"Go on the truck, get free!" Danny repeated, putting his glowing face out the back end.

"Yeah, you'll be free all right. Free to work!" said the yard boss. "Get back, get your hands in, or you'll lose 'em!"

The children's hands pulled back instantly. A grinding noise started up.

"No, NOT the red button, you doofus! The *green* button, on your left!"

"Sorry, boss!" Barney called cheerfully. "My bad!"

The ram panel crashed down. The truck started up with a roar. And as Taft stared helplessly from the ferns, the garbage truck carrying his friend chugged through the gates, up the forest road, and disappeared from sight.

"No," said Christina firmly. "We're *not* going back to the ridge. I need to get home in time for supper, or they'll come looking for me, and I'll never get out again." She brushed back the green vines that covered the entrance to Leo Loompski's tunnel and gave Taft what she hoped was a stern look.

"But Danny—" said Taft as she nudged him into the tunnel.

"Look, it's getting late. We won't be any good to Danny stumbling around on the mountain in the dark, tired and hungry."

"He'll be tired and hungry, too," said Taft, very low. "And he won't understand."

Christina took his elbow and steered him down the long tunnel, beneath bulbs that seemed dim after the bright outdoor light. "Let's pack him some food. We'll find him tomorrow, and even if we can't rescue him right away, we can probably throw him something to eat."

Taft nodded, looking slightly happier. "He'd like that pie. Will there be any left, do you think?"

Christina considered telling him that pie didn't toss as well as sandwiches but decided against it. "If there isn't, Cook will have another dessert he'll like just as much. Have you ever had chocolate cake?" She rattled the big, square wooden door as she passed. Still locked.

"No," said Taft. "Is it as good as pie?"

"Better," said Christina.

Their footsteps echoed in the tunnel, up the dimly lit stair, and across the slanting graveled roof of Christina's house.

"Are you going to tell your dad about your mom's message in the test tube?" Taft bent to shut the attic's service door behind him.

Christina was already two rungs down the ladder to her room, but she stopped and rested her elbows on the attic floor. She had been thinking about that.

"No." She looked up at Taft's serious gray eyes with their oddly thick lashes. "Nobody can help her now. And if I tell him, he's going to know I got out, and you can bet I'll never get free again. Besides"—she hesitated. "Lenny Loompski lied about my mom dying in a laboratory explosion. He's probably lying to my dad about what's really happening to the orphans. But he's my dad's boss, and until we know for sure how much my dad really knows—"

"Ask your dad tonight at dinner," Taft urged.

"I can't ask him straight out. He gets mad if I even *mention* the orphans."

"Hint around, then. Get him to talk about his work. He likes that, right?"

Christina groaned. "He'll just start talking about math, and a million things I don't understand—"

"You are so lucky!"

"—and don't even *want* to understand—"

"That's your whole problem." Taft gazed at her intensely, his eyes dark in the dim attic light. "You think it's impossible to understand your dad, so you don't even try. It's like you shut a gate in your mind, or something."

Christina glared at him. "And it's staying shut, thanks. You have no idea how boring he is when he gets going."

"Okay, then, let *me* listen in. You can ask the questions and get him talking, and then you can just—I don't know, glaze out or whatever you do—and I'll do the listening and understanding part."

"What, you want to hide under the bed and hope my dad comes up again? He hardly ever does, you know."

"Then I'll listen in at dinner. There must be some place you could hide me."

Christina thought. There were lots of places she could hide him . . . the hollow bench in the dining room, for one, or the hall cupboard that was hardly ever used . . .

"It's too dangerous," she said. "Someone might see you. And then we're both in big trouble."

"Well, so what if we are?" Taft's voice scaled up. "Danny's up there on that mountain—and so are a bunch of other kids. Maybe your dad knows what Lenny Loompski is up to—"

"I bet he doesn't," said Christina suddenly. "My dad *can't* know how bad Lenny is, or he'd have turned him in to the police. And for sure he doesn't know what happened to my mother."

"But he knows *something*. If we can just find out a little bit more, it might help."

CHAPTER 15

A CRACKPOT THEORY

TAFT was very good at sneaking soundlessly around corners. He got past Nanny's room and the study where Dr. Adnoid, just home from the lab, was reading the paper. He was almost past the overstuffed chair in the front hall when Cook backed through the kitchen door, carrying a stack of plates.

Christina shoved Taft down. By the time Cook turned around, he was crunched behind the chair and Christina was staring fixedly at the portrait just above it.

It was just another Loompski, complete with a medal in a frame. Christina tried to look fascinated by the dough-faced man with the lumpy cheeks.

"That's Larry," Cook said as she passed. "Poor man."

"Was he one of the grandchildren?" Christina positioned herself so that Cook wouldn't see Taft on her way back out of the dining room.

"No—Larry was Dr. Leo's brother," called Cook, over a clattering of china in the next room. "He wasn't much of a Loompski, though."

Christina looked at the portrait with new interest. This must be the brother who wasn't scientific. But still, he had won a medal . . . she looked more closely at the copper-colored disc and read:

Tidiest Desk Award, Grade Three
Dorf Elementary—Everyone's a Winner!

Cook bustled past, digging in the linen closet for napkins. "Larry never had much of a head for science. He was a nice man, though—collected trash for the city of Dorf until he died. He was always very prompt, but I'm afraid all the admiration went to his scientific brothers."

Christina took the napkins from Cook's hands. "I'll fold those," she said. "*And* set the table."

Cook beamed. "I always said you were a helpful child!" She disappeared behind the swinging door.

Christina pulled Taft out, dusty and rumpled, and hurried him into the dining room. By the time Cook returned, Taft was wedged inside the long hollow bench under the window and Christina was setting out forks with a placid air.

At dinner, Dr. Adnoid had little to say. He ate quietly, looking worried and unhappy, and now and then he stared at his fork as if he had forgotten how to use it.

Christina, for her part, was trying to think of questions to ask her father. She couldn't ask about the orphans, or zoom, without making him suspicious. And *anything* she asked him was likely to turn into a discussion of math. But she could almost feel Taft's impatience from the hollow bench beneath the window, as Nanny made sprightly conversation about the difficulties of knitting striped socks and Cook brought up the interesting fact that she had used green peppercorns with the baked chicken.

"Dad?"

Dr. Adnoid looked up, his eyes unfocused.

Christina gave it her best shot. "I was just wondering. Why did you come to Loompski Labs in the first place? What exactly do you do there?"

Dr. Adnoid seemed to collect himself. "Well, Leo Loompski hired me. I'm a physicist, you know, and we were doing work on some rather startling theories of his in quantum mechanics. He hired your mother, too. She was a geologist . . ." His face sagged. The lines around his mouth deepened.

Christina hesitated. "What's quantum mechanics?" She braced herself.

Her father's face brightened. "Quantum mechanics is the study of matter and energy. It's a mathematical construct for predicting the behaviors of microscopic particles—"

Christina could feel her attention start to wander. She shook herself—this time, she was going to *try* to understand, at least—and put a hand on her father's arm. "Dad. Could you make it simpler, please? I'm only ten."

Her father looked surprised. "Oh. Right. Well, see, on a molecular level, things don't work the way you think they will."

Cook began to clear the table. Nanny took her knitting and sat in the next room.

"What do you mean?" Christina asked as Cook clattered the dishes in the sink.

Dr. Adnoid cleared his throat and leaned back in his chair. "You've learned about molecules, haven't you? And atoms?"

Christina nodded. "They're tiny bits, so small you can't see them, and they connect together to make up everything in the universe."

"That's right. And have you learned that matter is mostly made up of space? This table, for example." He smacked his hand flat on the wood.

"It sounds pretty solid to me," said Christina.

"Yes, but that's just because the tiny bits are attracted to each other. They want to stay close to each other—but not so close they touch—and in between, there's a *lot* of space. Trust me on this."

"Okay," said Christina. It was surprising, but so far her brain hadn't gone completely numb. Maybe it was because he hadn't gotten to the point of writing down numbers and making her look at them.

"Now, my hand has a lot of space in between its molecules, too. And every time I slap my hand on the table, like this—"

Christina smiled to herself. Her father's expression was happy and interested again.

"—all the tiny bits in the table bump into the tiny bits that make up my hand, and my hand stops." He looked up, his eyes alight. "But quantum mechanics tells me that if I keep slapping my hand against the table long enough—for billions of years, say—eventually all the spaces would line up just right and my hand would go right through."

Christina looked at the table, and then at her father. "But it probably won't, right?"

"Exactly! It *probably* won't—but it *could*. That's the point, don't you see?"

Christina didn't. She shook her head.

Her father gave a dry chuckle. "Well, quantum theory *is* pretty hard to believe. But amazing things like that happen at the subatomic level all the time. And that's what was so exciting about Leo Loompski's work. See, he believed—"

Dr. Adnoid glanced at Cook, who was just going through the swinging door, and Nanny, visible in the next room. He lowered his voice. "He believed that there were places where these wonderful and strange things were *much* more likely to happen. He looked for places where very ancient rocks had been thrust up from the deepest parts of the earth, places where the fundamental forces of nature—"

He glanced around again as Cook left the room.

Christina leaned forward. "The fundamental forces of nature?" she prompted.

"—were poised to create a critical frequency—"

What was he talking about? Christina wondered.

"—with the vibrations of specific notes of precise pitch, with certain harmonic overtones—"

Christina held her breath.

"—to activate an element that—believe it or not—responded to thought waves."

"*Thought* waves?"

"Well . . ." Dr. Adnoid looked a little embarrassed. "See, Leo Loompski was a genius, but he also was a bit of a crackpot. He liked to work on these crazy inventions now and then—a rocket-powered baby carriage was one, I remember—and he had these odd theories. One of them was the idea that *thought* had vibrations, too, just like light and sound. And if you could tune your thought frequencies, so to speak, to the other vibrations that were going on—if you could focus your thoughts very precisely in just the right way, then . . ."

Christina looked at him, waiting.

Dr. Adnoid fidgeted. "It's hard to explain. At first I kept telling him there was plenty to investigate here on the quantum level—there were lots of exciting new advances in *hard* science that we could make without having to go in for this metaphysical mumbo jumbo. But his nephew Lenny was egging him on, telling him he should write up his research and try to win the Karsnicky Medal a second time. Leo began to leave the main laboratory work for me to supervise and go off on his own. He had your mother helping him up on the ridge, too. She was the one with the specialized knowledge about rocks."

Christina concentrated. "So are you saying," she said slowly, "that in these certain special places, when you have certain rocks and certain sounds and certain very focused *thoughts*—"

Her father nodded encouragingly.

"—that you can just *think* something, and it will happen?"

"Well, if you put it that way, it does sound silly," said her father. "And it's never worked for me. But of course, I don't have perfect pitch—"

He stopped. He pushed back his chair. "Perfect pitching ability," he said loudly, "like in baseball, I mean. That's why I went into science," he added, avoiding her gaze. "I didn't have perfect pitching. Pitch*ing*, you understand."

"I get it," said Christina.

"Anyway, I have work to do," said her father, and went into his study.

Christina glared at his retreating back. Her father explained every incredibly boring detail about numbers and math, but when it came to something interesting, something important, something she actually wanted to *know*, he clammed up.

Perfect pitch, the orphans, her mother's death—he wouldn't talk about any of it, and he didn't want Christina to ask questions, either. He wanted to keep her curiosity shut up behind a gate, too, and for what? Safety?

Christina stalked past her father's closed door. She was getting very, *very* tired of being kept safe.

CHAPTER 16

A VERY SMALL EXPLOSION

"**W**ELL, *that* didn't help much," said Taft, flopping on the attic floor.

Christina plugged a small lamp into the extension cord she had hauled through the trapdoor, and the attic was suddenly lit by a warm glow. "It was interesting, though. I mean, how cool would it be to be able to focus your thoughts and just make things happen?"

Taft made a small, exasperated sound. "Leo Loompski might have been a genius, but your dad's right—he was a total crackpot, too. Just *think* and things will happen? That's not scientific. That's just make-believe." He rubbed his shoulders and scowled. "And did you have to wait three whole hours to let me out? I'm stiff all over."

Christina glanced at him in surprise. "I couldn't help it that Cook decided to polish the dining room silver. And I had to wait for everybody to go to bed, so I could get you something to eat. Or should I have let you starve?"

Taft rolled over and stared at the rafters. "We didn't find

out *anything*," he muttered. "Not about where Lenny takes the kids, or zoom, or anything we can *use*."

Christina stretched her legs into the circle of light on the worn wooden floor and took the plastic wrap off the plate she had fixed for Taft. She was risking a lot, raiding the kitchen all the time. Pretty soon Cook was going to start wondering where all the food was going.

"Here," Christina said, pushing the plate across the floor. "Eat something. You're too grumpy to live. And I thought I did a *good* job getting him to talk. I even understood him, for once."

Taft tore into a piece of chicken, clearly hungry—and then set it down, and looked at her miserably. "Sorry." He rubbed his sleeve quickly across his eyes. "I'm just—you know. Worried."

"About Danny?"

Taft nodded. "He's alone, and scared—"

"He's *not* alone," said Christina. "The other kids are with him." She nodded at Taft's plate. "Why don't you try the chocolate cake? You'll feel better."

Christina watched Taft eat, thinking that Danny was lucky to have a friend. Taft might be rude, at times, but it was easy to understand why, once you got to know him.

Taft set down his fork, took a last drink from the thermos, and lifted his sleeve to wipe his mouth.

"Here," said Christina, handing him a napkin. "Don't use your sleeve, it looks like you were raised in an orphanage."

Taft gave the napkin a startled glance, and took it slowly.

"And don't lick your plate, either," Christina added.

Taft frowned.

"Listen," Christina said, "I'm just telling you. It's good manners."

Taft wiped his mouth in silence and put the napkin down. "They didn't teach us manners at the orphanage," he said slowly. "There's probably a lot they didn't teach us."

Christina hadn't meant to embarrass him. "You're smart, though," she said.

Taft ducked his chin. "I wish I was smarter. I *hate* not knowing stuff." He ran his hands through his hair in frustration. "I wish we could figure out what Lenny is doing with the zoom. And I wish I knew why the kids never come back."

Christina nodded. "And how come they don't run out of kids at the orphanage, if they keep sending more and more of them up to the ridge?"

"I can tell you that," said Taft. "It's because we keep getting new kids from the big city."

"Seriously?" Christina frowned. "But how can kids keep disappearing without somebody wondering what's going on?"

"Good question. But have you noticed that practically everybody in Dorf thinks Lenny Loompski is wonderful? Maybe they just don't want to ask any embarrassing questions."

Christina shook her head. "I never meet anybody from Dorf, unless they come to the house. And I hardly knew there *was* a Lenny Loompski before yesterday."

Taft looked pleased to know something that Christina didn't. "Well, we collected trash all over Dorf—trash, and recycling, and lately we're even going to garage sales to buy up any little plastic toys they have—"

"Like the ones Danny was scrubbing?" Christina interrupted. "Are they for you guys to play with?"

Taft looked at her in disbelief. "Are you kidding? We just sort them and clean them and put them in boxes. Then somebody loads them in the truck's cab, and a bunch of kids climb in the hopper, and that's the last we see of the toys. *Or the kids.*"

Christina was silent, digesting this.

"Anyway, everywhere we collect trash, people talk to the driver and say how great Lenny Loompski is, and how he's the nicest Loompski of them all, and how lucky the town is to have such a generous benefactor."

"Generous?"

Taft nodded. "He makes us pick up people's garbage—and he doesn't charge them for it. And he gives to the policemen's fund, and he buys extra equipment for the firefighters, and he donates hundreds of books to the library. Not the *orphanage* library," he added bitterly.

"Didn't you ever tell anyone what Lenny was really like?"

Taft snorted. "Ever try to tell grown-ups something they don't want to hear?"

Christina laughed.

"And besides, anybody who talks to one of the townspeople gets put on the next truck to the mountain, whether they can sing or not." Taft fiddled with his fork and put it down again with a clatter. "But that's not important now. We've got to make a plan to rescue Danny."

"Well, we need to find him first. And we should figure out where you can take him afterward, too." Christina glanced quickly at Taft. She had talked him out of staying in the tunnel and brought him to the attic. But it would be terribly hard to hide Danny in the attic—he might not understand the need to stay quiet. "I wonder if Gus and Jake *would* need some help?"

Taft tapped his fingers against his knee. "When we go looking for Danny tomorrow, we should find out what they're doing with the zoom, too. Your father must know a lot about it—they're working with it in the lab, aren't they?"

Christina nodded. "They've known about it for years and years." She reached into her pocket for the test tube and shook out her mother's ring. "See? This has got a zoomstone. It was my mom's before I was even born."

Taft turned the golden circle in the lamplight. The pink and green streaks stood out beautifully against the polished gray stone. "Can you make the streaks melt again?"

"Maybe." Christina rubbed the stone with her finger. "I don't want to ruin the ring, though. I'm not even supposed to have it."

Taft handed her the ring. "I wonder if you can control it, though. What if you just turned it to gel and then stopped? If it didn't liquefy all the way, it wouldn't hurt anything, right?"

"Well . . ."

"Come on. It would be a scientific experiment."

Christina was tempted. She probably could do it. She would try to put a little fear in her voice, but not as much as when she had lost her grip in the tree. And of course she would have to do it softly.

"*Crieee-eee!*" she sang in a thin thread of sound, G-sharp, falling to F, as she thought about what would happen if she were caught sneaking food. That added some fear, but no actual terror, and she watched with pride as the streaks brightened, trembled, started to liquefy—and then gelled and hardened once more. Perfect.

"Let me try." Taft reached out. "What was that first note again?"

Christina sang a high G-sharp, very quietly and exactly on pitch.

Taft held the ring close to his mouth. "*Crieee-eee!*"

Christina shook her head. Taft's cry sounded lonely and fearful enough, but the pitch was off. "That's not—" she began, and then stopped, aghast. The stone was smoking.

As they watched in horror, it emitted a sharp *POP!* Christina flinched as tiny fragments hit her cheek.

The smoke cleared away, leaving a smell like burnt orange peels. Where the stone had been was now only an empty hollow, a charred oblong in the gold circle.

"I sang the exact same notes you did!" Taft sounded near tears.

Christina couldn't take her eyes from the ruined ring. "No. You were flat."

"I *wasn't.*"

"Yes, you were," said Christina with the calmness of despair. "You were a quarter-step below the tone. I could hear it."

"I didn't mean to," said Taft. He ducked his chin inside his collar and looked at her worriedly. "I must have gotten close enough to the right frequency so the vibrations started to work, but not quite in the right way."

Thought had vibrations—that's what her father had said Leo Loompski believed. And if you could focus your thoughts exactly right, you could . . . what?

Christina cupped the ring between her two palms. The empty blackened setting stared up at her, and an edge of uncharred gold winked in the lamplight.

Well, all the focused thoughts in the world weren't going to fix exploded jewelry, no matter what Leo Loompski believed. Christina slid the ring into her sweatshirt pocket. She could get mad at Taft, but what good would that do?

Taft hunched his shoulders. "Your dad told Lenny Loompski that zoom was unstable. This must be what he meant."

Christina nodded. No kidding.

"With the exact right pitch, though," Taft went on, "it would be safe."

"It's not *that* safe. The drops explode when they hit the ground, remember?"

"Yes, but if you were careful not to let the drops actually hit anything? What if you just let the liquid slide gently into a jar, or something?"

Christina considered this. "It'd be okay as long as you didn't drop the jar, I bet."

Taft gave a short laugh. "A whole jarful would probably be like a small bomb."

Christina caught her breath at the thought. A small bomb might explode with orange light. A small bomb would make a muffled boom, could even shake her house . . .

"I bet that's what happened on the ridge last night," she

began, and then saw by Taft's stricken look that he had realized it, too.

"I'm going to sleep now," said Taft, his voice strained. "I'm leaving first thing in the morning. I'm getting Danny off that ridge, no matter what."

Christina sat gloomily on her bed. She pulled the green scrapbook off the shelf and opened it. Just seeing her mother's handwriting made her feel better somehow. She turned the pages until she came to her seventh year.

That was the year she had started music lessons with Mrs. Lisowsky. She had learned to read notes and play some simple tunes on the piano and count the beat. Christina took out her markers and drew a piano, and a girl with blond braids sitting on the bench playing, and a tiny woman who looked a little like a redheaded bird off to one side.

She held the book at arm's length to admire her drawing. A piece of paper slipped out from the back, where it had been left loose, and Christina picked it up off the floor. It was a sheet of music, written out in blue ink, and the handwriting was her mother's.

The title at the top said simply "Lullaby," and the line below said "To be sung to 'Largo,' from the *New World Symphony*, by Antonin Dvořák." Christina read it through, following the notes on the staff with her finger.

Her mother had written it for her; that much was clear, for it began, *Little one, child of mine*. Christina hummed the tune, and then, in a whisper, she sang it all the way through.

She held the paper for a moment, smiling down at her mother's words. Then she tucked the lullaby back in the scrapbook, and with it the message from the test tube, carefully flattened. Last, she looked at her mother's ring once more.

She would keep it safe. Someday maybe it could be fixed, and in the meantime, perhaps her father wouldn't think to look for it.

She opened the big wooden box that held her mother's jewelry, and the three tiers popped up. Christina couldn't bear to put the ruined ring in one of the velvet-lined compartments—she would see it every time she lifted the lid. So she put it in the bottom of the box, along with the loose necklaces and fingernail clippers and various odds and ends. She tucked it way in the back, under a pile of old keys—house keys and car keys and small luggage keys and one big brass key.

Christina turned the brass key over on her palm. It was strangely heavy in her hand and edged with green where it had tarnished. It looked like the kind of key that could open the door of a cathedral or perhaps a castle—

Or maybe a large square door with an old-fashioned lock.

She sat perfectly still, feeling a sudden clutch of excitement high in her stomach. Tomorrow they were going to go rescue Danny—but tonight, right this minute, she could try the key. The tunnel was lighted, and even if it wasn't, she had a flashlight.

CHAPTER 17
AT THE END OF THE TUNNEL

TAFT came with her, of course. "It might be a good place for Danny and me," he said. "It could be like an air-raid shelter, or something."

Christina passed by her mother's old rocking chair on her way out of the attic and trailed her fingers over the carved wooden back. Secretly, she hoped that the door led to Leo Loompski's private laboratory. Her mother had been working with Leo, her father had said, and clearly her mother had a key . . .

Taft closed the service door behind them. "Hey, if it *is* an air-raid shelter, maybe it will be stocked with food!"

Christina shone her flashlight down the long stair from her roof to the tunnel. She had grabbed some emergency supplies on her way out—the jackknife from her mother's jewelry box, a pack of Life Savers—but a few pieces of candy weren't going to last long, the way Taft ate. She doubted that the underground room was stocked with food, but it would certainly solve one problem if it were. It was hard enough to feed one boy—she could only imagine trying to feed Danny, too.

They stood in front of the wide wooden door. A string of lightbulbs, some burnt out, stretched along the back wall of the tunnel on either side like a row of broken teeth. Christina pulled the tarnished key from her pocket and fumbled at the shadowed lock. The key slid in with a scraping sound.

"Hurry up, can't you?" Taft was hopping with impatience.

"Stand out of my light," said Christina, struggling to turn the key in the stiff lock. The resistance gave way suddenly, and there was a distinct, metallic *snick*.

She pushed the door all the way open and shone her flashlight inside. The narrow beam played along rough stone walls, quite unlike the smooth, manmade tunnel behind them. Christina stepped inside and ran her hand over the rock. Yes, someone had wired it for electricity—there was a light switch, in a metal box—but when she flipped it, nothing happened.

"It's not a room at all—it's a cave!" said Taft.

Christina hesitated. The cave was vast and dark, and the rock hung overhead in great, wicked lumps that looked as if they might fall at any moment. And there might be bats. Her hand wavered slightly, and the shaft of light danced along the stone, throwing huge, trembling shadows.

"Can I have that for a minute?" Taft took the flashlight and moved forward.

Christina glanced back through the door. Behind her, the familiar corridor with its regularly spaced lightbulbs looked safe and beckoning.

"Hey! Are you coming or not?" Taft called. He stopped, half turned, yellow light illuminating the underside of his chin. "This cave goes a *lot* farther in!"

The cave went on and on. It twisted here and there, as if it were a river, and every so often, smaller rivulets went off in side passages. But as they continued on, the main tunnel also began to be littered with interesting bits of clutter. It looked as if someone had used it for storage.

Taft, intent on exploring to the end, kept forging ahead, sweeping the flashlight from side to side. Christina followed closely, trying not to look up at the curving walls and heavy ceiling of stone. But in spite of the frightened feeling she got whenever she thought about how many tons of rock were suspended above them, a part of her still wanted, like Taft, to go on and see what was at the end. Maybe there would be something there that her mother had left long ago.

Taft stopped suddenly. Christina pulled up short just in time to avoid running into him. "Why did you stop?" she began, and then she saw.

The cave had widened into a vast room, and all around them were more of the leftover objects: bulky forms half covered with sheets, high metal benches with test tubes and microscopes stacked on them, and everywhere piles of paper, old and brittle, with curling, broken edges.

"My turn for the flashlight," said Christina, and she shone it behind canisters and jars, under benches and on drawings of inventions inked in thin blue lines on large sheets of paper. "Hey—this *was* Leo Loompski's old laboratory!"

Taft lifted one of the drawings and held it to the light.

"That guy was *nuts*," he said. "Look at this. A rocket-powered baby carriage. Some baby was going for a *ride*."

"Dad talked about that one, remember?" Christina shone the beam on another piece of paper. "Look at this. 'Zoom Skates.' And this." She pointed at a drawing of a large catapult with what looked to be a child with a backpack sitting in the basket.

"Kidapult," read Taft. "Avoid the crowded school bus. Fling yourself to school and float down for a soft landing every time!"

Christina laughed. "It's like he remembered what he wanted when he was a kid and then he invented it." She studied the careful printing in the lower right-hand corner that read *Leo Loompski*. "I can see why my dad got impatient with him, though. This isn't exactly important scientific research."

"Maybe old Leo got tired of serious science all the time," Taft said. "I mean, look at this stuff—it's crazy, but it's *cool*. A hovercraft merry-go-round. A little plane . . ."

Christina walked ahead. Where were her mother's drawings? Where had her mother done her experiments?

The dust, suddenly thicker than ever, swirled at her feet, sandy particles with a soft, ashy feel. Christina coughed. She put up an arm to cover her mouth, and the flashlight's beam swung wide, illuminating not cavernous space but solid rock. The cave had ended. A pile of rubble filled it from floor to ceiling.

"Wow, a cave-in!" Taft darted forward. "Look, the ceiling came right down on top of everything, equipment and all—"

Christina suppressed a shudder. Her arm sank down.

"Oh," said Taft, from the darkness ahead.

There was a long silence. Far in the distance, there was a

faint murmuring gurgle that might have been water passing over rock.

Taft stepped back through the ashy dust and took the flashlight from Christina's hand. He played its dimming beam over every foot of the rock slide, then handed it back, gently.

"There's no way through," he said.

Christina did not answer. She did not want to talk about what might lie on the other side of the cave-in.

Taft seemed to understand, for he turned and began to poke around the sheet-draped equipment, lifting corners to see what was underneath. "I wonder if Leo Loompski ever built any of those inventions he drew, or if they're all just on paper?"

Christina shone the flashlight on Taft. "Let's go back now."

"Okay," said Taft. He let go of a sheet corner that hung above a curve of burnished metal and sneezed as the dust flew up. "Anyway, this is a bunch of old equipment. Nothing too interes—"

The sheet slipped to the floor.

Christina took in a sudden breath. Before her, gleaming in the tea-colored beam of light, was a silvery, smooth, perfect little craft.

It rested on small rubber wheels. Its body was like a polished metal watermelon, extra-large. It had two red-leather seats, one in front of the other, and a windscreen, and tail fins, and two beautifully curved wings. It was the plane in Leo Loompski's drawing, and it was just their size.

"*Wow*," breathed Taft. "Do you suppose it can really fly?"

There were no real controls. There was a speaker phone sort of thing—a funnel on a tube—and a cap that unscrewed and seemed to lead to a fuel tank, but no throttle, no rudder pedals, no joystick.

"And no airspeed indicator," mourned Taft. "It's not really meant to fly. It's only a model."

Christina sat down to leaf through the drawings that Taft had let fall, found the diagram of the plane, and shone her flashlight on the instructions.

"After initial activation," she read aloud, running her finger under the first line of print, "sustain tone until replicated."

She glanced at Taft, but he looked as puzzled as she felt. She went to the second line. "Lights. Fundamental Frequency." She moved her finger again. "Hold the light for me, will you?"

"It's getting dimmer," said Taft.

Christina peered at the next two lines. "Prime Fuel Chambers: Raise to the Third. Set Internal Switches: Raise to the Fifth."

Taft moved the flashlight so it almost touched the writing. Its fading beam illuminated the fifth line. "Hey, it says 'Ignition'!" cried Taft. "It *does* fly! We just have to figure out how—"

His voice broke off as the feeble light in his hand diminished sharply, gave a last weak flicker, and blinked out. They were plunged into darkness.

CHAPTER 18

LIGHT IN THE DARK

IT was more than darkness, it was blindness. It was blacker than anything Christina had ever known, and it had weight that pressed on her eyeballs. She moved her hand in front of her face—she touched her nose—and saw nothing at all.

Something came down on her arm. Christina nearly screamed.

"It's just me." Taft's hand groped for her wrist. "Get out the spare batteries and we'll switch."

Christina felt her face flush red under cover of darkness.

"No," said Taft. "No, no, no. *Don't* tell me you didn't bring any fresh batter—"

"I didn't bring any." Christina tried to speak lightly, as if this were an amusing mistake. She gripped her knees with her hands to keep them still. She tried very hard not to panic.

Taft didn't sound panicked—he sounded mad. "Even *I* know you don't go into a dark tunnel without extra batteries for your flashlight." He sighed deeply. "All right. We'll just have to walk out. We'll keep the wall on our left and keep touching it."

"But there were side tunnels, *lots* of them—"

"Look, I know. But what else can we do? Stay here forever? It's not going to get any lighter."

This was not a cheering thought.

"Anyway, the side tunnels were smaller. We'll be able to figure it out. Come *on.*" He felt for her hand and tugged.

Christina tried to get up, but her knees would not hold her. "Just—give me a minute," she said, breathing quickly.

"What's the matter? Scared?" Taft sat down beside her.

Christina didn't want to answer. The solid darkness seemed to press on her shoulders. She had been afraid ever since she had seen the heavy rock hanging overhead, but now that there was no light at all, it was even worse. She imagined the rocks settling, giving way, crashing down on her . . .

"Listen." Taft squatted next to her, his voice calm and steady. "The way to keep from being afraid is to think of something else. I should know—I've had lots of practice."

Christina was at the ragged edge of terror, but Taft's matter-of-fact tone did her good. She sat on the cave floor, holding tightly to his sleeve, and shut her eyes. If she shut her eyes, she could pretend it was night in her room. She could think of something else besides the fact that they were stuck in a cave, deep underground, with no light—

It was impossible to think of anything else.

All right, then. The other way to keep from being afraid was to face what you were afraid of. Christina tipped her head back and stared into the darkness above, sweating. She couldn't see them, but she knew the rocks were there. Let's see . . . she could think of them as strong, instead of heavy. As if they were holding everything up, instead of ready to fall. As if—

She blinked. There was a pinprick of light, directly above.

Was it her imagination? She moved a few inches to the left, and it disappeared. Back to the right, and there it was again.

"Taft. Look up."

"What?"

"Do you see it? The light?"

Taft's clothes rustled and he grunted slightly as he got into position. He put his head next to hers. "Nope."

"Move over a little. Here, like this." Christina moved farther to the right to give him room.

"Holy cats," said Taft, low and with feeling. "It's a *star*."

"You sure?" Christina squinted.

"Look at it. There's got to be some kind of opening, high up in the roof of the cave. And in the morning there'll be sun coming in."

Christina watched the star, mesmerized. It pulsed faintly, twinkling an immeasurable distance away.

"It's like my mother's song," she said, almost to herself.

"What song?"

"Just this lullaby she wrote for me . . . I found it in the scrapbook."

"Oh." There was a pause. "So, was it just for babies? Or was it for kids, too?"

"Kids, too, maybe," said Christina, trying not to sound as surprised as she felt. It was funny how Taft could be so calm in a crisis and, in the next minute, sound like a little kid who missed his mom.

Well, maybe he did. Maybe she did, too, for that matter. In her mind, Christina held again the sheet music and looked at the notes. Quietly, shyly, she began to sing:

> *Little one, child of mine, safely rest tonight*
> *Through the window, shining star touches you with light*

She stopped. "It *is* kind of for babies, I guess."
"I like it," said Taft unexpectedly. "Is there more?"

> *Someday you may wander far, someday you may roam*
> *Someday you may find yourself lost and far from home*

Christina paused and swallowed hard. In a moment, she went on, her voice stronger:

> *Never fear, Mother's near, though just out of sight*
> *Look above, find your star, in the darkest night.*

The last line echoed in the cavern, almost as if another singer had chimed in a fraction late. As the echoes died, Christina could hear a tiny, burbling sound, like that of running water or a small stream.

"Christina," breathed Taft, "look."

Christina turned. A rosy glow, beautifully warm and pink, showed briefly in the dark, not far away. It faded as she watched.

"Sing it again," said Taft urgently. "The whole thing. All the same notes."

Christina did. And saw what Taft had seen.

"It happens when you sing 'star' in the last line." The curve of Taft's cheek was briefly visible in the glow that came again, then dulled. "Sing it again. Just that one note."

Christina took a breath, sang a high G-sharp, and held it for as long as she could. The glow began, softly pink, and quickly intensified to a deep, rich color, gleaming dully through the silvery metal of the plane's body, leaking out in bright fingers from around the edges of the fuel cap. In a side pocket in the rear of the plane, a canister the size of a milk carton glowed pink, too. And then, just as she was about to run out of air, the plane itself began to hum.

They walked back through the length of the cave with the plane rolling between them, each pushing on a wing. The soft glow of the fuel tank through the plane's body, together with the canister in its rigid pouch, threw just enough light for each step forward, and the droning sound that came from the plane was loud enough to discourage conversation.

Christina glanced at the rolled-up drawing she had tucked in the back seat. She would take a closer look at it once they had more light, but for now she was just as glad to think without interruption. The deep hum of the plane, two octaves lower than the note she had sung, vibrated through her finger-tips as she worked out the problem in her head.

First, the plane must run on zoom.

It was too much of a coincidence that a harrier's cry, starting with a high G-sharp, should melt the pink and green streaks in Starkian rock—and that a high G-sharp should, apparently, get the fuel in the tank going, somehow.

And yet the plane *wasn't* going. It was humming—it was glowing—but they still had to push it. It was as if the plane was just getting ready to go, just barely—

"Activated!" she said aloud.

"Huh?"

The plane's drone was dying down, the glow fading.

"I think you've got to hold it," said Taft. "Hold the note long enough so the hum starts."

Christina took a deep breath and sang a long, sustained note, thinking hard. Her father had talked about frequencies—vibrations that were heard as sound—but she had ignored him. It had just seemed like more math that she didn't want to learn. But it had to do with music, too, clearly. And there was something nagging at the corner of her mind, if only she could remember . . .

When they got to the big square door and the lighted tunnel, Christina unrolled the drawing and read the instructions again.

"After initial activation, sustain tone until replicated." Well, she had already done that; the plane was humming nicely.

"Lights. Fundamental Frequency." What on earth was a fundamental frequency?

"Prime Fuel Chambers: Raise to the Third. Set Internal Switches: Raise to the Fifth."

She paused. She *knew* she had heard those terms—a third, a fifth—used together recently. Where? When?

She looked down at the paper and read the next line: "Ignition: Raise to the Minor Seventh," and then she knew.

It was a chord!

"Hey!" She thumped Taft on the shoulder. "I've got it!"

"Got what?"

"The instructions. It's a chord. The fundamental frequency is the root, the first note in the scale—like *do* in *do, re, mi, fa, sol,* you know. The third is three notes up, the fifth is five, and then the seventh tone, down one half step, is the minor seventh—"

Taft looked annoyed. "You are making *no* sense at all."

Christina grinned. Taft looked as confused and bored as she felt every time her father talked about math. But this wasn't math, it was music; it was fun, it was *easy.*

Christina shut her eyes, the better to think. Okay, she had the plane activated. Which note would be the root of the chord? She went right up the scale, singing C, C-sharp, D, D-sharp, E—

The plane bucked slightly, as if it had a hiccup.

"Maybe you're supposed to sing into this." Taft grasped the funnel on its striated metal tube and pulled it toward her.

Christina bent over and sang an E into the funnel. The control panel lit up like a Christmas tree. Two lightbulbs in the tunnel went dark.

Of course. Just like her mother's lullaby was written in the key of E.

"Hold that note!" Taft shouted. "Keep singing!"

She couldn't get enough air for a strong tone, bending at the waist. Christina threw a leg up over the plane's curved silver side and scrambled into the front seat. The speaker-funnel was in front of her. She pulled it toward her mouth, sat up straight, and held the note, loud and long. Just as she was about to run out of breath, the plane's hum became two-toned, taking over Christina's E and making it stronger, deeper. The plane's rosy glow changed to a fiery orange.

Taft laughed out loud. "Now the next note!" he crowed, and Christina sang it. The orange color shifted subtly into golden, with a gurgling sound of liquid. Three more lightbulbs blinked out.

"Now sing the fifth," Taft prompted. "Set internal switches."

Christina took in another deep breath and sang a B. She could hardly hear anything over the deep sonorous humming, but she could feel through the leather seat a multitude of simultaneous clicks. The yellow color turned greenish. The plane's hum took on a third note, high and harmonious. The tunnel grew darker as the string of lightbulbs flickered one by one down the line, but Taft didn't seem to notice or care.

"Now ignition—the minor seventh!" Taft crackled the paper in his hand, his eyes wide with excitement.

Christina gasped for breath, but she sucked in yet another lungful of air and let loose with a high D.

The chord took on an added tension, a piercing musical

urgency that made Christina long to sing a final E for resolution. The plane trembled beneath her knees, gave back her note with deeper resonance, and the green color shifted to blue. With a soft *whoosh* of air, the craft rose gently and hovered a foot off the floor, in a shimmer of color and expectant sound.

CHAPTER 19

FLY BY NIGHT

"**D**ON'T leave without me!" Taft scrambled over the tail fins and slid into the back seat with a thump. "Okay, I'm ready. Let's go."

"Go where?" Christina raised her voice over the plane's musical drone. "Anyway, I don't know how to fly this thing."

Taft leaned over her shoulder and pointed. "Use the instrument panel. Punch that button."

Christina pressed the circular spot of light with GO across its face, but nothing happened.

"Maybe we missed a step." Taft bent over the drawing again, following the numbered lines with his finger in the vivid violet light.

"Lights, fuel chambers, check. Switches, ignition—ditto. Here we go—Takeoff." He was silent for a moment as he read, and his expression changed.

"What does it say?" Christina turned in her seat and tried to read it upside down.

Taft's mouth twisted sourly. "It says, 'Thought vibrations

complete the fuel circuit. Place helmet on head and strap securely.' *Thought* vibrations," he repeated in disbelief. "It's nothing but a *toy*. It goes up and down, it has pretty colors—and that's all."

Christina didn't want to believe it. She searched the cockpit. There was no side pocket, no glove compartment, and no place big enough to hide a helmet, anyway. Maybe the helmet—if there was one—was still back at the far end of the cave.

She suppressed a shudder. She didn't want to have to go back *there*. It might be easier to just assume Taft was right.

But her father had said that Leo Loompski had been working on the frequency of thought. Maybe he had done it. Maybe he had actually figured out a way to make a person's thought vibrations line up with sound vibrations, and together with the liquid zoom create some sort of power.

She reached under her seat. Were there more instructions there? Yes, there was something; she could feel it but she only succeeded in pushing it farther back.

"I see it." Taft pulled out the object and gave a derisive snort. "Yeah, this is *just* what we need for all our happy thoughts!" He held up a soft, padded helmet, with a strap that went under the chin and two clear, flexible tubes that hung down, ending in couplings.

"Maybe it's for real," Christina suggested. She grasped the ends of the tubes and looked for a place to plug them in.

"Of *course* it's real!" Taft said grumpily, from the back seat. "And so is fairy dust and talking rabbits and magic lamps that grant wishes—"

"Just try it," said Christina. She had found two slots at the base of the speaker tube and pushed the ends in.

"If you insist," said Taft, strapping on the helmet, "but it'll never work. Go. Go. Come *on*, you stupid plane, GO!"

Christina held on, just in case.

Nothing happened.

"See? I told you." Taft took off the helmet. "I mean, give me a break. *Thought* vibrations?"

"Oh, be quiet," said Christina. "Give it to me if you think it's so stupid."

"It *is* stupid," said Taft, unbuckling the strap. "Leo Loompski might have been a genius, but he was off his rocker with *that* theory."

Christina looked at the clear plastic tubes. Thought vibrations did sound pretty lame. How could your thoughts have power? For power, you needed things that moved, like water or wind, or things that were explosive, like gas and gunpowder . . . or zoom.

But sound had power, too—they'd just proven that. Why not thought? Her father had said that, on a molecular level, surprising things happened all the time. She hadn't understood everything he'd said about quantum physics, but certainly thought waves, if there were such a thing, would be made up of even tinier particles than anything else in the world. And if incredible things happened all the time on a molecular level, then how much more amazing and strange would be the things that happened if you went to the level of *thought*?

She strapped on the helmet. All right. If something in the

zoom could respond to the invisible vibration of her thoughts, then she was going to think about nothing but flying. She didn't understand how to do it, not yet, but she wasn't blocking it out of her mind—she wasn't starting by saying it was impossible. She plugged her ears against the sound of Taft's laughter, and focused.

And then Taft stopped laughing. He tapped her on the shoulder and pointed at the flexible tubing hanging from the left side of her helmet.

Christina watched wordlessly as a deep blue liquid moved slowly up its length. She felt the fluid spread through the helmet's padded pockets, cool and with a slight additional heaviness that was not unpleasant. Then, slowly, the blue liquid flowed down through the tube on the right, and back into the plane.

"Try it out," whispered Taft. "Think something."

Christina looked at the control panel, at the button she had pushed. *Go?* she thought tentatively.

The plane stayed still, floating gently above the tunnel floor.

Taft rustled the drawing behind her, holding it open with his elbows. "Wait. Here's one more thing at the end. It says, 'To engage, resolve the chord.' What does that mean?"

Christina knew. She had been longing to finish the chord ever since she had sung the D. She opened her mouth and sang a high E. The blue liquid turned violet. With all her might, she thought, *Go.*

And the plane *went.* It zoomed along the tunnel—blink,

blink, blink-blink-blink went the rest of the lightbulbs, fizzing out as they passed—faster and faster, a rushing wind in their faces and the walls screaming by.

"STOP!" cried Christina, panicked, and almost flew over the windscreen as the plane halted suddenly in midair, just short of the tunnel's end.

There was a sound of rapid breathing behind her as Taft fell back in his seat. "Don't think anything else for a while," said Taft, "okay?"

Christina unstrapped the helmet in a hurry. Just ahead of them was the dark opening into the forest, covered by vines, etched now with violet light. If she hadn't stopped, they would have gone crashing through, maybe lost a wing.

She took a deep breath and studied the instrument panel again. She wasn't limited to just GO and STOP. There were buttons that said SLOW and UP and DOWN, and directional arrows, too.

Maybe those buttons were just to show the possibilities. She hadn't had to push the stop button to stop. She had just shouted it, instinctively.

Slowly, tentatively, she strapped the helmet back on. She patted the side of the plane with a soothing hand.

"It's not a dog," said Taft's strained voice from behind her.

"I'm just getting used to it." Christina looked at the mouth of the tunnel and the hanging vines ahead. *Go on*, she thought gently. *Go slow, don't bump yourself. Give me time to move the vines aside.*

The plane moved forward slowly. On the instrument

panel, a button glowed suddenly brighter—RAISE LANDING GEAR.

Christina repeated the words in her mind and felt a little hitch as the wheels lifted into the body of the plane. She smiled to herself. Maybe the plane itself would teach her what to do, if she paid attention.

The airplane inched through the vines and out into the night, lurching slightly as it cleared a last stubborn branch.

Seat belts? thought Christina, and from the inside wall of the plane, a plastic belt came curving over her midsection and snicked into a port on the opposite wall. Behind her, a second *snick* followed.

"Unreal," murmured Taft. "He thought of everything."

Christina grinned. Inside the cockpit, the instrument panel glowed violet. The plane itself gleamed silver in the moonlight, hanging weightless in the air a few feet above the forest floor. The wood around them was alive with soft night sounds—an owl's distant call, a tiny scurrying in the underbrush, the hushed whisper of leaves rustling in a quiet breeze. The sound of the humming plane was not nearly so loud as it had been in the tunnel.

But it was still too loud for safety. Christina glanced through the trees at the yard light of the orphanage, fifty yards away past the high electrified gate. *Could you be any softer, please?* she thought at the plane, and immediately the hum diminished to a musical purr.

She almost laughed aloud. She could hardly believe her luck. A little plane just her size that would do anything, go anywhere—and a friend to share it! They could fly over the town, they could loop over the river, they could land on the playground at the elementary school and jump on the swings . . .

"I don't *believe* this," Taft said. "It's some kind of weird dream. And why does it work for you and not for me?"

Christina had a moment of doubt. Was it just a dream? It did seem as if it couldn't be real—

The plane dipped suddenly. The pulsing hum skipped a beat. Behind her, Taft sucked in his breath.

No, she couldn't think it wasn't true. The zoom would react.

Christina shook off her doubts. The plane drifted upward. Its hum gained in strength.

She half turned in the red leather seat. "Don't say that again. Don't even think it. This plane runs on my thoughts, and if I think it *can't* fly—"

Taft nodded, still gripping the back of her seat. "Sorry."

"Okay, then." Christina glanced at the orphanage yard, lit and fenced. No one seemed to be coming to investigate, but she had better not push her luck. "Where do you want to go first?"

Taft leaned forward, his face pale. "The Starkian Ridge, of course."

Christina felt a little ashamed. How could she have forgotten?

Her stomach clutched as she thought the plane straight up through the trees, startling a row of sleeping birds. Pine needles brushed her arm as she and the plane searched for clear spaces between branches. Christina glanced down once and saw that the tunnel opening had all but disappeared, the vine-covered hole merging into dark leafy forest.

It might be a little hard to find again. But the opening was close to the orphanage yard lights. And no one would see them searching—after all, who would be out at this time of night?

We would, she thought gleefully, and soared above the tops of the trees, not tired in the least.

The great wedges of rock that made up the Starkian Ridge were distant at first, then grew larger, slanting across the night sky like giant teeth turned to stone. As they loomed so tall they blocked the moon, Christina reduced airspeed.

Even softer, she thought to the plane, and the chord diminished to a muted melodic drone. Watching carefully, flying slowly, she flew ever closer to the crest of the ridge.

Taft tapped her shoulder and pointed down.

Christina nodded. She had already seen the leaping fire, the rough guardhouse, the silhouettes of burly men. Now, circling above, she could see that the jagged teeth of the Starkian Ridge were like a high fence, enclosing a rough and lumpy basin. In places the basin had been chiseled away into terraced steps, with ramps leading up and down the sides, as if someone had been quarrying rock. In other spots, cone-shaped lumps rose up, looking for all the world like giant anthills that had turned to stone.

Behind a bank of scrubby trees was a blocky shadow the size of a garbage truck. And still farther away was a tiny camp-fire, just a flicker in the dark. Nervously Christina edged the plane well into the shadow of the ridge. She couldn't be sure but it looked as if there might be people around the fire, too. Small people.

Christina's braids lifted in the wind from their flight. She banked the plane in a long, slow curve just outside the ridged stone teeth, slid in between two prehistoric slabs set on edge, and set down in a sheltered corrie.

The plane's bottom scraped with a harsh sound of metal on rock. Taft pointed over her shoulder to the control panel. LOWER LANDING GEAR, it read, dark letters against bright violet.

"*Now* you tell me," whispered Christina, turning around. Her knee bumped the control panel.

"It wasn't *my* job to fly the plane," Taft retorted, and then suddenly the panel went dark and the humming stopped.

"What did you do that for?" Taft demanded, his voice low.

"I didn't do anything!"

"Yes, you did, you pushed the stop button somehow—"

"Shhhh!" Christina hissed. "Listen!"

They sat perfectly still in the darkened plane. A muted humming came and went, rose and fell, carried softly on the night breeze.

"Wait!" whispered Taft. "I'll go, you stay with the plane—"

But Christina was already over the side and moving cautiously toward the gap between the two massive slabs of rock.

Taft came up behind her, muttering under his breath. Christina ignored him. Instead, she slid sideways along the rock, her body flattened against the cool, smooth stone. Just as her fingers reached the far edge, she stopped. She poked her head around.

There, a little distance away, was the tiny campfire, surrounded by a hundred small shadowy figures, sitting with shoulders hunched and heads back. They were singing, very softly, and swaying as they sang.

The tune was familiar. The words Christina knew by heart.

The orphans were singing her mother's lullaby.

CHAPTER 20

COLLARED

"LET'S go find Danny," said Taft.

Christina stared at him blankly. She was still thinking about her mother's song—how had the orphans learned it?—and could hardly take in what he was saying.

"I think I see him," Taft added, and stepped out of the rock's shadow.

Christina clutched at his sleeve. "Wait. There might be guards."

Taft shook off her hand. "They're all back at the guardhouse. Besides, what do you want to do? Just stand here?" His face was pale and anxious in the moonlight.

"Listen." Christina spoke low and rapidly. "We don't want to get caught—that's the first thing. Because if we're caught, we can't help Danny, or anybody else. Right?"

Taft's mouth drew down at the corners. "I guess."

"Okay. And second, you don't want Danny to see you."

"Yes, I do!" Taft's whisper was fierce. "Then he won't feel so scared!"

Christina shook her head. "Think about it. What's he going to do when he sees you?"

Taft was silent.

"He's going to say, 'Taff! Taff!' and he won't understand why he should be quiet. And then he won't understand when you have to leave him, either."

"I'm *not* leaving him," Taft said, his chin jutting. "He's not some piece of trash to throw away."

"There's no room for him in the plane."

Taft turned on her angrily. "So you want to abandon him? What did you even come up here for, then?"

"Will you please just listen?" Christina glared at him. "I want to rescue Danny, too. I wish we could rescue *all* of them. But let's stay under cover. We need to watch until we know more."

Taft leaned his weight on one foot, then the other. "All right. But I'm going closer, anyway. I can't see their faces from here."

Taft and Christina moved step by step in the dark, working their way silently around a large rock outcropping and down wide terraced steps before they finally settled in a shadowed niche behind a square metal vat the size of three garbage cans. In the meantime, the orphans had switched from the lullaby to a new tune, sung even more quietly.

Beside her, Taft grinned, his teeth catching the reflected firelight. "That's the song I made up," he whispered. "The one they never sing in front of Lenny."

Christina pressed against the vat's metal side, still warm from the day's sun, and listened as the orphans sang under their breaths.

Lenny makes us say we love him
When we'd really rather shove him
Off a Starkian mountain cliff
Do we love him? Hah! As if!

"There are nine verses," said Taft in Christina's ear. "Do you see Danny anywhere?"

Lenny wants to win the Karsnicky
(Since he's dumb, it would be tricky)

Christina flinched at a sudden sound. And then she heard it again—the sharp scrape of a boot on stone.

"All right, you little worms!" The voice of the guard was loud as he mounted the terrace. "You'd better not be singing what I think you're singing!"

The quiet, bitter song died instantly. The shadows froze.

"Well? Who's going to answer me? Number Seven? Number Thirty-one?" The guard, a man with a broad face and a squashed-looking nose, rather like a bulldog's, hitched his thumbs in his belt and looked around.

"We were just practicing," said a clear, anxious voice, and one of the shadows stepped forward.

The guard bent down to look at the front of the child's shirt. "Number Seventeen, is it? And what are you practicing?"

"We're practicing our ... um ... welcome songs. For Lenny Loompski."

"Good answer, wormlet. Only I don't believe you. What, exactly, were you singing? Let's hear it. *Now.*"

The child took one more step forward—Christina could see it was the girl called Dorset—and began to sing.

> O, happy day, when Lenny came
> The Loompski of the greatest fame
> To care for us, poor orphans dreary
> To wipe our eyes when we are teary—

"But that's not what we were singing," said a slow voice from somewhere in the crowd. "We were singing *Taff's* song."

Taft sucked in his breath. His back went rigid.

"Taff's song, eh?" The guard swept his bulldog head from side to side, scanning the seated orphans. "Keep singing it, whoever you are."

"No!" Taft whispered. "Don't, Danny—they'll beat you—"

Danny's clear, sweet tones filled the hollow.

> Lenny makes us want to vomit
> Take this orphans' home, and bomb it—

"All right, whoever's singing that, stand up!" roared the guard.

Taft gripped Christina's arm. "Stay *down*." He peered around the corner of the vat, crouching, as Danny began to struggle to his feet.

Christina nodded frantically—of course she was going to stay down, what else would they do?—when all at once her heart catapulted. Taft was up and trotting into the circle of orphans before she could stop him.

"It was me!" he said loudly.

"*Taft!*" cried Danny, rising all the way. "You came!"

Five pairs of orphan hands immediately pulled Danny back down. Taft ran to the guard, opening his eyes wide. "I'm sorry, really I am. I just sang it because that's what you *said* you wanted to hear."

"I didn't want to hear how Lenny Loompski makes you want to vomit, you disgusting caterpillar!"

Taft spoke up as two more guards, attracted by the commotion, came striding along the gravel path from the guardhouse. "But you *asked* for the song about bombing the orphans' home. I *heard* you." He blinked several times, looking particularly innocent.

The first guard glanced uneasily behind him. "That's not what I meant—" He spun to face Taft. "You trying to get me in trouble, maggot?"

"Who, me?" said Taft.

The guard grabbed his shoulder and shook it. "And where's your number, you little grub? And your collar?"

"What happened? Attempted escape?" asked a fourth guard, coming up.

"Look," growled the first guard. "Somebody let this one off the last truckload and forgot to put a collar on him. No number stamped on his shirt, either."

"Wasn't me."

"Wasn't me, neither."

"Well, it sure as night crawlers wasn't *me.*"

"I don't care who it was, you leeches, let's get a collar on him now! Mr. Big Boss Loompski could come back anytime, and I don't need to tell you what *that* means!"

Christina stuffed her knuckles in her mouth to keep from crying out in protest. Taft looked as if he wanted to put up a fight, but in an instant his arms were pinned behind his back and a collar was fished out of a pocket and snapped onto his neck with a crimping tool. The last guard marked the number 101 onto his shirt, gave his forehead a noogie for good measure, and quick-stepped him toward the vat where Christina was hiding.

"No!" Taft shouted. "I mean—wait! Look!" He twisted under the guard's hand, and pointed. "Over there!"

Christina froze. What was Taft doing?

"Behind the rocks!" Taft was pointing away from the vat, but his eyes slid sideways to where Christina hid in deep shadow. "Go behind the rocks!"

"You giving me orders, boy?" The guard was incredulous.

Christina edged backward. Taft wanted her to get behind the rocks, that much was clear . . . but why? She couldn't help him from there. She moved slowly, quietly, back up the terraced steps, past the rock outcropping. The guards, their eyes used to the firelight, did not seem to notice her quiet movements in the shadows of the night.

Christina made the safety of the standing stones and peered through to the corrie behind. The little plane, silvery in the moonlight, waited like a promise.

One of the men near the fire guffawed. "Go ahead, Torkel, show the kid what's behind the rocks."

Christina watched with dread as Torkel, looking more like a bulldog than ever, marched Taft straight toward her, up to the tall stones that ringed the terraced basin.

"Go past that rock." The man gave Taft's collar a violent shake. "Go on, get going."

Taft took a step forward and hesitated. "Are you saying you want me to . . . try to escape?"

"Yeah," said Torkel, sounding bored. "Now, move it."

Taft took another step, and another. Christina bit her knuckles. Could she sing fast enough to start up the plane and get Taft out before the guard caught them? Probably not—but what else could she try? Taft was almost to the nearest upright slab. She backed up—she took a breath—

"AIIGGHH!" Taft's cry was choked. His hands flew to his neck; his knees buckled. He fell to the ground and lay helplessly, his legs twitching.

Torkel guffawed. "Got a shock, did you?" He grabbed Taft's arm and hauled him to his knees. "Now you know what happens if you go past the circle of stones. And there's an alarm that goes off in the guardhouse, too. So we'll be hot on your tail if you try it, fishbait."

Taft knelt, swaying. Torkel began to pull him up, but Taft shuddered and lifted his head. "I bet," he said, his voice faint, "you'd like me to sing the Happy Lenny song instead of the song I made up."

"You got that right, wormboy."

"I bet," Taft went on, his voice a little stronger, "that you want me to sing it loud. Loud enough to drown out a Starkian harrier, if it started screeching."

"Yeah, yeah. On your feet, Number One-oh-one."

"You probably want me," Taft said even more clearly, turning toward the rocks as he was led staggering away, "to sing so loud that you couldn't even hear somebody singing *six notes!*"

"You're a musical little squirmer, aren't you? You can start singing right now, if you're so excited about it. Go on, sing!"

Christina watched in agony as Taft was marched away, hunch-shouldered and skinny, his hair sticking up in little tufts over his ears that caught the moonlight.

Taft's voice came howling back to her, loud and raucous: "Oh, happy day, when Lenny caaame . . . Help me sing, you guys!" he cried as the guard propelled him toward the circle of staring children. In an instant, more voices were raised. "The Loompski of the greatest faaame!"

Christina took her fist out of her mouth and gave the plane an agonized glance. She couldn't abandon Taft, and Danny, and the rest—she *couldn't* leave them here—

No. She wasn't abandoning them. She was going to get help, and that was exactly what Taft was hoping she would do. He was covering for her, making enough noise so that she could sing the plane's engine through all the steps to ignition and takeoff. She couldn't waste what he was doing, or he'd never forgive her.

"*To care for us, poor orphans dreary . . . to wipe our eyes when we are teeeeary . . .*"

She gave a harrier's cry. She had the plane humming.

"*Oh, happy, happy, happy weeee . . .*"

Root. Third.

"*Will always happy, happy beeee . . .*"

Fifth. Minor seventh.

"We'll never whimper, never cry—"

The plane was droning beneath her, glowing blue, hovering. Christina sang the last high E, the note that resolved the urgent, singing chord, and the plane glowed violet and was aloft, speeding away by the power of thought. And as she skimmed the treetops, the wind in her face bringing tears to her eyes, she heard a last gallant, defiant shout—

"WE WILL BE HAPPY TILL WE DIE!"

CHAPTER 21

A DANGEROUS MAN

MIDFLIGHT, Christina realized that she hadn't thought things through.

The plane still hummed its musical chord, the violet light was magical in the dark, whooshing air, and high above, the moon shone golden—but flying had lost its first ecstatic thrill for Christina, and she was worried.

Who was she going to get help *from?* The only one she knew who could possibly assist was her father, and if she told him where Taft was now, she'd first have to explain who Taft was. And that meant she'd have to tell her father that she'd gone against his direct orders.

For although she had obeyed Dr. Adnoid, strictly speaking, when he said not to go into the yard—she hadn't, she'd gone *under* it—she had known quite well that he wouldn't have wanted her to do that, either. And he would be even more unhappy to know that she'd hidden an orphan in their attic, almost killed herself falling out of a tree, exploded her mother's ring, trespassed in a locked cave, and flown a plane full of zoom up to the Starkian Ridge.

Still, what else could she do but tell him? It wasn't as if she could leave Taft on the ridge at the mercy of the guards and Lenny Loompski, too.

An uncomfortable thought intruded, reminding her that she had once been perfectly willing to leave all the other orphans stranded on the ridge.

Well, that was before she had seen them up close. Now they had faces and names—now they were real to her, and she couldn't forget that they were in danger.

Christina frowned and aimed the plane at the lighted square that was the orphanage yard. The entrance to the tunnel was somewhere near there. She hoped it wouldn't be hard to find . . .

But it was impossible. Everything was the same deep, leafy dark, and she had no time to land and search.

Fine, then. Christina swooped the plane up through the trees and away, and straight toward her own house. That was a better thought, anyway. She could land the tiny plane on the roof behind the gargoyles, and no one would be the wiser.

She adjusted the helmet strap, which had loosened in the sudden turn she'd made above the tunnel, and zeroed in on the high gables of her own rooftop, dark but still visible against the moonlit valley below. Flying was beginning to get chilly. If only she had brought a jacket! She was thirsty, too, and so tired she didn't even *want* to know how long past her bedtime it was.

But although the roof of her house was dark, as Christina flew closer she could see that people must still be awake, for the windows in the lower levels were bright with lamplight. In fact, the whole first floor was lit up, and this seemed very odd. It was certainly after midnight; why would people still be up?

She soared in as quietly as she could and lowered the plane gently into a flat space behind one of the gargoyles. The bottom scraped on the roof—why didn't she *ever* remember to put down the landing gear? Christina glared at the control panel. Now that it was too late to do any good, it said LOWER LANDING GEAR. It said SET BRAKES, too, but she didn't bother. The plane wasn't going anywhere, stuck on its belly behind a gable.

She reached out a finger to push the stop button and paused. Maybe she'd better make sure everything was all right before she killed the engine. The plane would wait, idling, while she checked things out. She unstrapped her helmet and climbed over the side of the humming plane. Its soft violet light shone on the parapet, on the stone gargoyle that was still twisted open, revealing the stairs that descended to the tunnel.

Christina seized the stone wings and pushed hard. The gargoyle scraped shut, and she breathed again. If anyone in the forest found the tunnel, at least they couldn't follow it to her roof now. She dusted off her hands and turned to the small service door to the attic—and stopped. Two police cruisers were parked at her front gate. And behind them, almost invisible behind the hedge, was another car, long and black.

"And I'm telling you, Wilfer, your synthesizer experiment is over. You know as well as I do that to extract the zoom we must have a *living* sound; a child's throat or a bird's. The resonance is all wrong otherwise."

Christina sat at the top of the staircase, listening intently. Below, in the kitchen, Lenny Loompski's voice was loud and emphatic. "I'm far more interested in what you've been working on lately, you know, the polly—pollysticky—oh, you know, the stuff they make those little plastic toys out of?"

"Polystyrene," said Dr. Adnoid.

"Yeah, that stuff. Anyway, you did good work on that, Wilfer, I must say. The plastic soaks up the zoom and then you can transport it and it won't explode—and better yet, nobody thinks you're carrying anything but a little, cute, plastic—"

"No, no, we found out it was far too dangerous," interrupted Dr. Adnoid. "The polystyrene acts as a catalyst, and if the zoom is absorbed and then melted again, it becomes a hundred times more explosive than nitroglycerin. Simply out of the question—at least until I can create an artificial sound that mimics the harriers. No matter how good an energy source zoom might be, you *cannot* use children for something so dangerous."

"Why ever not? Children *like* to be useful."

Christina clenched her teeth in an effort to keep silent. Kids might like to be useful, but that didn't mean they liked to be *used*. Did Lenny Loompski think that little girls wanted to drag big heavy garbage cans to the curb, or that a boy like Danny would rather scrub plastic toys instead of going to school? And whatever it was that the orphans were forced to do up on the Starkian Ridge, she was pretty sure they weren't volunteering for it.

There was a silence. "Listen, I'm sure I can manufacture an artificial sound that works," came the strained voice of

Christina's father. "I just need a little more time. And meanwhile, I think you should try again with the harriers. Maybe if you just tethered them? I know you said that cages didn't work, but it seems to me that you should try everything possible rather than using children—"

"You're still concerned about the orphans, are you?" Lenny sounded amused. "You know, they're *happy* working for me. Why, they actually compose poems in my honor—'Lenny, oh, Lenny, we love him so'—you know the sort of thing. Primitive, but really quite touching—"

"I'm sure." Dr. Adnoid's voice was dry. "But *why* didn't the cages work? You could bring the birds right down into the mines, get them close to that new vein of zoom you want to open up, and leave the children out of it. It's too dangerous for them, anyway, underground."

"Still, we have the most advanced safety precautions in place," said Lenny smoothly. "And strangely enough, we've found that if we want the birds' cry to have the right tone, they must be soaring free. There's something missing in their cry when they're restrained—something wild. But children—now *their* cries work best when they're afraid. And so we find it useful to keep a certain level of fear going. Very mild fear, I assure you; almost like Halloween, you might say. Trick or treat, you know."

Christina stiffened in outrage, remembering the garbage truck's rusty hopper, and the small desperate faces looking out, and the steel panel crashing down. She was filled with a passionate longing to squish Lenny into the hopper with its smelly garbage and see how he liked it. Anyone who made kids afraid on purpose deserved that, and worse.

Besides, he was wrong about Halloween. Christina had watched through her telescope as kids in costumes went running through their neighborhoods with flashlights, and the one thing she knew for sure was that they weren't afraid—they were having *fun*.

"I wish I had asked these questions years ago." Dr. Adnoid's voice was expressionless, but Christina, who knew him, realized with a shiver just how angry he was. "And where do you find all these orphans, anyway? I only know of one case in town where a child was left without both parents, and we sent the boy off to his relatives. What do you do, import them?"

Lenny Loompski chuckled. "There's no shortage of unwanted kids in this world. I can name you a hundred cities right now where I could just walk in and have my pick. Not all in this country, of course, and the trick is getting them past the borders . . . but I'm not going to tell you my secrets, Wilfer. Why do you ask? Are you thinking of going into the orphan business yourself?"

"I wouldn't touch your filthy business with a thousand-foot pole. If I had known this before, I'd have left long ago."

"*Filthy* business?" Lenny Loompski's voice grew soft and cold. "I'm not clean enough for you pure scientists, is that it, Wilfer?"

"Well, if the shoe fits—"

"Just like the garbage business is filthy, is that what you're saying? Just like my father, Larry, wasn't as good as his famous and important scientist brothers, is that right?"

"Now, listen—"

"Of *course* you didn't mean it, Wilfer. I'm *sure* you understand. You have a child yourself; you comprehend the bond between parent and child . . . Where *is* your daughter, by the way?" he added casually.

Christina held her breath in sudden terror.

"My daughter is none of your business." Dr. Adnoid's voice trembled.

"Are you sure, Wilfer? She could help those orphans you're so concerned about. Their pitch isn't always exact, sadly. We had an explosion just last night—"

"You keep your hands off her, you hear me? You try to even *speak* to my daughter and I'll tear you apart with my bare hands!"

A warm feeling spread through Christina's chest. Her father didn't just care about her math grades, or keeping her behind a fence—he would *defend* her—

"Do you hear that, officer?" Lenny Loompski raised his voice. "Officer! You, there, outside! This man is threatening my life!"

Heavy footsteps sounded on the kitchen tile.

"Threatening?" cried Dr. Adnoid. "I'll do more than threaten, you pasty chunk of bologna—"

"Now, sir," came the officer's voice, "there's such a thing as terroristic threats—"

"And he's certainly making them," said Lenny. "Oooh, I'm so *scared*—"

"I'll rip out your heart and stomp on your liver before I let you near her!" cried Dr. Adnoid, in a high, enraged voice that Christina had never heard before.

"Heart ripping, officer? Liver stomping? How much more evidence do you need that this is a truly dangerous man?"

"Sir, I'm afraid I'm going to have to take you in," said the officer. "Now, are you going to come quietly, or do I have to use the cuffs?"

"*Handcuffs?* For what? Trying to protect my own *daughter?*" screamed Dr. Adnoid.

Christina pressed a hand to her mouth, frantic with worry. Should she go down to help her father? Should she tell the officer what Lenny Loompski was really like? Would he even believe her?

"And by the way, officer," came Lenny's voice clearly over the sounds of a scuffle, "I not only have a search warrant—I have here a temporary order, signed by the magistrate, to take his daughter and place her in the orphanage, if it turns out that we have to arrest him. And, tragically, that *does* seem to be the case."

Christina's heart gave a sudden beat, high and hard in her throat.

"Temporary is right, you hind end of a pork chop! This order won't stand—what did you do, bribe the clerk? I'll get it straightened out in the morning—you're going to *pay* for this—"

"Tell it to the judge, mister," said the officer firmly, and the scuffling sound moved from the kitchen to the front entrance and out the door.

There came a sound of thick fingers snapping and a shuffling of several pairs of feet into the kitchen.

"All right, the rest of you," said Lenny Loompski, his voice low and forceful. "Search the house. I want that girl."

CHAPTER 22
A DIFFICULT SITUATION

SNICK. The trapdoor in the floor of the attic closed and latched. Christina, carrying her shoes in her hand, hurried silently across the wooden floor, bumping her mother's rocker into motion as she passed.

For an instant she paused, hearing the sound she dimly remembered, the creak that had once matched the rhythm of her mother's lullaby. *Little one, child of mine, safely rest tonight . . .*

Christina turned away. She unlatched the service door and was on the roof in two seconds flat.

She climbed into the still-humming plane, dropped her shoes in the passenger seat, and strapped on the helmet with fingers that fumbled. Her father had been willing to go to jail to keep her safe. But she had not been able to help him at all . . .

A cool breeze touched a tear on her face, and she realized that she had lifted off and was flying toward the Starkian Ridge once more.

She didn't look back. She couldn't bear to see them take her father away.

There was a scent of pine as Christina skimmed the treetops near the great slabs of rock. On the way to the ridge she had figured out what she should have realized before; she could rescue Taft without any trouble at all. All she had to do was swoop down in the plane. He could leap into the back seat and they'd be up and out of reach before anyone knew what was happening.

And where would they go then? And what about Danny and the other orphans?

Christina squinted, focusing on the ridge ahead. If she rescued Taft first, then together they could figure out a way to set the others free.

But to do that, she had to locate Taft and see if the guards were still with the orphans. Perhaps if she flew high enough, she could spy out the situation without anyone noticing the glowing violet craft.

She climbed higher into the night sky. A harrier soared up with her, close enough that she could see its fierce yellow eye and soft ruffled wingtips tinged with color from the plane's violet-blue glow.

Christina glanced at the control panel, puzzled. Suddenly there was more blue than violet. The piercing high E faltered, resumed briefly, and then was lost to the chord. The plane dipped, sputtering. The blue light took on a tinge of green.

Christina stared at the dashboard. What was going on?

The green color became more pronounced. The minor seventh tone faded in a series of soft *pops* and then disappeared entirely.

All at once Christina knew exactly what was happening. She was running out of fuel. And unless she managed to land in a great hurry, she was going to crash.

Christina gripped the armrests, her hands sweaty. She couldn't think about crashing—not with the zoom responding to her every thought. She had to keep focused on flying, she had to keep thinking she could make it—

The plane plunged through the night like a small chunky comet, first green, then yellow, then orange. Christina's breaths came short and fast as the plane dove spiraling down. At the last moment, in the light of the plane's dying pink glow, she spied a rock ledge jutting out from the cliffs. It was small and slick with damp, but it was almost flat, with room enough for the plane and a little to spare.

The plane stuttered through the mist of a thin waterfall that splashed down the rock face and disappeared into the darkness below. With the last spurt of liquid draining from the helmet, Christina remembered to put down the landing gear. The tiny rubber wheels bumped on the wet rock, the plane's glow faded, and the melodic hum went silent.

Christina slumped with relief. She had done it!

But there was no time to waste. She had to refill the tank from the canister in the back, and she had to do it at once. Who knew how long she had to rescue Taft and the others?

Maybe the guards had seen the plane diving and were already climbing down the side of the cliff to investigate.

The moon gave just enough light to see by. Christina unplugged her helmet and clambered out to pull the spare canister of zoom from its slot. She popped open the fuel cap, fumbled for the funnel, and began to unscrew the canister lid with nervous fingers.

Her arm was already wet to the shoulder from the waterfall's spray. She glanced up, annoyed—if she wheeled the plane a little farther along the edge, could she refill the tank without getting drenched?—and stopped in midmotion.

There was something glinting up there in the waterfall, caught and wedged against a lip of rock; something that stuck out and sent a fine spray curving from the cliff's face.

Christina set the canister down and climbed back into the plane to stand on the red leather seat. The object was half hidden by the tumbling water, and yet she could see its smooth, glassy surface, its rounded tip.

It was a wonder that it had stayed stuck there all this time. Christina stretched—could she reach it? Not . . . quite . . .

She stared at the test tube, her heart thumping. Her mother must have sent the messages out for as long as she could, hoping that one of them would be picked up. What would this one say?

Christina stepped up onto the plane's curved metal back and stretched higher.

The water cascaded along her upraised arm and down the back of her neck, soaking her shirt. She touched the smooth glass tube with her fingertips. Only a little farther, just enough to get a grip on it. She was almost there—

She gave a spring with her toes and grasped the test tube, wrenching it from the rock. It shattered in her hand, but she didn't let go as her feet slipped on the wet, curving back of the plane, as she caromed off its rounded side, as she landed with a cry of pain on the damp rock ledge, just barely missing the canister of zoom.

Christina lay in a heap, breathing hard. She had almost blown herself up.

Her hand was bleeding, too. But things could have been worse. She was safe, and she had her mother's message, and—

And the plane was rolling. She had forgotten to set the brakes.

She lunged, she grabbed, but she was too late. The plane tipped for a long, agonizing moment at the corner of the ledge and then fell, hurtling nose first down the mountainside with a shriek of twisting metal and a rending crash.

Christina sat hunched on the ledge in the pale, cold light of a quarter moon. For some bizarre reason, the dancing chickens from Chickie-Go Math came to her mind, with their signs that read GOOD EFFORT! and NICE TRY!

She stared out into nothingness. It didn't matter in the least how hard she had tried or how good her efforts had been. She had failed. And if she were the crying sort, now would be the perfect time to burst into tears.

Her father was in jail.

Her only friend had been captured.

A horrible man wanted to turn her into one of his orphan slaves.

And to top it all off, she was soaking wet, bleeding, and stranded on the side of a cliff—plus she had just watched the coolest kid-sized plane in the world roll over the edge and vanish forever.

Shivering, Christina picked shards of glass out of her palm and tried to think of something good about her situation.

Well, she had her mother's message. Of course, the moon didn't give enough light to read it by.

On the other hand, she did have perfect pitch and a canister full of zoom.

Carefully, delicately, Christina unscrewed the canister's lid all the way. She flattened out the crumpled, blotted paper with her good hand and opened her mouth to sing a high G-sharp.

But instead, she found herself singing her mother's lullaby.
Someday you may find yourself lost and far from home . . .
The canister of zoom glowed beautifully pink as Christina reached the high G-sharp and held it. She smoothed the message with a trembling hand—and almost cried aloud in disappointment. The message was blotted on every line with her blood.

A word here and there was readable. Danny's ABC, for one—she could make a guess at *Adnoid, Beth, Christina*—but besides that, just a few more random words, senseless without the other words around them. About the only thing that wasn't defaced with a red smear was the date, in the upper right-hand corner . . .

The date.

Christina blinked twice and read the clear script again.

The year was this year. The date was last week.

Her mother was still alive!

CHAPTER 23

THE CRACK OF ZOOM

HER mother was still alive, and trapped in the mountain. She might be on the other side of the rock wall, right now.

Christina's mouth went dry. She stared wildly at the blood-soaked message. Only a few days ago, her mother had touched this very paper. Only a few days ago, Beth Adnoid had been thinking of her daughter—she had written Christina's *name*.

Christina pressed the note to her chest. She was getting blood all over her shirt, but she didn't care. The thought of her mother, alive, so close, filled her with an ache so acute she almost couldn't breathe.

Words drifted through her head, accompanied by a haunting tune. *Never fear, Mother's near, though just out of sight . . .*

She swallowed hard and shook herself. She had to get a grip. Her mother needed rescuing, and *now*.

But how to start? What to do?

Christina gazed at the sheer cliff with its translucent

streaks of zoom, still faintly shining from the note she had sung.

She put her face up close to the rock. The fine tracery of pink and green webbed over the surface like a veil. The color was fading, dying away as she watched.

She sang a G-sharp, exactly on pitch. The thin veins of zoom brightened, and strengthened in hue. They were mere threads, not pencil-thick strands of zoom as she had seen before, but there was something different in the rock behind them. The rock surrounding the zoom did not stay dark, but seemed to blush in wide swaths of muted color.

It was almost as if, somewhere deeper inside the rock, there was a strong, broad vein of zoom lying hidden.

How deep did it go? Could she melt it and just walk right in?

But there was a layer of stone over it. How could the zoom respond to the vibrations of her pitch, with all that rock in the way?

Christina looked at the mountain before her. Leo Loompski had said that thoughts had vibrations. Would it help if she could somehow focus her *thoughts* while she sang?

She shook her head, setting the helmet's tubes swinging. Of course Leo had figured out a way to make it work for the plane, but that didn't mean it would work without inner mechanisms and the—

The helmet. The plane was gone, but she still had the helmet.

She touched the long flexible tubes hanging down; she

looked at the couplings on the ends, and suddenly felt like a fool. What did she think she was going to do—plug them into the *mountain?*

She felt a sudden urge to laugh hysterically. Of course it wouldn't work. How dumb, how ridiculous, how absolutely *stupid*, it was as stupid as dancing chickens, as stupid as *math*.

Christina paced three steps in one direction and three steps back, grazing her knuckles against the rock as she turned. She sucked on her hand where it had started to bleed again and put her back against the cliff wall. All right, what else, then? What other options did she have?

She stared blankly into the dark. Nothing came to mind.

Below the cliff, pine boughs shifted uneasily in the night breeze, making a lost, forlorn sound. Christina's wet clothes stuck clammily to her skin, and she wrapped her arms around herself, shivering as the wind picked up.

The thought of Nanny suddenly filled her mind: Nanny, large and huggable, running a hot bath, tucking her into a warm bed piled high with quilts . . .

Christina felt like slapping herself. What was she doing, thinking about warm quilts when her mother was trapped inside a mountain, needing her?

She clenched her hands together and shut her eyes in concentration. She needed a great idea, and she needed it *now*.

After a moment, she found she was thinking of blueberry pie and dry clothes.

Christina felt a slow flush spread from her neck to her cheeks, and she slid down to sit with her face buried in her arms. Of *course* she couldn't think of a great idea. She wasn't used to real problems, in a real world. She was used to being babied and taken care of and kept safe behind a fence.

Not like the kids she watched through her telescope, who figured out things on their own all the time—new rules for games, stunts on their skateboards, how to find their way in the dark on Halloween.

Not like Taft, who had learned math in spite of poor teachers and hardly any school and had taken care of Danny besides.

Not like her mother, who was trapped but had still sent message after message, never giving up hope. Now it was Christina's turn to do what she could. Which, unfortunately, turned out to be nothing at all.

Christina tried very hard not to cry. She was mostly successful. After a while she wiped her nose and looked up.

The night sky was salted with stars. Somewhere in that bright scattering was a star that had once shone through her nursery window, a star her mother had put in a song. There was no way to tell which one it was, but it was still shining on her, that much was certain.

A lovely thought. Completely useless at the moment, of course. But it gave her a little spark of courage.

Was her first idea worth trying? Plugging a helmet into a mountain sounded like the brainless idea of a very stupid person, but then she had thought she was stupid at math, too, and Taft had shown her that wasn't true.

And even the dancing chickens, annoying as they were, had *never* held signs in their beaks that said WAY TO GIVE UP! and HOORAY, YOU QUIT!

Christina gazed past her knees, thinking. The pine tops spread out below the cliff like a restless dark sea, and far beyond, down in the valley, she could see the winking lights of Dorf, like a bowl of fallen stars.

Okay, so maybe she *could* try her idea.

But could she use the power of zoom if she didn't first believe it would work? She couldn't be sure that her song would work through solid rock, or that she could rescue Taft or her mother or the other orphans, or that she could even save herself.

She blinked up at the stars, considering this. And then her little spark of courage flared into a tiny bit of hope.

She could *act* as if she believed it. She could begin by doing the first thing, and she could go on to the next. And maybe, if she kept on going, the belief, or the focused thought, or *whatever* it was she needed, would come to her. At any rate, she didn't intend to fail for lack of trying.

She looked at the stone wall, now completely dark again. Step by step, Taft had said when he taught her math. All right, then. What did she know for sure?

Well, she knew that zoom worked. It was mysterious, but it worked all the same.

She looked at the dangling tubes. The zoom had been drawn up from the fuel tank, through the tube, and into the helmet, where it had been as close to her brain as was possible. Then the zoom had gone back down the other tube and back into the plane.

The mountain had no fuel chambers, no internal switches, no delicate mechanisms. It was crude, raw—just rock and zoom and nothing else. If the helmet was going to work, the tubes had to go straight into the zoom.

Christina sang a soft, high G-sharp, and scanned the surface of the rock as the threads of zoom grew luminous. Was there any place where the threads seemed to be a little thicker? Could she just shove the tube in somewhere? The couplings would have to come off first.

Christina pulled out the jackknife from her pocket and cut off the ends of the tubes with two sharp motions. The couplings went flying. One hit the canister of zoom with a small *ting*.

She looked at the canister thoughtfully. Yes, that might work. It would be just like the plane, only simpler.

Christina's hands trembled slightly, whether from cold or excitement she didn't know. She dangled the helmet's left tube into the canister's gelling zoom. She pressed the open end of the right tube against the rock wall, a quarter inch into the thickest spot of zoom she could find. And then she began to sing.

A high G-sharp pierced the air, clear and pure, and the zoom began to gleam and soften. Beneath the surface of the stone, thick veins of pink and green started to glow, faint at first and then with more intensity. The liquid from the canister moved slowly up the tube like a milk shake through a straw; it coiled heavily through the helmet and then through the other tube and into the mountain.

The threads of zoom opened up, melted, began to stream down the rock face in a shining skein. Christina pushed the right tube farther in, took a fast breath, and sustained the tone. She focused her thoughts the best she could, on the melting zoom, on the zoom deep within the rock, on what she hoped was on the other side—her *mother*.

And with that thought came a wave of longing so sharp, so strong, it filled her mind just as the sound of the G-sharp filled her ears, and she shut her eyes and tipped back her head and sang with every ounce of air in her lungs, with all the power and passion and belief that she had.

The mountain trembled beneath her. There was a series of abrupt noises, like pistol shots, and Christina opened her eyes to see bits of the rock flaking away, and the green and pink glowing liquid pouring out, flooding out, it was a *river* of zoom—

CRACK. The cliff split. The gap widened, lengthened, spread down and across, opened under her feet. The rock crumbled beneath her.

She fell into darkness.

CHAPTER 24

THOUGHTS MADE REAL

SHE was screaming, she was sliding, she was moving with terrible speed down a glowing, brightly colored vein of zoom. It threaded her into the roots of the mountain like a sock through a winding laundry chute and dumped her out at last on a sandy floor, where she rolled and bumped and skidded and finally rammed into something extremely hard. Her head promptly snapped sideways and bashed itself just above her left ear, and everything went black.

Sometime later she opened her eyes.

The face over her was wrinkled, with a faded blue gaze and a kindly, befuddled smile. Above the bushy eyebrows was a nimbus of white hair, and below the dumpling chin was a dirty white lab coat and a name badge.

Christina blinked twice and the name came into wavering focus.

"Have we met?" asked Leo Loompski.

Christina felt the lump under her hair and thought that she must have banged her head pretty hard.

And then another figure came into view, silhouetted by a lantern that hung behind. Christina heard a sudden intake of breath and then a thin arm reached swiftly back and unhooked the lantern, raising it high.

Leo Loompski turned with evident relief. "There you are, my dear. Is this little girl someone we know? I seem to have forgotten her name."

Christina, flat on her back, looked up and saw a woman's face.

It was a familiar face, one Christina had seen before. It was older now, and pale and unwell looking, but the eyes were just like the photographs, and the hair was still the color of honey.

"Mom?" whispered Christina. She swallowed past the pressure in her throat and struggled up onto her elbows. "I got your message."

For a long time, all Christina's mother did was hug her daughter and cry. But at last they began to talk and share bits and pieces of their lives.

"I thought of you every single day," said Beth Adnoid. She wiped her eyes, coughing, and dropped a kiss on the top of Christina's head. "How old you were, what your interests might be, what made you laugh. Some days, it was all that kept me going."

Christina leaned against her mother's side. She pressed her cheek into the hollow formed between shoulder and collarbone, and listened to the quiet wheeze of her mother breathing in and out. It was odd to suddenly have a mother after all these years, but Christina was sure she could get used to it. Something inside her was deeply contented in a way she couldn't remember ever being before.

She looked up at the ceiling of the vast cavern. She didn't feel quite as closed in and claustrophobic as she had in the other tunnel, but maybe that was because this cave was huge and vaulted like a cathedral. High, high above was an opening, and through it poured the light of the moon.

Around the edges of the cavern hung shaded lanterns, turned down low for the night. Equipment, stacks of papers, counters full of test tubes—all reminded Christina of the cave she and Taft had explored, and indeed this was part of the same system. Her mother had shown her the other side of the cave-in that had buried half of Leo Loompski's secret laboratory.

"There was some kind of explosion aboveground. Lenny had been working up there—who knows, he might have caused the explosion himself—and the rock slide cut off our way out. There was no food, but luckily there was an underground stream that gave us fresh water. You can imagine how thankful we were on the third day when we heard Lenny Loompski shouting to us through the hole in the roof."

Christina looked up. Moonlight streamed through the hole in a shaft of pure light, pooling on the floor of the cave. Her mother followed her gaze.

"That's where I stand every night and sing," she said, nodding at the moonlit sand.

"A lullaby," said Christina slowly. "To the tune of 'Largo,' from the *New World Symphony*. I saw the sheet music in the scrapbook you started."

"Did you?" Beth Adnoid gave her a fond smile. "I knew you couldn't hear me—not really—but all the same, I would sing as strongly as I could, straight up at that opening. I liked to think that the breeze would carry the tune to your window."

So that was how the orphans had learned it.

Christina found it hard to speak. Her overwhelming weariness combined with powerful emotion made her feel as if she were a very small child again. She pressed her face against her mother and shut her eyes. Her mother was so warm.

"Now where was I? Oh, yes—Lennard Loompski. Well, I don't know what he was doing aboveground those three days—"

"He was blowing up your other laboratory and telling everyone you had been in it," said Christina, her voice muffled.

"No doubt." Beth Adnoid coughed, turning her face away. "But of course we didn't know that. He lowered a basket to us with food and said he would bring rescuers and lifting equipment and get us out. He told me to send up my wedding ring—it would give Wilfer something to hold on to, he said—and then we waited."

"And waited," said Christina, guiltily passing over the subject of the wedding ring.

"Yes. From time to time he'd bring more food and more excuses. And then he started to lower supplies so that we could work. Discover the secret of zoom, he said. Learn to control its power, write up the results of our research, give him a paper he could submit for the Karsnicky Medal, and he would make us rich. As if we cared about that!" she added scornfully.

"So what did you do instead?" Christina twisted a braid around her finger.

"I kept working on exactly what Lenny wanted me to. But I wasn't doing it for him. I was trying to discover how to use it myself. With a dependable power source, I could have figured out a way to get out of here. And even without it, I tried and tried. But Lenny always managed to thwart my attempts. And we came near to blowing ourselves up a few times, too."

Christina chewed on the end of her braid. Something wasn't making sense. "But I thought that Leo Loompski had *already* figured out how zoom worked," she said. "Didn't he tell you? Weren't you working together?"

Her mother shook her head. "I'm afraid the cave-in unsettled Leo's mind. And living here for years has only made it worse. He keeps *saying* he's discovered how to make it work, but he can't actually *do* it. It's sad to watch him, but if I try to argue, he just gets agitated. I've found it's best to give him the materials he asks for and let him go his own way."

Leo Loompski, pottering nearby with a bit of tubing, looked up at the sound of his name. "It's thinking that does it," he explained. "Thinking and singing and making waves in the air. Put it all together and you'll go ZOOM! At least . . . I think so . . ." His smile faltered. "Must keep working," he muttered, turning back to fiddle with the tube.

Beth Adnoid watched him, smiling sadly. "You see?" she said to Christina. "His inventions never quite work, but he keeps thinking that if he makes just one more, this time things will be different. They never are, but making things keeps him happy and quiet, and that's something."

"But his inventions that use zoom *do* work," said Christina. "At least one of them did. A little plane. I flew it myself, with thought and song."

She looked away, embarrassed to admit the next part. "If I had it here, I could show you. But it crashed."

Beth looked down at her daughter. She seemed about to say something, but instead she held out her hand and led Christina to the mouth of a wide tunnel that branched off from the main cavern.

Leo Loompski trotted after them. "Are we going to visit my fleet?"

His fleet? Was he making little models of boats, and playing with them in the stream?

But no. Christina saw what he meant as soon as her mother raised the lantern high. There before her, rank upon rank, was an entire fleet of little planes.

CHAPTER 25

UP AND OUT

CHRISTINA sat in the plane, looked up at the moonlight streaming through the hole high above, and adjusted her helmet.

They had rolled out the first plane in line to the center of the cavern floor and filled its tank and spare canister with zoom. "We have lots," said her mother, pointing to the rows of canisters against one wall. "Lennard sends it down for our experiments. It stays liquid as long as it's not exposed to air."

"Someone very smart must have discovered that," said Leo Loompski, bobbing up.

"You did, Leo, remember? Long ago." Beth Adnoid clasped her hands and looked at Christina worriedly. "Go ahead, dear, show us how it's done. But be careful not to crash. Are you warm enough? Do you need another sweater?"

Christina grinned. It was a new experience to have a mother worry over her, but it was kind of nice, too. "No thanks," she said, and sang a high G-sharp into the funnel-shaped speaker.

The zoom responded promptly, glowing a deep pink

through the metal of the plane. Christina held the note. The plane began to hum.

She glanced at her mother, who looked startled.

"That's right," said Leo Loompski, his eyes wide and excited. "Sing! Think!"

Christina did just that. Beth Adnoid's mouth dropped open as the plane glowed orange, yellow, green . . . then droned back a deep and powerful chord, turned a luminous blue, and with a soft *whoosh* rose to hover a foot in the air.

"Oh, be careful!" begged Christina's mother.

"Fly high!" cried Leo Loompski, clapping his hands.

Christina sang the last high, resolving E. The liquid zoom turned violet in the tube that stretched from her helmet to the control panel. She thought, *Up*.

The little plane rose in gentle spirals, higher and higher beneath the domed roof. Below were gasps and shouts, but above, Christina could see the hole to the outside growing larger. Her heart pumped more strongly. At last she was getting closer to Taft—but maybe to Lenny, too.

She drifted slowly upward—she didn't want to bump on the ceiling of the cave—and edged toward the opening.

Softer, she thought to the plane. *And dimmer, too, if you can.*

The plane's hum diminished to pianissimo, and the bright violet muted to a soft, deep plum. Far below, she could hear the sound of two voices cheering.

Thank you, thought Christina—it only seemed polite, the plane was doing its best for her—and she inched it upward toward the opening that, she now could see, was wide enough to allow her to fly through, with care.

She didn't fly through. She nudged the plane up little by little and hovered in the shadow of the rim, her head just barely clearing the hole. She looked around, her eyes adjusting to the darkness. Where was Taft? Where were the rest of the orphans?

She was a little higher than the flat central area where she had seen the orphans sitting around their small fire. The opening was at the peak of a rounded cone; it was as if some kind of pressure under the earth had once pushed up the rock and then drained away, leaving a hollowed hill with a hole at the top. It looked a bit like a small, round volcano, and Christina wondered if perhaps that was what it was. The caves might have been hollowed out by lava, too, once upon a time.

The sound of dragging feet caught Christina's ear, and she turned. The children were coming back from the mines. Weary, slump-shouldered, carrying their tin cans, the gray shadows filed up from the terraced pits in a silent, stumbling column.

Christina recognized the two guards herding them. When the men gave the order, the children dropped where they stood, their zoom-collecting cans clanking at their belts.

The guard with the squashed-looking face gave a sharp bark of laughter. "Learned your lesson, have you, wormlets? The next time you sing that vomit-bomb-it song, I'll know you're just asking for another midnight shift in the mines!"

The two men turned away from the exhausted children and walked slowly down the gravel path to the guardhouse. The other guard, Barney, shook his long bangs, looking more like a sheepdog than ever. "I dunno, Torkel. I almost feel sorry for them."

"Don't let anyone else hear you say that," warned the first guard. "We're going to get rich off those kids someday soon."

"Huh? How?"

"I hear the scientists finally figured out how to make zoom into fuel." Torkel lowered his voice. "Instead of barrels of oil, you only need one drop of zoom!"

Barney scratched his chin. "That's good, right?"

"Good? That's fantastic, you moron. Lenny Loompski is going to sell zoom for billions, and we're going to be rolling in dough, see? And all because of Loompski's Happy Orphans!"

Barney bent over to tie his bootlace. "They don't look so happy to me."

"Listen, they're *orphans*." Torkel thumped him on the back. "Nobody expects them to be happy. And anyway, people need fuel to drive cars and keep their houses warm and all that. We're doing everybody a *favor*."

Barney looked up. "Really?"

"Well, except for the orphans. But seriously, who cares if we sacrifice a few kids that nobody wants?"

Barney straightened, his bootlace tied. "What happens to them in the end, though?"

The heavy boots of the guards scuffed past the cone-shaped hill and down the path to the squat wooden building that housed the guards. Christina, in the plane with her head barely poking aboveground, strained every fiber to listen to their fading words.

"If I told you *that*, Barney, you'd feel even more sorry for the orphans than you do now," Torkel said cheerfully. "Come on, let's go find the cards and play a game of Slap 'Em."

The silhouettes in the guardhouse window moved about, pulled out chairs, sat down. Christina turned to look farther away at the lumpy forms of the sleeping children. Taft was in there somewhere.

Did she dare fly the plane out to pick him up? Its glow was subdued but still noticeable. If the guards happened to look out the window just once, they would see it. Of course if anyone came after her, she could easily escape in the plane, but then where would that leave Taft? And she couldn't fly back inside the cone to her mother and Leo, not with guards on her tail.

No. She would have to find him the old-fashioned way—on foot.

Stay, she thought at the plane. It gave a little dip and hummed. *Good plane*. She patted it absently, unstrapped the helmet, and stood up, grasping the edges of the volcanic cone. The plane rocked a little under her, but she got a knee up and climbed out with no trouble at all.

The hill was rough beneath her hands, rock covered by a thin layer of soil, a multitude of pebbles, and a few scrubby plants. She slid down the slope on the seat of her jeans, dusted off her scraped palms, and stood up cautiously. To the guards, if they happened to glance up, she would look like just another orphan. But she didn't dare make any noise. Noise was something the guards would investigate. Maybe it was a good thing that her shoes had gone over the ledge with the little plane.

Sock-footed, Christina picked her way soundlessly among the sleeping forms. The orphans looked like heaps of rags, with here and there an elbow jutting, or a calloused bare foot, or a thin arm flung over a face. The smell of unwashed children rose to her nostrils, and the sound of their breathing was uneven, marked with scattered coughing and quiet, dreaming whimpers.

What had Taft been wearing? She couldn't remember. Anyway, after a night in the mines, his clothes were probably as gray as everyone else's.

She glanced nervously back at the hill. The plane would wait awhile, she knew. But how long would it be able to hover? That might take more fuel than just idling.

The tank was full, Christina reminded herself, but all the same it made her nervous. She quickened her steps. No one heap of rags looked any different than the next. She would have to roll every one of the orphans over to check.

"Taft?" she whispered, bending low over a sleeper of about the right size. "Wake up!"

The boy rolled over and looked up. He had a snub nose and freckles underneath the dirt on his face, and his eyes were dark and lost looking. "Mama?" he murmured thickly.

Christina shook her head.

"Go away then." He flung an arm over his eyes.

The next one was a girl with short hair, and the one after that had a scar on one cheek. One by one, Christina checked them, but none of them were Taft. The last boy she tapped gave a loud cry and flung out his arm, hitting another orphan, who cried out, too. Christina sank instantly to the ground and pretended to be asleep, her heart pumping like a piston in her chest.

After long minutes, when she was sure the guards weren't coming, Christina's heart slowed enough to allow her to think. And suddenly she had it.

"Go-Go," she sang softly, "Chickie-Chickie, Chickie-Go Math." She knew the irritating little tune by heart, it had played across her computer screen for interminable years. "Chickie-Chickie, Go-Go—"

Five yards away a gray-clad figure sat up abruptly, tossed the hair out of its eyes, and stared at Christina with an extremely dirty face.

"Taft?" Christina peered at him.

"Of course it's me, you doofus. Did you bring the plane?"

Christina nodded. "Come on," she whispered, "hurry. And be quiet!"

Taft glanced over his shoulder and seemed to hesitate.

"We'll come back for Danny and the others later. I can only rescue one at a time. Hurry!"

Two stealthy figures crept up the cone-shaped hill. If a guard had glanced out at that moment, he would have been mystified to see them drop suddenly out of sight. And had he followed them up the hill and looked down through the hole that appeared at his feet, he would have seen an enchanting, glowing, beautifully violet plane circling down and around with two filthy children inside, and two anxious faces watching from below.

CHAPTER 26

PETER

"CHRISTINA, you shouldn't have gone so high!" Coughing, Beth Adnoid put a hand to her chest as if it pained her. "It's much too dangerous!"

"But, Mom, there are all these orphans up there—Lenny's working them like *slaves*—"

"Orphans?" Her mother glanced up at the hole in the cavern. "Above us, now?"

"They've been there for *years*, Mom—"

Beth Adnoid's eyes were dark and troubled. "Just before the cave-in, I'd been asking questions . . . Lenny worked aboveground, while we were below, and I'd begun to suspect he was using children in a way he shouldn't."

"He probably *caused* the cave-in," said Christina hotly, "just to stop you from finding out!"

Her mother nodded. "But I had no idea the children were right above me all these years." She reached for her daughter. "It was good of you to try to help them. All the same, what if Lenny had caught you? I just want to keep you safe, sweetheart."

Christina glanced at Taft, who was standing in the shadows, unnoticed. How did it feel to him, she wondered, to know she had *two* parents who were desperate to keep her safe, while he and the rest of the orphans had no one at all? It hardly seemed fair.

All at once Beth Adnoid was bent double, coughing violently. Christina stepped back. What was wrong? Was her mother sick?

Taft was on her other side, now, and Leo hurried to the far end of the cave, where trickling water ran over rock and out through a crack in the floor, and cupboards made of packing cases stood braced.

He came back at a trot. "Here," he said, holding out a flat glass bottle and a spoon. "Her medicine."

Christina looked at the bottle's contents and then at Leo. Behind her, Beth Adnoid was wheezing.

"Come *on*!" cried Taft. "Why don't you pour it?"

Christina handed the bottle to Taft without a word.

Taft shook it, held it upside down over the spoon. A few dried flakes of something brown fell out. He looked up.

"Here, like this." Leo took the bottle, poured an imaginary dose, and pushed the empty spoon at Beth Adnoid. "Take your medicine, my dear." He leaned in, agitated. "It will do you good! Take it, take it, take it!"

Christina's mother reached out blindly for the spoon and tipped it against her mouth, as if swallowing.

Leo nodded happily. "She'll be better soon, you'll see." He fished a wrench out of his back pocket and trotted off toward the wide tunnel that branched from the main cavern. In a few moments, a gentle clinking could be heard and a tuneless whistle.

Taft's eyes slid sideways to meet Christina's. "Who was *that*?" he whispered.

"Leo Loompski."

"No kidding?" Taft nodded toward the sound of clanking metal. "He's gone a little nuts, though, hasn't he?"

"More than a little." Christina looked worriedly at her mother, who was gasping for breath. "Come on, Taft. She needs to lie down, maybe."

The cavern was lined with flat couches made of the same red leather that was used for the plane seats. Christina helped her mother lie back, and Taft found a blanket that he mounded into a pillow.

Beth Adnoid had stopped coughing at last, but her breathing was raspy. She raised her shoulders as Taft tucked the makeshift pillow underneath and looked a question at her daughter.

"Mother," said Christina, "this is my friend Taft."

Taft stood in the light of the wall lantern. He looked strangely old and gray—his hair dusty from the mines, his face gray with smudges and fatigue. His eyes, too, were gray, with their unusual rim of thick lashes, and when he turned his gaze on Beth Adnoid, she reared back on her couch, visibly startled.

Taft took a step back into the shadows. "I know I'm dirty," he mumbled, swatting the dust from his pants.

Beth Adnoid held out her hand, smiling faintly, and after a moment's hesitation, Taft leaned forward and grasped it.

"I'm very glad to meet you," Christina's mother whispered. "Taft—surely that isn't your whole name?"

Taft flushed. "I'm from the orphanage. They only use our last names there. Or our numbers," he added, looking away.

Beth Adnoid gazed at him, her eyes thoughtful. "Tell me about yourself, Taft. Do you have a favorite subject in school?"

Taft kept his head down. "Math," he mumbled. "But I haven't gotten very far."

"Don't believe it," Christina interrupted. "He helped me, and I learned more from him than I ever did from the dancing chickens."

Beth Adnoid raised an eyebrow.

"It's a computer program," said Taft. He looked up once more. "I just taught her some of the basics. She learned fast."

Christina's mother raised herself on one elbow. "And what is your first name?"

Taft blinked. "I'm pretty sure—I mean, I think it might be Peter."

Christina's mother nodded, as if she had expected this. "Do you remember your parents at all, Peter?"

Taft rocked a little, back and forth. "I remember someone tossing me up and catching me. He was big—he had black hair—"

"That was your father."

"—and someone who sang me a song about a little white duck, sitting in the water—"

"That was your mother."

"—and I remember falling in a lake and someone got me out. And bright-colored stars. And some little kid was crying."

"That was the picnic on Mossy Hill. You would have been about four, I think. You wandered too close to the lake, and your father fished you out, and there were fireworks when it got dark. Christina wasn't quite three, and she cried at the noise when they went off."

Taft's eyes were dark and unbelieving in his grimy face.

"I remember your parents very well," said Beth Adnoid gently. "John and Andrea Taft were scientists and our good friends. When they died in a car accident shortly afterward, Lenny Loompski made arrangements to take you to your nearest relatives. He *said* that's where he had taken you." Her face grew stern. "We had no reason to disbelieve him . . . then."

"But how can you be sure? How can you be *sure* it was me?"

Christina saw with dismay that one of his shoulders was beginning to hunch. She cast a pleading look at her mother.

"You have your mother's eyes," said Beth Adnoid firmly. "Those gray eyes and thick, dark lashes are unmistakable. And your parents were both *very* good at math. I would have known you anywhere, even"—she paused and took out a handkerchief—"even with a dirty face." She wiped at a bit of wetness that had just appeared on his dusty cheek.

"You made it worse," said Christina, watching with a critical eye.

"I probably did," said her mother. "You'll both need to wash. Go on—you'll find a bucket and soap and a place for washing behind the cupboards over there."

Taft ran off at once. Christina lingered. "Do you," she said, tracing a welt on the couch with her finger, "do you cough like that very often?"

"Oh, now and then. But don't worry, sweetheart." Beth Adnoid laid a thin hand on Christina's arm. "When Lenny does supply drops, he brings medicine."

Christina looked down. Her arm felt hot where her mother's hand touched it. Her mother had a bad cough, her breathing was too quick, she had a fever . . .

"How often does Lenny bring supplies?" Christina asked abruptly.

Beth Adnoid's eyes were shadowed. "Oh, often enough. Now go take your turn at the bathroom, and then you can stretch out on one of the couches. You must be tired to death."

Christina *was* tired. She stood in front of the packing-case cupboards, waiting her turn with the bucket and soap. She wasn't used to staying up until the middle of the night.

Supper seemed a very long time ago. Were there any snacks in the cupboards? She lifted the flap over the first packing case and then the second. The third. The fourth.

Taft emerged from behind the cases with a clatter and set down the bucket. "I saw where your mother must have sent the messages from. There was this crack in the rock big enough for a test tube, but not much more—what's the matter?" he asked suddenly.

Christina jerked her chin at the packing cases. She couldn't speak.

Taft's gaze swept over the empty cupboards, bare of everything but dust. He jammed his hands in his pockets and whistled.

Christina pressed her lips in a straight and furious line. No wonder her mom and Leo were so thin. Lenny Loompski was *starving* them.

"I'm feeling much better now," said Beth Adnoid. She sat up, swaying slightly. "I was just wondering, Christina . . . do you think that plane would carry me, too?" The lamp's flicker caught at her eyes, and they gleamed. "I know you must be tired, but if I could get out tonight, I could go straight to the police and tell my story. We could get your father released and by morning we could have the whole town up in arms against Lenny, and rescue the orphans, as well."

They tried it at once. Her mother wedged herself into the back seat, her legs dragging over one side, her eyes feverish and bright. Christina, desperate to get her mother home where there was food, sang the notes in order and got in the cockpit. She thought as hard as she could in her tired state—but the plane wouldn't even lift enough to hover.

Taft pointed to the control panel, which now read WARNING! WEIGHT LIMIT EXCEEDED!

Beth Adnoid struggled to her feet, wheezing. "Well, it was worth a try. Tomorrow, Leo can make some modifications. Or we could somehow use two planes—"

"Stay here and rest, Mom. I'll ask him!" Christina ran to the tunnel where the fleet was kept, but Leo had climbed into a plane in the second row and fallen asleep, snoring gently. Though it was clear he had made the plane for someone his size—and he was very small for a man, hardly bigger than Taft—Christina thought it was still a tight fit. Maybe he had intended the planes for children? Or maybe it was just easier to work on a smaller model. Someday, if his mind steadied again, she would ask him.

"Wow!" Taft lifted a lantern off its hook and held it high.

The small perfect planes stretched back into the darkness of the cave, looking like a patch of large silver watermelons that had sprouted wings. The red leather seats were free of dust, the windshield glass was clear and spotless; even the spare fuel canisters were in their holders near the tail. Christina was careful not to bump them as she went to shake Leo's shoulder.

But Leo proved impossible to awaken. Christina gave up and turned to Taft. "I could fly out now, by myself. I could find the police station and tell them everything."

"They won't believe a kid, though." Taft frowned. "And they'd probably call Lenny to come and get you, anyway. He had a court order, you said."

Christina whirled and stalked across the sandy cavern floor. "Well, at least I can fly to my house and get a sack of food. They're *hungry*, Taft!"

Taft followed, looking troubled. "Except your mom will never let you go. She'll say it's too dangerous."

Christina glanced at her mother, who was stooped over, unfolding two extra quilts on the red couches. "That's why I'm not going to even ask her," she said, very low.

"Not going to ask me what?" Beth Adnoid turned, and put a hand on the wall to steady herself.

Christina froze. Her mother must have ears like a rabbit. "Um . . . sorry, but we couldn't wake Leo up," she said at random.

"That's all right. We'll ask him to modify the planes in the morning. What was it you wanted to ask me, though?"

Christina's imagination failed her. She looked at Taft.

Taft grinned. "I *was* actually wondering something. If this was Leo Loompski's private lab, why doesn't it have electricity?"

Christina cast him a grateful glance.

Beth Adnoid sat down at the edge of Christina's couch and took off the rubber bands that held her daughter's hair in braids. Christina stiffened automatically—she hated having her hair combed, Nanny always yanked too hard—and then relaxed in surprise as her mother began to brush with gentle, rhythmic strokes. This was actually kind of nice. If only her mother's hands weren't so terribly warm . . .

"We had it in the main laboratories, of course." Beth Adnoid smoothed Christina's pale hair and parted it in the middle. "The aboveground buildings where I worked with your father were wired for electricity. But the zoom was so powerful an energy source that, whenever we managed to activate it, there would be a sudden surge of localized power and all the electrical circuits would blow." She turned aside to cough, from deep in her chest.

Christina remembered how the lightbulbs had fizzed and gone dark in the tunnel, but she was more concerned about her mother. Shouldn't she be lying down?

"In the end," continued Beth Adnoid after a moment, braiding up one side, "we had to use such extremely small amounts of zoom in our experiments that Leo got frustrated—"

"And he built the underground labs so he could work on more zoom at a time, and he used oil lamps because they wouldn't go out, I bet!" Taft stretched out on one of the couches.

Beth Adnoid finished Christina's second braid and wrapped the end with a rubber band. "I helped him. I know about rocks, you see, and it was clear that this was a site of a former volcano—and honeycombed belowground with lava tubes."

"Lava tubes?" Taft poked his nose out from his brown striped quilt.

"You might call them caves, or tunnels." Christina's mother set down the brush as if it was suddenly too heavy. "You're in one right now. Lava flowed through here long ago. Then when it drained out, the empty tunnel was left." She drew a gray patchwork quilt up under Christina's chin with fingers that trembled. "But enough questions. Growing children need their sleep."

"I'm practically asleep already," said Taft.

"Me, too," said Christina.

"Good night, darlings," said Beth Adnoid.

Christina lay still, reveling in the new sensation of being tucked in and hugged. She wished she could just go to sleep like a regular girl and let her mother take care of everything.

But the sound of coughing echoed suddenly from the washing area. Christina waited, tense under her quilt, until it was over. No, she couldn't rest.

She turned to Taft and spoke under cover of the quilt. "Listen. We'll fly out as soon as she's sleeping. I bet I can find some cough medicine in the bathroom cabinet at home."

"And then let's find Danny and bring him down here."

"Food first," whispered Christina. "If we brought him down here but there was no food when he got hungry—"

"Okay," Taft said reluctantly. "Quiet now—she's coming back."

Christina nodded. And then she felt the touch of a warm hand on her hair and heard the sound of her mother's voice, singing a familiar lullaby. She shut her eyes . . . She would only pretend to sleep . . .

CHAPTER 27

SAFETY SECOND

CHRISTINA woke to a hand shaking her roughly and Taft's voice insistent in her ear.

"Hurry! We don't have much time!"

She opened her eyes. Far above, the hole to the sky showed the dull gray of the hour before dawn. She fought her way out of a tangle of quilt and stumbled to the plane she had used the day before, parked near the rest of the fleet.

"Sing *soft*," said Taft.

Christina didn't need reminding. But as the plane bloomed into its final, muted chord, Leo Loompski lifted his rumpled head from the second row.

"Where are you going?"

Taft put a finger to his lips. "To get food," he whispered. "Since Lenny didn't bring you any."

Leo sat up, a small man with confused eyes beneath wispy hair. "Lenny?" He gazed at the luminous violet plane, his eyes reflecting its glow. "Are you going to see my nephew?"

Christina, in the cockpit of the plane, sat perfectly still.

Would he wake her mother? Would he tell them they couldn't go?

But Leo just dug in his pocket. "You need a wrench. For fixing."

Christina took the proffered wrench. It clinked against the jackknife in her back pocket.

"But what do you want us to fix?" Taft asked gently.

Leo stared at them both, his eyes more focused than Christina had ever seen them. "*Lenny* needs fixing. Go. Fix him *now*."

As they neared the top of the cavern, they heard voices.

Christina circled around the dim, gray light that washed in through the opening and hovered in the shadows, beneath a hanging lump of rock. The plane's humming was drowned out by the sound of an idling engine nearby, and the arguing voices were deep and loud.

"But I've got the winch on the back of the truck," said a voice that Christina thought she had heard before, "and the supplies all ready. Just let me lower the food, at least."

"No," snapped the second voice—which was clearly Lenny Loompski's.

"But that's the second supply order you've canceled!"

Christina recognized the first voice now—it was the yard boss from the orphanage. She glanced back at Taft. He sat rigidly, his shoulders hunched nearly to his ears.

"So?" Lenny's voice held a shrug. "I supplied everything Uncle Leo and Beth Adnoid wanted for years, but not once did they give me what *I* wanted. Nothing I could submit for the Karsnicky Medal! Nothing I could use to make zoom into fuel!"

"But the scientists at the main lab just figured that out."

"Right. So what do I need these two for? Nothing, that's what."

There was a pause. "What are you going to do? Starve them to death?"

"I'm not *starving* them. I've just . . . lost interest in feeding them." Lenny's voice sounded annoyed. "Anyway, what business is it of yours, Crumley?"

"Er . . ."

"If you feel that sorry for them, why don't you join them? I can lower you on the winch right now."

"Boss, I never said—"

"You're paid to do as you're told and keep your mouth shut, remember? Now turn off that truck and leave it."

"Yessir."

The idling engine was cut. Suddenly everything was much quieter.

"Hey," said Crumley, "do you hear somebody humming?"

Softer, softer, softer, thought Christina in a panic, and the plane's hum diminished to the merest breath of sound.

"I don't hear anything," said Lenny. "Come back to the guardhouse. We just got in our first order for zoom, and I want to go over the procedure with everyone."

Lenny's sentences began to break up, coming to Christina's ears in fragments.

"Tonight . . . visitor . . . doesn't know . . ."

Lenny's voice faded into an indistinct murmur. The sound

of footsteps died away, and a door slammed in the distance. Christina edged the plane up just until her head cleared the rim, and she and Taft looked out.

Directly before them was a large pickup truck, backed up to the hole. The predawn air was gray and murky, but there was enough light for Christina and Taft to see that the pickup was loaded with food.

"Jackpot," whispered Taft.

Stay, Christina thought. *Good plane*. She took off the helmet, stood on her seat, and climbed out over the lip of the cone. She slid a little—the cone sloped—and stopped herself against the truck's rear right tire, which smelled of asphalt and rubber. She peered around it to the guardhouse at the bottom of the hill. A window showed the silhouettes of Lenny and the bristle-haired boss, backlit by yellow light, as they sat down and leaned toward each other.

"Look, there are even gunnysacks!" Taft was already up on the truck's flatbed, poking amid the stacked boxes and baskets. "We can pack them with whatever we want!"

Christina was filled with a powerful sense of satisfaction as she scrambled onto the pickup. She *would* be able to get food to her mother and Leo, lots of it, even sooner than she had thought. And the truck would block them from the view of anyone who looked out the guardhouse window.

"Hey!" Taft stopped in the midst of loading a gunnysack with bread and fruit. "Why don't we make more than one trip? There won't be room for me in the plane anyway, if the food's in the back seat—"

"And while I'm unloading, you can be filling another sack!"

Christina flew down into the cavern with the first sackful of food, flushed with triumph. In a few more trips, they'd have enough food to last them for weeks—time enough for Leo to design and build a plane that could carry more weight. And then—why, then her parents would be reunited, the orphans would be freed, and Lenny Loompski would be thrown behind bars, where he belonged.

Yes, everything was going perfectly. By the time her mother woke up, the cupboards would be completely stocked with food.

And medicine? Christina flew softly past her sleeping mother and blew her a kiss. It would be in one of the boxes on the truck. The question was, could she find it in the dark?

"I've been thinking," said Taft. He paused to wipe the sweat from his forehead; while Christina was gone, he had filled six gunnysacks and lined them against the side of the truck. "Why not bring Danny down, right now? Once we get enough food, I mean."

Christina climbed onto the open tailgate and dug in the first box she came to. Was that a bottle of cough medicine? She held it up and squinted in the gloom. No, only mustard.

"I know we can't rescue all the kids yet," Taft went on. "But Danny needs me. I could go find him and send him down in the plane with you."

Christina ripped open the next box with her pocketknife. "That won't work. Once he sees you again, do you really think he's going to get in a plane and let me take him away from you?"

"But I'd *explain*—"

"You'd have to explain over and over again, and he would make a fuss. And he's never been in a plane, I bet. He might be scared. He might yell."

Taft looked at his feet. His shoulders slumped.

"Of course," Christina said, "he'd go with *you*."

Taft looked up.

"If *you* were flying the plane," she continued, warming to her idea, "he'd go with you in a heartbeat, no fuss at all."

Taft frowned. "I can't fly, remember? I tried."

Christina felt inside the second box. Duct tape, pens, scissors, paper. Cough medicine had to have been on the supply order—where was it? "You *can* fly," she said briefly, opening a third box. "But you have to believe you can, first. It's just like me and math."

"Math is different," said Taft. "Anyone can do math."

Christina sat back on her heels, exasperated. "Well, *I* couldn't. And you'll never focus your thoughts enough to fly, either, until you stop focusing on how you *can't*."

Taft looked doubtful.

"Come on, try it. You can practice without Danny, and while you fly the food down, I'll try to spot where he is." Christina jumped off the truck. "Here, let me have your shirt—and let's cut off your shock collar. I can tape it together around my neck. Then if somebody sees me, I'll look like just another orphan. Now get in the plane, and put that helmet on—unless you *don't* want to rescue Danny."

Taft climbed into the plane, protesting all the way. "Listen, Christina, it's different for me. I really can't fly this plane—it won't let me. I bet it can tell I'm just an orph——"

"Stop *saying* that!" Christina saw with fury that his shoulders were beginning to hunch. "You're brilliant at math, and you didn't panic in the cave even when the flashlight died, and you're my best friend, and Danny's, too." Christina knelt at the edge of the hole and glared down at Taft, shivering bare-chested in the plane's front seat. "You're not just an orphan, you're *Peter Taft*. Now think! Think hard! Think GO!"

There was a *whoosh* of air and a swirl of violet light as the plane beneath her took off with a jerk. Christina suppressed a whoop—he'd really done it!—and turned to look around the edge of the truck.

Yes, the two silhouettes were still in the guardhouse window—and now they had been joined by more, all lifting glasses and drinking. They looked as if they were settling in for a long, long time.

Even better, Christina found the cough medicine in the fourth box. She wanted to make sure Taft took it in his very next load, so she set it front and center on the tailgate of the truck, where he would be sure to see it.

She couldn't help but feel a little proud of herself as she prowled the ridge, looking down at the orphans' camp below. She had figured things out, she had made her own plans, and now she was even going to rescue Danny.

But Danny was nowhere to be seen.

For sure he wasn't among the sleeping orphans that lay about the smoldering embers of the fire. The length of his body and the size of his head would have made him easy to spot.

Where could he have gone?

She was getting close to the guardhouse. Christina slipped

from shadow to shadow, careful how she placed her feet. Had they taken Danny inside?

She crouched down under the window. The voices inside were loud and confusing, talking all at once, but she could pick up random snatches of conversation.

"Yeah, nobody cares what happens to orphans, so we're safe—"

"—the Karsnicky Medal comes with a hundred-thousand-dollar prize—"

"We've got to ship a kid out tomorrow with the plastic toys—"

"—singing wrong notes on purpose, I swear—"

"But weren't you going to get some kid with perfect pitch, boss? For the underground mine, where they can't hear the harriers?"

"Yeah, well, she made a run for it." The babble quieted as Lenny Loompski's voice grated with suppressed rage. "We'll find her, though. I found a picture of her in her dad's office, and I put up 'Missing Child' posters all over town—the police station, the library, the school . . . I want everyone here on the lookout for a scrawny girl with blond braids. Answers to the name Christina."

CHAPTER 28

THREE SIMPLE RULES

CHRISTINA could scarcely breathe. No place was safe. Even in the town, people would be looking for her. And at Dorf Elementary, where she had hoped to go to school one day, her face was plastered on the door . . . like a criminal's.

She tried to stand and walk away, but her legs felt strangely watery. She crawled instead, trying desperately to make no noise at all. When she reached the first bit of adequate cover—a large bush at the base of a tree—she stopped and hugged her knees to keep from shaking, and tried to think what to do next.

Lenny was looking for a girl with braids.

Well, she could fix that. Christina reached into her back pocket, past Leo's wrench, and pulled out her jackknife.

She hesitated a moment. It had been so lovely when her mother brushed her hair.

Of course if Lenny caught her, she might never see her mother again. Christina gripped her left braid and sawed away with the knife. The night was quiet; she could hear an irregular squeaking, like an odd sort of cricket, and the soft, rasping sound of splitting hair next to her ear.

The braids were off, and heavy in her hand. She rubber-banded them together and tucked them in her waistband. There was no sense leaving them around for someone to find.

She needed to look more like an orphan and less like the girl in the picture. She picked up a handful of dirt and rubbed it on her face. There. She'd done what she could for now.

Christina looked up toward the cone where the pickup was parked. It was getting lighter, and now she could see the flitting shadow of something moving, legs perhaps, between the truck chassis and the ground. If she squinted, she could see a faint glow seeping over the cone's top like a pale violet fog.

No, it was gone again. Taft must have put in another gunnysack and gone down to unload.

All right. She hadn't been able to find Danny. But clearly she had to get back inside the mountain. And there was no time to lose . . . The sky had changed from dark to pearly gray. She couldn't move about, hidden, for much longer.

That cricket was squeaking in the strangest manner. The sound seemed to be coming from behind a large upthrust rock.

Christina crept stealthily toward it. She could hide behind it if anyone came, and it was fifty feet closer to where she needed to go.

Only it was not a cricket. It was Danny.

The moon had set long since, but the sky was growing lighter, and she could see his tall, dejected form slumped against the rock, tear streaks on his dirty face. He was cradling something in his arms—the rubber cow—and as Christina watched, he squeaked it again.

She *couldn't* leave him here alone . . .

But Danny didn't know her. Even if he *would* come with her, even if he *didn't* make a fuss, he would still be slow and clumsy climbing up to the cone. Her chances of getting caught were at least doubled with Danny along.

The door of the guardhouse slammed. Heavy boots clattered down the wooden steps. There was a sound of matches flaring and then a wafting scent of tobacco.

Christina hunkered down in the shadow of tall weeds, her heart beating wildly. If she stayed very still—if they didn't glance this way—

One of the guards scuffed at the dirt. "Did you get all that, Torkel?"

"Sure, Barney. What didn't you understand?"

"Well, those plastic toys are too hard to soak up zoom."

"Nah, plastic soaks liquid up just like raisins do. Ever soaked hard raisins in water? Give it a day and they're juicy again."

"But I still don't get *why* . . ."

Christina slid her eyes sideways. She could see the ends of the guards' cigarettes glowing briefly as they inhaled.

Torkel blew out a stream of smoke. "I guess if zoom's in plastic, and solid, you can bring it anywhere, no spills, no explosions. But melt it, sing it out again, and *wow*!"

Barney scratched his head. "Wow, what?"

"Something happens to it when it's in the plastic. It's a cat—a catal—"

A catalyst, thought Christina. She had heard that word from her father. But she couldn't remember exactly what it meant.

"Anyway, all of a sudden it's, like, a thousand times more explosive!"

"Wow, dangerous!"

"More like, wow, more energy, more power for fuel, and a lot more money for Lenny Loompski!"

There was a silence. From behind the rock there came another squeak.

"Is he going to give any of that money to us, Tork?"

"If we do a good job, Barney. See, you drive the garbage truck, right?"

Barney swelled up his chest. "I sure do."

"Well, then. You're the one who's going to drive the kids and the toys. Just pretend you're picking up garbage, and drop the kids off instead, and you're done."

"But where are they going on the garbage truck, Torkel? I won't feel sorry for them, I promise."

Danny was still squeaking his rubber cow, oblivious to the rumbling voices of the guards. Christina could only hope they thought it was just another insect. But simply for her own sake, she wished he'd stop. She might miss hearing something important.

". . . lots of places still heated with oil. If they can be heated by orphans singing zoom out of plastic toys, it's a ton cheaper. The clients save lots of money, Lenny gets even richer, and everybody's happy, as long as they follow three simple rules—oh, come *on*, that cricket's driving me crazy!"

Torkel picked up a stick and threw it in the direction of the rock. There was a cry.

"That's no cricket!"

The guards thundered past the patch of tall weeds where Christina lay hidden. There was a sound of scuffling and a whimper from Danny as he was dragged to his feet.

"All right, hand over the squeaky toy." Torkel stood over Danny, legs apart and arms folded.

Danny clutched the cow to his chest. "Taff gave it to me," he said, his voice ragged.

"I don't care if Santa Claus and all his elves gave it to you. Hand it over."

Slowly, reluctantly, Danny stretched out the hand that held his toy.

"Oh, for crying—" Torkel made an impatient noise and grabbed the cow. He flung it away, and Christina followed its high, curving arc with her eyes.

"Now get on out of here!" Torkel gave Danny a push with his boot, and the tall boy went stumbling off, his large head low.

Barney shuffled his feet. "Guess you gotta be hard on them, huh, Torkel?"

"It's for their own good." Torkel threw an arm around Barney's shoulder as they walked back toward the guardhouse. "See, if we're soft with them now, it'll just be harder for them later. Life isn't easy for orphans, and the sooner they learn that, the better."

"So that's why everyone tells them they're stupid and dirty and won't ever amount to anything?"

"Yep. Then they won't be disappointed when it turns out that way, see?"

Barney followed the other man's bulky form up the steps to the guardhouse. "But, Torkel, you said there were three simple rules to follow. What are they?"

Torkel paused at the door. The lantern shone full on his squashed, bulldog face. "Rule number one: Keep the orphans a secret."

Barney looked up. "Is that why I have to deliver them in a garbage truck?"

Torkel nodded. "And then the client puts them in a little room with no windows—"

"And locks it, I bet!"

"That's right. And they never leave, until their voices get too grown-up sounding to work."

Barney twisted his hands together. "I suppose rule number two is to keep them hungry, or they won't sing when it's time to."

"Well, of course."

"I don't know if Momma would have liked that," said Barney, half to himself.

Torkel socked Barney playfully on the arm. "Your momma's dead, though, right?"

"Yeah," said Barney earnestly, "but what if she's looking down on me from somewhere?"

"Listen, Barney, was your momma a normal person? Or a crazy bleeding-heart type?"

"Um . . . normal. I guess."

"Well, then, she'll understand it's just business. Nothing personal."

"Oh," said Barney. He looked up. "And what's rule number three?"

The guardhouse door opened. Torkel and Barney backed down the steps as Lenny came out, took a deep, vigorous breath of the early morning air, and looked over at the sleeping orphans, some distance away.

"I've got to get these kids earlier," he said, rasping the stubble on his chin. "I hear the younger you teach them their notes, the more likely they are to develop perfect pitch." Lenny gazed at the sleeping orphans some distance away. "I'm sure I can find a few babies across the border—hey, you there!"

Christina looked in the direction of Lenny's glare. A little distance away, Danny was on his hands and knees, searching for something in the weeds.

"What do you think you're doing?"

Danny lifted an anxious face. "My cow is lost."

The sky grew lighter in the east as dawn neared. On the rocks above, a harrier cried out its first greeting to the day.

"Hear that?" Lenny raised his voice. "Forget the cow. Just remember that pitch, if you know what's good for you, or . . . KABOOM!"

Danny ran back to the sleeping orphans, whimpering.

"Hee hee!" Lenny clapped his thick palms together.

"I wish you wouldn't say that, boss," said Barney plaintively. "That *kaboom* part gives me the willies."

"It's fun, though." Lenny opened the guardhouse door. "Anyway, if they're not afraid, they won't get the right sound in the note."

"And that's rule number three," said Torkel, as the door slammed shut.

Barney frowned. "Keep them secret. Keep them hungry. And . . . keep them scared?"

Torkel nodded. "And when their voices change, of course, get rid of them."

"You mean . . . *permanently?*"

"Sure. We just drive up in the garbage truck like we're going to pick up trash, only we pick up the kid. And then, well, you know. We push the red button."

"We *mash* them?" Barney swallowed hard. "Isn't that a little . . . harsh?"

Torkel shrugged. "Maybe, but how else are we going to keep rule number one?"

CHAPTER 29
STRANDED

CHRISTINA stumbled across the rocky ground in horror, hardly able to take in what she had heard.

This was why her father had tried so hard to keep her safe. Because he had known what she had not—that there were terrible people in the world who didn't care about keeping children safe at *all*.

The guards were back inside, but not for long. Christina made a last dash for the relative safety of the pickup truck and collapsed behind it, her breath uneven.

There were no gunnysacks left. So Taft had made five trips, up and down—and now he would come back for her. She hoped he would understand why she hadn't brought Danny.

She scanned the back of the pickup truck. Would Lenny notice that some of the food had been taken? Maybe she should rearrange the boxes. Quickly, she scrambled up—and saw the bottle of cough medicine still there, front and center.

She snatched it up and tucked it inside her waistband with the braids. No harm done. She'd bring it down with her.

Christina quietly moved some full boxes to the fore and hid the empties behind them, glancing over her shoulder now and then to see if Taft had returned.

He should have come back by now. How long did it take him to unload one sack? She scroonched on her stomach to the lip of the cone and hung over the edge. Yes, there was Taft, already flying up, the plane glowing a beautiful blue . . .

She blinked. That wasn't right.

The plane struggled higher and took on a greenish tint.

Christina cupped her hands around her mouth. "You're running out of zoom! Use the spare canister!" She glanced back over her shoulder. Had anyone heard? She hoped the sound had all gone downward.

She looked back into the cavern and saw Taft still ascending, his face upturned, the plane now greenish gold.

"What did you say?" he called, his voice anxious.

"The spare—" Christina began, and then clapped her hands over her mouth. No! He couldn't refuel midflight—the plane was far too wobbly. If the zoom spilled, it would explode when it hit the ground. And her mother and Leo were down there.

The plane turned golden. Suddenly Christina saw that Taft would never make it. He needed what zoom was left to make a safe landing—if he could do it at all. It would take less fuel to go down than to keep rising.

She still had her mother's cough medicine. She pulled it out along with her braids—yes, she could rubber-band the hair around the bottle to cushion it.

"Catch!" she cried, and dropped the bottle.

Taft caught it with both hands and pulled it to his chest. He looked up at her as the plane turned a bright pumpkin color.

Christina could read his face like a headline. He understood what was happening. But he couldn't make himself abandon her.

"You've got to!" cried Christina. "Go down now, or you'll crash!"

Taft cast her one last anguished look. The plane began to descend, faster, faster.

Christina clenched her hands, her fingernails biting into her palms, and waited tensely for the sound of smashing metal. But all was quiet.

She looked down. Far, far below, there was a faint glow of pinky rose—and then it winked out.

Taft was safe. And she was on her own.

There was a crunch of boots behind the pickup. Christina, startled, shoved herself quickly away from the lip of the cone.

It was a little more force than she needed. The cone was steep and the pebbles loose, and she was skidding, sliding, making far too much noise. She scrabbled to a stop at last and opened her eyes. There, inches from her nose, was a pair of polished black boots.

Christina's heart jackknifed like a fish leaping. She sucked air as a ham-sized fist gripped her arm and hauled her upright.

"And what have we here?" Lenny Loompski bent over Christina, his face shadowed. "Is this one of my happy orphans who loves me?"

Christina pressed a hand to her heart, whose beat had steadied to a taut, fearful pounding. She looked up at the man's dark, broad face.

He didn't recognize her with her dirty face and short hair, but she recognized him. This was the man who had imprisoned her mother, jailed her father, enslaved a hundred orphans, and driven his own uncle insane. She could not think of anyone she despised more.

"Yes," she said through her teeth.

"And what were you doing way up here, all by yourself?" Lenny's eyes darted suspiciously to the truck.

"Er . . ." Christina thought fast. "I was practicing my song. I didn't want anyone to hear it until it was ready. It was a Happy Orphan kind of song," she added in a burst of inspiration.

Lenny Loompski's face relaxed into a smile. "Really? A song for me? A new one?"

Christina nodded. She was pretty sure Lenny Loompski hadn't heard verse two of Taft's vomit and bomb-it song. But she thought she had better change a few words.

Lenny's sure to win the Karsnicky
Since he's smart, it won't be tricky
Yes, it's clear, it is not murky
Lenny's not a big fat turkey . . .

She sang it slightly off-key. Lenny didn't seem to notice.

"Marvelous, marvelous! You'll have to sing that one for our visitor tonight. And make sure you sing your very best." He pointed down past the sleeping orphans to the terraced mines, open to the sky. From this angle, Christina could see what she had never noticed before—a blackened hole in a rock wall, the height and width of a man. The top seemed to have been recently collapsed.

"That," said Lenny, chuckling, "is where orphans go when they're *not* so happy. Sometimes, bad orphans don't sing their very, very best for Lenny. But if their pitch is off in the underground mine . . . Well, let's just say, small loss. And the roof of the mine gets opened up a little more, so it all works out in the end, see?"

Christina looked at him in horror. She backed away.

"Bad orphans go *kaboom*, see?"

Christina turned and ran. Down the hill, toward the orphan camp—anywhere to get away from that smiling, evil man. She crashed through tall weeds, her feet kicking up everything in their path—dirt, gravel, rocks, rubber cows—

Christina stopped. She walked back a few steps and looked carefully at the ground. She bent swiftly and tucked something inside her shirt.

The orphans sat in the dust, all eyes fixed on Christina. She had told them very little about herself—who knew if one of them might accidentally blurt something out in front of a guard? But they seemed most interested in the fact that she wasn't an orphan.

"So . . ." Dorset traced a line in the dirt with her finger. "What's it like to have a father?"

Christina looked around the circle of children. The faces

were all different, and yet every child had the same look: unwashed, uncared-for, eyes large and hungry.

The small boy at Christina's side tugged at her sleeve. "Not a Happy Orphan Daddy," he whispered. "The real kind."

"Well," Christina began, and stopped. What could she possibly say?

The orphans inched closer, leaning in to hear.

Christina tried again. "I guess . . . a real father keeps you safe."

A soft sigh went up from each orphan throat.

"What about a mother?" asked a small girl with tangled hair and an upturned nose. "What does she do?"

Christina gazed at the girl thoughtfully and reached out a hand. "A mother does a lot of things. Like this, for one." She pulled the girl in close and began to comb gently through the tangled hair with her fingers.

"Does she use ribbons?" asked the girl dreamily.

"Sometimes," said Christina. "If she has them."

"*My* mother would always have them."

A boy in a gray undershirt stirred restlessly. "She would not. *Your* mother abandoned you."

The girl under Christina's hands snapped straight. "Well, so did yours!"

"No," said the boy, shaking his head. "I think maybe I was stolen."

"Me, too!"

"That's what happened to me!"

"It did *not*, you bragger."

A babble of voices rose in heated discussion. A guard

stepped outside the guardhouse, yawned and stretched, and began to stroll toward the orphan camp.

Dorset stood up and rattled her tin can. "Come on, it's time."

The children scrambled to their feet, picked up their cans, and shook awake the few orphans who were still asleep. In a moment, they had formed a ragged column and begun to march off the flat sleeping area and down the terraced steps to the mines.

"Maybe when I was little, my mother was going to give me a ride in my stroller," said the boy in the gray undershirt, hooking his can to his belt. "But then she had to go inside for something she forgot, and Lenny Loompski came along and stole me."

The girl who had wanted ribbons looked serious. "She shouldn't have gone back inside."

"It was just for a minute," said the boy. "She didn't mean to."

On the edge of the orphan camp, behind a stone slab on the first terrace down, Christina found Danny sitting in the dust.

She spoke softly, so as not to startle him. "Hi, Danny. My name's Christina."

The big boy raised his face, his eyes dark brown pools of misery. "Steena?" He blinked and looked down again at his hands.

"What's that you have there?" Christina took a step closer.

Danny opened his cupped hands to reveal a stone the size of a small egg. "Rocky." He moved his big thumb over it, back and forth, as if he were petting something very fragile.

Christina watched him for a moment. "I found something of yours," she said. "Here."

Danny stared at the rubber cow, unbelieving. The rock fell from his hands as he reached for the toy, his face changing from hopeless misery to delight. "Bubby!" he cried. He pressed the cow to his cheek, his neck, his chest, and turned bright eyes to Christina. "Taff gave her to me!"

"I know," said Christina gently. "Taft is my friend, too."

"You know Taff?" Danny gazed at her. "Is he coming to get me?"

Christina hesitated. Taft was stuck inside the mountain just as certainly as Leo and her mother were. He couldn't sing the notes needed to get the planes activated again, even if the fuel tanks were filled to overflowing with zoom.

"*We* are going to get *him*," she said at last. "But not right this minute."

Danny scrambled to his feet. "When?" he asked urgently.

"Soon," said Christina, desperately hoping it was true. "Very soon."

CHAPTER 30
ONE TIN CAN

"**H**EY! You, there!"

Christina looked up to the rim's edge where a guard, bored and sleepy, was scratching himself.

"Get a move on!"

Danny crammed Bubby the cow into the front of his shirt and obediently shambled down the stair-stepped path to the mine's lower levels. Christina followed more slowly.

The mines were like a big rough bowl beneath an endless gray sky. The top level was fissured with cracks where the zoom had been sung out already, by children or birds. Here and there, Christina could see a blackened crevice, where perhaps the children's notes had been slightly off.

She picked up a pebble and rapped sharply at a bit of lichen on the terrace wall, flaking it off. Would it look like she was working? She had no tin can.

Just above her, amid the rocks that fenced the Starkian Ridge, something moved and ruffled. A harrier poked its smooth feathered head above its nest, roused, and opened its yellow beak, crying a protest at being disturbed.

Below, the orphans' voices all lifted together in an imitation of the cry, and Christina could hear the clink of tin cans as they were pressed against the rock. At her fingertips, a spot of zoom that had been beneath the lichen suddenly glistened, melted, and fell in drops to the ground with a *pop! pop!*

"I heard that!" shouted the guard. "Someone's wasting zoom!"

The sun bumped above the mountains, throwing instant shadows, blue-gray and sharply edged. Christina moved like a cat into the deep shade of the rock wall, glanced over her shoulder, and slipped down to the next terrace, and then the next. She couldn't afford to be noticed, if she ever wanted to rescue Taft and Leo and her mother. And she *had* to rescue them; she was the only one who even knew where they were, apart from Lenny and his guards.

But how, how? She was just one girl against an evil man who seemed to have almost everyone on his side. She didn't even know how she could rescue *herself*.

A low-lying fog had settled in the deepest level of the mine, and Christina could see the heads of the orphans moving above it, ghostly in the swirling vapor. She hurried down the last few steps and ducked into the cold and clammy mist.

Child-shaped forms moved past her like smudges in a cloud. Sound was echoed, magnified—harriers calling one to the other, children crying out like frightened birds, metal tapping stone. Christina huddled out of the way, her back against the terrace wall. She had to think. She had to plan.

Instead, pictures of her father rose in her mind's eye.

Her father, rumpled and absentminded, patting her shoulder as he passed.

Her father, rustling the morning paper, setting down his coffee to draw out a math problem on his napkin.

Her father, anxious to do the right thing, carefully writing down her height, weight, dental appointments in the green scrapbook—knowing it wasn't enough, but trying his best; her father, whose greatest desire was to keep her safe.

Christina wanted nothing more than to run into the safety of his arms. If only he were here, right this minute, she would tell him everything and then he would come up with a good solution.

She blinked until the moisture was gone from her eyes. All right, then, so her father *wasn't* here. What would he do if he were?

Well, he wouldn't be sniveling uselessly. He would be looking at the problem step by step. Don't worry about the final answer yet, he would tell her. What do you know right now that you can build on?

Christina drew in the dirt with her finger. She knew a lot, actually. She knew all about Lenny Loompski's horrible plans for the orphans. And Lenny didn't know that she knew.

That was an advantage.

What else did she know that Lenny didn't?

He didn't know who she really was. A dirty face and no braids had fooled him completely. Christina's hand went to the back of her neck, touching her cropped hair, brushing against Taft's shock collar . . .

Wait! She had forgotten the biggest advantage of all! Lenny and his guards didn't know that her shock collar, the thing that kept the orphans penned up on the ridge, had been cut through and no longer worked!

She fingered the duct tape where it joined the two ends. She had to keep the guards from noticing it. Luckily the tape was gray—everything in this place was gray, it seemed—and her hair was just long enough to cover it, if she didn't bend forward.

That was her solution. She just had to wait for a moment when the guards weren't paying attention and then slip over the ridge and hike down the mountain. She would go for help—she would find her father—

She would have to be careful not to go off the cliff, though. The side of the mountain where she had been stranded in the plane was way too steep for anyone but a mountain goat. No, she would have to look for a safer way down. Of course she couldn't use the road.

But what if her father was still in jail?

And what if Lenny had guards waiting at her house?

Christina poked at a hole in the knee of her jeans. She did not want to think about guards that might be waiting for her somewhere.

There was a second hole on the other knee, and a jagged

rip just above it. Christina brushed the frayed edge back and forth, marveling.

She had never played hard enough to get holes in her clothing before. After all the times she had watched other children on the playground, skinning their knees and wearing holes in their pants playing Chase and Tap, *she* had finally gotten outside and done things, too—climbed trees, run after garbage trucks, explored caves, slid down into mountains.

But she had not wanted to be chased, or grabbed, or kept prisoner for real. And the kids at Dorf Elementary had a teacher to run to if they got hurt or were scared.

Christina lifted her head, struck by this idea. If she could find the school, could *she* run to a teacher for help?

Yes—yes, she could! She could ask for old Mrs. Lisowsky! Her music teacher would believe and help her, surely. All she had to do was find just one grown-up who would listen, who would tell the police and everyone else that Lenny Loompski was not what he pretended to be.

The fog was thinning. Christina stood up. She would keep her eye out for the best way off the ridge, but in the meantime, the most important thing was to blend in with the orphans. She had to get a tin can.

"Dorset!" she hissed, recognizing the girl passing a few yards away. Christina strode quickly toward her—and stumbled on a rock she didn't see. She staggered, twisting, and fell heavily on her right shoulder.

"Are you all right?" Dorset's concerned face appeared above

her. "You can't move fast in fog, you know." She peeled back Christina's shirt and examined her shoulder. "You have to feel with your feet before you step. You'd better learn, because we get a lot of fog here, with all the streams running through the rock."

Christina tried not to moan aloud. "Now you tell me," she managed, gritting her teeth against the pain. "I think I broke my whole shoulder."

Dorset's fingers pushed and prodded. "You're bleeding. And you'll have a good bruise. You might have pulled a muscle, too. But I don't think you cracked anything."

"Stop—*moving* it," Christina gasped. "I believe you."

Dorset sat back on her heels. "If you tell a guard, they might give you an extra rag for a bandage."

"No." Christina struggled to sit up. "No guards. If they get that close, they might notice—"

"Notice what?"

Christina hesitated. Then she bent forward, lifting her hair off the nape of her neck.

Dorset took in her breath sharply. She touched the duct tape with reverent fingers. "Can you cut mine? Do you have a knife?"

Christina nodded. "But no duct tape. It's back on the truck."

Dorset leaned forward. "What are you going to do?" she whispered. "How can I help?"

Christina told her. It took some time.

The last rags of fog drifted away. Dorset, her whole face alive with excitement, helped Christina to her feet. "I know where there's an extra tin can."

"But that's Joey's can!" said a boy with a snub nose and dark thick hair. "She can't take it. You said we'd leave it there to remind us."

More orphans gathered behind Christina and Dorset, staring mutely at the blackened entrance to the underground mine. To the left was a box of candles and matches; to the right, a small pile of stones, carefully stacked, and a battered and dented tin can. Someone had put the flowering tops of a few straggling weeds in it and filled it with water.

"Hey! Orphans!"

Every face looked up. The shouting guard, silhouetted at the mine's top, put his hands on his hips. "Breakfast!"

"Listen," said Dorset to the gathered children, rapidly and low. "We'll *always* remember Joey. Every one of us piled a stone here in his honor. But this girl needs a tin can so no one knows she's a spy."

"A spy?" The word went from mouth to mouth like a whispering breeze.

"And she's going to help us get off this mountain. But we have to help her, first."

"Orphans! NOW!" yelled the guard.

"Go, go!" urged Dorset. "And don't look so happy or the guards will know something's up!"

The children filed up the stairs, pulling their mouths down as best they could. But their eyes were bright and their backs straight with joy.

"Better tell them to slump," murmured Christina. Dorset nodded, looking worried, and ran up the side of the line, whispering as she went.

Christina picked up the tin can. Gently, she laid the flowers to one side, poured out the water, and turned to go. Then, hesitating, she turned back.

She laid one more stone on the little cairn. She said a brief prayer.

She ran up the stairs after the orphans, a lump in her throat.

CHAPTER 31

AN UNEXPECTED VISITOR

CHRISTINA cleared the rim and saw before her the flat sleeping space of the orphan camp and the dead remains of the night's fire, a pile of white flaky ash that smelled of smoke. She joined the line of orphans forming near the guardhouse, where a rough wooden table held a large, steaming pot and a stack of bowls. The garbage truck, parked in the small lot at the end of the road, added its own distinct aroma to the air.

Christina shuffled forward as the line moved, carefully shifting her eyes from side to side. Up above the cone with the opening to the cavern, the tall slabs of rock ringed the camp like prehistoric fangs. Beyond, she knew, was the cliff. She couldn't escape that way.

Of course the gravel road was on a more gradual slope and curved down into the forest. But she would be all too easy to catch on the road.

Splat. Christina looked down at the thin, lumpy, whitish gruel in her bowl. It looked like library paste.

She dipped her spoon in. It *tasted* like library paste. No wonder Taft had been so enthusiastic about the blueberry pie. She gave her bowlful to the child next to her—the garbage truck had taken away her appetite, anyway—and glanced back over her shoulder.

On the far side of the terraced mines, the rocks weren't so high, and beyond them she could see trees sloping down. That would be the best way to go, if only she could get there without attracting notice.

But it was impossible to get to the far side with the guards watching at the rim.

The children worked the mines all day long, the heat baking off the bare rocks in shimmering waves. In her efforts to blend in, Christina sang just like the other orphans, collecting only a little zoom. She didn't want anyone to notice anything special about her.

Her shoulder ached steadily. Her socks were shredded from the hard, stony ground, and her feet, unused to going barefoot, were tender. At noon, she washed the blood off her shirt in one of the little rivulets that trickled through the rocks. Blood might draw someone's attention.

She got hungrier as the day went on. The half slice of stale bread at lunchtime was not what she had been hoping for, and by suppertime she was ravenous.

But it was almost sunset before the children were finally allowed to trudge up the wearisome steps, half asleep and faint with hunger, and told to line up in rows.

The pickup truck full of food—well, partly full—was now parked in the lot next to the garbage truck. Christina stared at it with a mixture of dread and longing. Would anyone notice that some of the food was missing? And, more important, would she and the others get anything decent to eat, at long last?

The guard Barney was in and out of the garbage truck cab, cleaning the windows and side mirrors. He whistled between his teeth, first sloshing a rag into a sudsy bucket, then pulling a rubber squeegee across the windshield with a satisfying squeak.

He looked positively carefree. But as Lenny Loompski's long black car pulled up the gravel road, he stopped whistling. He polished a little harder.

Was he getting the garbage truck ready for tomorrow? Christina tried to remember everything she had heard. They'd had an order for zoom . . . It would be sung out of the plastic toys . . .

A car door opened with a creak. "Oh, wonderful!" cried a gentle, quavering voice. "An orphan choir on a mountaintop!"

Startled, Christina whipped around. Emerging from the car was a small, wrinkled woman, a little hunched over, with a fuzz of light red hair and the look of an inquisitive bird.

What on earth was *Mrs. Lisowsky* doing here?

"But I'm afraid I've lost my glasses." The music teacher ducked into the car again and felt around with her hands.

Christina chewed on her lip. She had wanted to find her music teacher and ask for help. But she couldn't possibly say anything in front of Lenny and his guards.

"Attention, Happy Orphans!" Lenny got out of the car and stood with his arms open wide. "Now I know you have undoubtedly stuffed yourself full of supper—"

"We haven't had *any*," said a small voice, instantly shushed.

Lenny gave a fierce scowl and a jerk of his chin, and one of the guards instantly clapped a hand over the speaker's mouth, hefted him like a sack of potatoes, and carried him off, struggling silently.

"As I was *saying*," said Lenny. "I have brought you a whole truckload of food! *Extra* food! As a special treat!"

Every orphan was suddenly attentive. A hundred pairs of eyes swiveled in unison to the basket Lenny held up, full of bread. "Anyone who sings well, according to our distinguished guest—the lovely and musical Mrs. Lisowsky—will get a little snack. And anyone who sings *extra* well will get even more! Now, who wants to be first?"

One hundred orphan hands went up instantly.

Lenny spread out his hands. "You see, Mrs. Lisowsky? These children *love* to sing for their Happy Orphan Daddy!"

There was a murmur among the orphans. Something squeaked loudly.

Christina looked over at Danny. Was that his rubber cow?

"Who made that noise?" Lenny's face darkened. "I'd better not hear that again, or—"

"My *dear* children, I'm delighted to meet you all!" Mrs. Lisowsky peered about her. "I only wish I could see you better. Young man, would you look one more time for my glasses, please? I'm sure they're in the car somewhere."

Lenny turned. "You don't need glasses to hear, do you?" He toyed with something in his shirt pocket.

"Well, no . . . but I love to see their happy faces. Now," she said firmly, "let's hear them sing."

The tuning fork was struck; Mrs. Lisowsky gave her instructions. The children's voices were raised, one by one, in short vocal exercises that had been familiar to Christina since age seven. The music teacher was half blind without her glasses, Christina knew, but still her palms grew moist as she waited her turn.

But the pale blue, rheumy eyes passed over Christina's dirty face and chopped-off hair without recognition.

Christina sang the notes a half pitch flat, with a few a quarter tone sharp for variety. Mrs. Lisowsky tilted her head alertly, looking puzzled.

"What?" said Lenny. "That sounded off, to me."

"Yes . . . ," said the music teacher thoughtfully.

They moved on. Christina relaxed.

"Why do we need to have them sing all those notes?" said Lenny Loompski, impatience clear in his voice. "Just one is enough to see if they can sing on pitch, right?"

"Yes, pitch is important," said Mrs. Lisowsky, "but so is timbre, and intonation, and breathing—"

"All I'm interested in is pitch."

"But I am interested in listening to a choir. Which is what you asked me to do, correct?"

Lenny pulled something shiny out of his pocket, and dropped it. "Yeah. Right." He ground the object under his heel. Christina heard a crunch.

Mrs. Lisowsky moved slowly on down the line, striking the tuning fork for each orphan. "Now, you said I should identify children with perfect pitch. But you really don't need that for a choir; the children will have a piano to follow. What you want is merely accurate pitch."

"I want to know which ones are the best singers," said Lenny bluntly. "I want a kid who can listen to a tuning fork in one room, and then go into another room and sing the same note. I can't have the tuning fork in the second room—it would be too, uh, explosive. Wrong overtones, you see. We have the same problem underground."

The music teacher cocked her head. "I'm afraid I don't know what you mean."

"It doesn't matter. Just tell me the best singer."

The child in front of Christina shifted slightly, and suddenly Christina could see the thing that Lenny had dropped. It was a pair of glasses, now crushed and broken.

Her lips tightened. Naturally Lenny wouldn't want Mrs. Lisowsky to see the orphans clearly. She might see how dirty, and thin, and neglected they were.

Mrs. Lisowsky paused suddenly, clapping her slender hands. "Now, here is a very sweet voice, and really quite accurate pitch!"

Christina looked over. The tiny woman had stopped in front of Danny and was looking up at the tall boy in delight.

Lenny scowled. "*That* one? Are you sure?"

"Of course I'm sure. I know voices, my dear Mr. Loompski. And it's always possible that he has perfect pitch; do you know your notes, dear? Can you sing me an E-flat?"

Danny looked worried. "I only know A ... B ... C," he said.

"Well, no matter." She turned to Lenny. "This voice clearly has the best pitch, and with a very lovely quality, too!"

Lenny Loompski peered at the number on Danny's shirt,

and wrote something on a yellow pad. "All right. And the next best voice?"

There was another loud squeak. Lenny Loompski snapped upright.

"Bubby," said Danny, blue-eyed and smiling. "Bubby has a very good voice." He squeezed the cow a third time.

"Bubby, eh?" Lenny's thick lips curled into a terrifying smile. He bent back Danny's wrist and plucked the cow out of his hand. "I think Bubby wants to go for a *ride!*" He tossed the cow into the garbage truck's hopper. It landed with a squeak.

Danny gave an inarticulate cry and started forward.

"Close the ram panel, Barney!" called Lenny. He grabbed Danny by both arms. "Now listen up, boy. We'll open the panel in the morning, and you can climb in and play with your little toy. And then"—he paused and gave a tremendous wink over Danny's head at the guards—"you can go for a nice, long ride with Bubby. Won't that be nice?"

Barney climbed into the cab and pushed a button. The rear panel grated down into a closed position with a clank. But it didn't stop there. The hydraulic hoses kept up their long, slow whooshing, and the panel bent at its middle hinge, scraped along the curved bottom of the hopper, and scooped up and back, pushing what had been in the hopper into the main holding tank for garbage.

The ram panel straightened, slid back, and stopped in the open position. The hopper was empty.

Lenny's eyes narrowed. "Hey, you dumb guard! I said *close*, not scoop!"

Barney tumbled out, tripping over his feet. "Gee, I'm sorry, boss."

"*Green* to close, *brown* to scoop, *red* to—well, you *know* what red's for. Get it straight, or you won't be my driver."

"Yes, boss. Won't do it again, boss. I must have misheard you."

Lenny bent over, looking under the ram panel to the dark narrow opening above and behind the hopper. "Bye-bye, Bubby!" He grinned back at Danny, his teeth gleaming. "But don't worry—*you'll* still go for a ride in the morning."

Danny's eyes filled with silent tears. His arms hung at his sides.

Mrs. Lisowsky cleared her throat. "Now, Mr. Loompski, I'm not sure what this is all about, but I have to teach a music class in town. So before I go, I want to hear all the voices together. Is there a song that everyone knows?"

Lenny puffed out his chest. "Of course! Happy Orphans know lots of songs about me. Go on, pick one to sing for the lady!"

The children turned to one another and conferred in low, dull voices.

"There's that cheer we sang yesterday. That one wasn't too bad."

"Or Dorset's song. If we *have* to sing."

"Let's pick a short one, at least."

Christina looked at Danny's miserable face and felt a burning sensation in her stomach. She was tired, and hungry, and scared—but she was also *mad*. And she didn't intend to sing one note of a song that praised Lenny Loompski.

She reached for Danny's hand. She began to hum.

The children's faces brightened. They joined in, singing the words quietly, and then a little louder. Facing one another, their backs to Lenny Loompski, they held hands and *sang*. Christina's voice soared, exactly on pitch, and her mother's lullaby echoed among the jagged rocks.

The song ended. The children turned, reluctantly. Lenny's face was dark and full of rage.

But Mrs. Lisowsky's mouth was open in astonishment. "Christina Adnoid!" she said. "What are *you* doing up here?"

CHAPTER 32

BUBBY

"**W**HERE? Which one is she?" demanded Lenny Loompski. The veins in his neck stood out like rope, and his voice grated with threat.

"Why, I don't know." Mrs. Lisowsky stared blindly in his direction. "I thought I heard her voice."

"Sing, all of you! One by one. Now!" Lenny towered over the front row, spit spraying with every word. His big-knuckled hands worked, kneading the air, and his breath hissed between his teeth.

The terrified orphans squeaked out their notes, one by one. Christina longed to sing out clearly, to let Mrs. Lisowsky know who she was . . . But what could one little old lady do against Lenny and his gang of men? They would certainly make sure she never told anyone what she knew.

Christina made sure to sing even more off-key than before.

Mrs. Lisowsky blinked. "Yes, I can see now that I was wrong." She turned to Lenny and patted his arm. "I must have been confused when they all sang together. Christina

Adnoid has much better pitch. I can't imagine what I was thinking."

The dark purple color of Lenny's face faded to a brick red.

Mrs. Lisowsky dithered on, pressing his hand. "Oh, Mr. Loompski, you're so *good* to these orphans. I can just hear in their voices how much they all love you! Why, I even heard you planning a pleasant little ride for the best singer and his favorite toy . . ."

Christina gagged. Was she serious? Could Mrs. Lisowsky really be that clueless?

"And it was so *very* kind of you to ask my advice," the music teacher went on, "but I *really* should get back. I have a music class, and then I simply *must* knit a new pair of slippers for the church bazaar. But best of luck with your orphan choir; the children's voices are lovely . . . just lovely."

She wandered off, smiling and talking to herself. "Now, which way is the car? Which one of you nice young men is going to drive me down?"

Torkel sidled up to Lenny. "Do we need to take care of her, boss?"

Lenny's skin had lost its deep red shade, and the veins in his neck were flat once more. "No, let her go. She's just a little old lady, not too much upstairs."

Christina privately agreed with him, after the nauseating display she had just seen.

"Okay, boss. But I've got some bad news."

Lenny clasped his hands behind his back, watching as the car carrying Mrs. Lisowsky disappeared down the gravel road. "What's that?"

Torkel whispered in Lenny Loompski's ear.

"Whaaaaat?" Lenny Loompski whirled to face the pickup truck. "How much?"

"About half."

"Half the food is *gone*? *Who took it?*"

Torkel backed away. "I dunno, boss. Must've been the orphans."

Lenny Loompski swelled like an inflating balloon. His features grew puffy. He stared without expression at the trembling children.

"I've got a *new* song for you." His voice cracked with menace. "It's not some fairy tale about mommies who love you, and it's not about stupid shining stars. It's the song we sing in the guardhouse when you're not listening." And in high falsetto he sang:

> *Kid, you're mine, don't you forget*
> *Love has never saved you yet!*
> *You're forgotten, lost and lone,*
> *Any chance you had is blown—*

The guards, who had been drawing nearer, grinned and sang along to the chorus:

> *Keep a-workin', harder, faster*
> *Sing for Lenny, HE'S your master!*

Lenny's lips stretched over tombstone teeth. "You're nothing but a pack of dirty orphans. Even your *parents* threw you away. You're worthless, not even good enough to pick up garbage—you ARE garbage!"

Christina lay at the far edge of the glowing fire, looking up at the stars. She was weary to the bone, and her heart felt as sore and bruised as her shoulder.

She could still escape. She could leave the camp tonight, when all were sleeping, and get safely away. If she traveled all night, and if she did not fall in the dark and break a leg or lose her way in the forest, she might find someone to help. She might be able to convince the police to let her father go, and come up here before Lenny sent Danny away to . . . where? She didn't know, and once Danny was gone, Lenny Loompski would never tell.

Oh, who was she kidding? She'd never make it in time. She would have to take Danny with her.

Christina shut her eyes. Even that wouldn't be any good. If Danny was gone, Lenny Loompski would just put the next best singer on the truck. Unless she took every single orphan with her tonight, tomorrow one unlucky child would be thrown in the hopper.

And then? And then a long, terrible ride in a garbage truck, and a box of dangerous plastic toys, and a locked, windowless room. And after that—mashing.

Christina sat up. There was no way around it. They would all have to leave tonight.

She checked for guards. Except for the one stationed in the pickup truck—and he didn't show any signs of life—all were in the guardhouse. Lenny's car was gone from the lot again, and she felt a grim relief. He must have gone back to the orphanage.

Quietly she crept to Dorset's side and tapped her. Dorset's eyes flew open.

Christina said a few words in a low voice. Dorset nodded.

One by one, they woke the children. One by one, the orphans lay still and pretended to be sleeping.

"Wait for my signal," said Christina, and the orphans passed the word quietly, mouth to ear.

Dorset was counting on her fingers. "We're missing one," she whispered, and counted again.

Christina looked over the ragged orphans, lying like heaps of old clothes. She had no idea who most of them were. She could recognize a few—the little boy in the undershirt, the girl with the tangled hair, Danny of course . . .

"Where's Danny?" Christina asked abruptly.

Dorset looked around. "I don't see him." She paused, frowning. "I haven't seen him for hours, actually."

Christina sat back on her heels. They couldn't leave without Danny. "I'll look for him," she said, handing Dorset the pocketknife. "You cut the collars."

Christina moved stealthily across the camp. If she was stopped, she could always say she was stretching her legs—but she wasn't stopped. And she had an idea where Danny might be.

The guardhouse was quiet, except for someone inside who seemed to be pacing back and forth. In the pickup, the sleeping guard snored blissfully. Christina moved on cat-soft feet to the far side of the garbage truck, where she scanned the bushes and listened intently.

She heard what she had expected to hear. Danny, weeping low.

Christina smiled sadly. Danny had wanted to get as close to his cow as he could. It sounded as if he was right next to the truck.

But he wasn't. She walked around the whole garbage truck, holding her nose against the smell, but Danny didn't appear.

Christina listened more carefully, trying to judge direction. He was close, she could tell. Had he gone inside the cab?

She cracked open the driver's side door and jumped as the overhead light came on. She glanced inside—there were the buttons Barney had such trouble with, green, brown, red— but no Danny. She shut the door with a quiet click and watched the light go out.

Danny sniffled and hiccuped. He sounded terribly near. Christina circled the truck once more, looking in all directions, and finally ducked down under the hopper to look beneath the truck. It was dark.

"Danny?" she whispered.

Something squeaked.

Christina blinked, confused. The cow was squeaking— but how could that be? The toy had been scooped into the body of the truck, where the garbage was packed . . .

She stiffened in horror. Danny had crawled up inside the truck itself.

CHAPTER 33

A TERRIBLE DECISION

CHRISTINA couldn't seem to breathe. She squatted down, hunching over her knees. The ripe odor of garbage curled around her like a fog.

Danny must have wedged himself up through the narrow gap while it was still half light. He had felt around until he made something squeak and found his rubber cow. And meantime, it had grown dark outside . . . and he couldn't find his way out. That was what must have happened.

She looked up at the fire of the orphan camp glowing fitfully on the flat, elevated space where the children slept. There were a hundred children—well, ninety-nine—who were waiting for her signal. How long would it take to get Danny out? What if she accidentally woke the guard who was sleeping in the pickup truck only ten feet away?

The orphans' collars were all cut by now. If they didn't escape tonight, they would have lost their chance; the guards would see the collars in the morning.

Christina made herself stand up. Trying not to touch

anything, she bent over the hopper and craned her neck, so that her whisper would go straight through the gap. "Danny?"

A scrambling sound came from within the truck. "TAFF!"

"Shhhh!" Christina dropped to the ground behind the truck's massive tire. She waited for shouting, for the sound of boots, for a guard to drag her from her hiding place.

There was only silence. After a long moment, she breathed again and got up shakily. "Don't be loud, Danny—whisper. Can you get out? Can you come this way?"

Danny whimpered.

Christina's cheek twitched. This was maddening. The rest of the orphans needed her *now*, and she was stuck here with this boy who couldn't understand anything at all.

Disgusted, she gripped the slimy metal and got a leg over the side of the hopper. She pulled the other in—she slid down, pressed her knees against the curved back side, and reached up through the gap, gagging.

"Take my hand, Danny." Her whisper was urgent. She couldn't hold her breath much longer against this horrific smell. "Come on, I'll pull you through!"

The cow squeaked again, a forlorn, hollow sound. "Taff?" begged Danny.

Oh, for crying out loud. "I'm not Taft," Christina snapped. "Come *on*, already!"

There was a slithering sound of motion, a thump on the steel floor, and a low cry. "I can't *find* you, Taff! TAFF!"

Christina leapt out of the hopper in a fury of desperation. The stupid kid was going to get her killed if he didn't shut up . . .

She scrunched down behind a bush and listened bleakly to Danny's piteous sobs.

No. *She* wasn't the one who would get killed. It was Danny who would be killed, unless she went in and got him out.

Christina drew in her arms to her chest, suddenly cold. Was she brave enough to go into that dark, horrible place?

She wasn't sure. And even if she did go into the truck after him, what if Danny's noise and clumsiness ruined the whole plan for everyone? Then ninety-nine children—not to mention her mother, Taft, Leo, and Christina herself—would lose their best chance to escape. And if they didn't escape, some of them would die.

Christina sat without moving. They might not die right away, of course. It would take weeks before the food in the cavern ran out. And not all the children would be sent away in the garbage truck.

But if she tried to save Danny and things went badly—if she was caught, and the cut collars were discovered, and the guard on the orphans was doubled and tripled so that there was no chance of escape at all—then, eventually, people *would* die. How would she feel then, watching children loaded into the hopper, knowing that all too soon they would be mashed? How would she stand it, knowing that beneath her feet, near and yet impossibly far, her mother and Leo and Taft would slowly starve to death?

Christina stared up at the orphan fire, and her mouth went dry as she faced the alternative.

She could leave Danny where he was.

She could go now and lead the other ninety-nine orphans

off the ridge. People would call her a hero, and sometime tomorrow when they got off the mountain, the townspeople would come and lift out her mother and Leo and Taft, too. It would be too late, then, for Danny, but she would have saved everyone else.

A soft night breeze lifted the cut ends of her hair and blew them back against her mouth, and stirred the leaves of the bush that sheltered her. It swirled up dried weeds, a sprinkling of dust, and bits of torn paper from the garbage truck's hopper, and then it wafted back down and cooled the hot tears on Christina's cheeks.

It was too hard to make the right decisions, out in the real world. No wonder her father had kept her behind walls, safe and protected. She couldn't do it.

What if she did save ninety-nine orphans while leaving Danny in the garbage? Could she really pretend to be a hero? Could she even look Taft in the eye, knowing she had done that?

Christina bowed her head. Ninety-nine wasn't going to be good enough. It had to be one hundred. And it had to be now.

She stood in the hopper, twisted away from the yawning open slot, and took a last deep breath of sweet air. Then, before she could change her mind, she stuck her shoulders through the gap, heaved up a leg, and scrambled in.

She was on her hands and knees in something that oozed. Retching, Christina tried to stand upright but stopped while she was still bent over, her stomach heaving in dry convulsions. Something squelched underfoot.

"Taff?" said a frightened voice from a back corner.

Christina shook her head, then realized Danny couldn't see her. "Not Taft," she managed before she choked, strangling on the fetid air.

The smell was beyond belief. It was ripe, it was rotten; it was old bananas and sour milk and rancid cheese and spoiled meat. It had the sharp, acrid scent of mold, and the rich, fruity odor of decaying plums and fresh vomit, and everything was slimy and wet and unspeakably foul.

"Steena?" said Danny, and then she had found him; her hands were patting his face, and he was gripping her arm, weeping in terror and relief.

"Hush, Danny. It's all right. I'm here now."

"But it's dark, Steena," Danny said, trembling. "I can't get *out*."

"I'll help you. Come on, hold my hand. But, Danny, listen. Be very, very, *very* quiet, all right?"

Danny's body joggled, and Christina realized that he was nodding vigorously.

"All right. I've got you. Now get down on your knees and crawl . . . Wait. What's that?"

The children froze at the sound of heavy boots crunching across gravel. There was the creak of a steel door and then the garbage truck bounced. A dim light flicked on in a thin line, where the back and side walls met.

"Okay, Barney," came Barney's voice, faint but clear through the crack. "You are not as stupid as they think. You are going to figure these buttons out if it takes all night."

CHAPTER 34

SILENT SCREAM

THE engine roared into life, rumbling and loud, the whole truck throbbing like a hollow steel drum.

Christina thought: This isn't happening.

There was a sudden hiss of hydraulic hoses. Something shifted and clanked. The rear ram panel shut with a boom.

Christina clutched Danny, her mouth open in a silent scream.

A gleam of pale light appeared at the middle hinge of the rear panel, accompanied by a grating, sliding noise Christina had heard before. The ram panel was scooping, up and back, into the body of the truck.

Christina staggered away from the moving steel, dragging Danny to the far wall. She flattened against it, her heart hammering like a piston. She fixed her eyes on the yellow crack of light from the cab as if it were her last hope.

The crack thinned—dimmed—and winked out. The wall was moving, it was *moving*, she could feel it at her back, pushing them toward the rear panel, the panel that was scoop-ing, ramming, coming at them—

Barney had pushed the red button. They were going to be mashed.

Christina became aware of a thin, high screaming and a rapid-fire metallic banging. At the same time the engine noise shut off abruptly, and over it all an angry male voice shouted, ". . . IT OFF, YOU DONKEY BRAIN! PEOPLE ARE TRY-ING TO SLEEP!"

Christina's throat was sore and rasping. The scream, she realized, had been her own. She lowered the hand that had been frantically banging Leo's wrench on the steel wall. Next to her, Danny was moaning quietly. She put a hand over his mouth and listened, weak at the knees.

"Sorry—sorry, Torkel. I just wanted to practice pushing the buttons so I didn't mess up tomorrow—"

"You don't have to start the engine to do that, you moron! Just turn the ignition halfway, enough for lights and such. The buttons will still work. Anyway, what's the big deal? Look, it's simple. Green to close, brown to scoop, red to mash. What's the matter—can't you tell them apart?"

"Of *course* I can, Torkel. I'm not stupid!"

Torkel snorted. "Right. Listen, I'm going in to get some sleep. Push all the buttons you want, but keep an eye on the food truck, will you? I'm leaving—it's your shift anyway."

Christina heard a crunch of gravel, a creak of wooden steps, and the sound of a door closing. She had to stop this, they had to get *out*.

"Barney!" she shouted, putting her mouth to the crack in the corner. "BAAAARRNEY!"

Her voice echoed hollowly. The truck jolted as if Barney had jumped a foot and fallen back on the seat.

"Who—who's there?" Barney's voice quavered.

Christina was struck by a sudden thought. Barney sounded *afraid*.

"Baaaaaarrney!" she cried again, making her voice lower, more ghostly. "Don't doooooo this, Baaaarney!"

There was a long silence. "Who *are* you?" Barney said at last, his voice cracking.

This was better. As long as she could keep him talking, he wouldn't be pushing buttons. "Whooooo do you thiiiiink I am, Barney?"

Barney gasped. "*Momma?*"

Christina felt an almost uncontrollable urge to laugh out loud, but she squashed it back down. This was no time to get hysterical. Let's see—what would a real mother say? Danny moved restlessly under her hand, and she patted his shoulder.

"You were such a *good* boy, once, Barney."

There was a sound of sniffling from the cab. "I was, I *was*! Momma, I always tried hard!"

Christina had a moment of sympathy. Barney *did* try hard. But trying hard wasn't good enough, no matter what the dancing chickens on her computer liked to say. You had to get it *right*. "So why are you mashing children, Barney? Couldn't you find something better to do with your time?"

"Now, listen, Momma, you don't understand. It's nothing personal—it's just business."

The small bit of sympathy Christina had felt instantly drained away. "It's personal to the kids getting mashed, Barney."

The truck moved a little, as if Barney was shifting his weight. "Well, the mashing is really a very small part of it, Momma."

Danny leaned against Christina's side. She smoothed his rough hair and felt a growing anger, like a live coal in her stomach. "Sure, Barney, I know. There's also the part where you starve them and scream at them and keep them working like slaves all day and all night—"

"Oh, Momma, I'm sorry!" Blubbering sounds came from the cab.

This was more like it. "It's not too late to be a good person, Barney. Get away from Lenny Loompski and find a different job. But first, I want you to push the green button. No, wait—"

Christina concentrated. The green was to close the ram panel. What opened it? The brown button, perhaps? Yes. After it scooped, the panel went back to an open position. But Barney kept getting the buttons mixed up. And she couldn't risk him pushing the red button. Barney didn't seem to know his colors very well. The vision test she had taken on her computer only two days ago probably would have said he was color-blind.

Christina was suddenly alert. *That* was Barney's problem! And red and green color blindness was the most common kind. The two colors just looked like shades of brown.

No wonder Barney kept pushing the wrong buttons. They all looked exactly the same to him.

"Momma?" said Barney anxiously. "You said you wanted me to find some different work. What should I do?"

"*Don't* fix traffic lights," Christina said instantly. "You're color-blind."

"I am?" Barney's voice scaled up in surprise. "I thought I was just dumb!"

"Well, that too . . . no, no, I didn't mean that. Listen, I want you to press—" Christina thought of the panel of buttons. She could see them in her mind's eye—green on the left, then brown, then red. "Press the middle button, Barney."

The truck jolted. Danny began to whimper.

"Shh, shh, shh," Christina whispered in his ear, over and over, like a lullaby. "It's okay, I'm right here with you . . ."

The ram panel scooped and grated and clanked back into position. A puff of air wafted in through the open slot.

"Momma? Did I do that right?"

Christina thought of the dancing chickens. "Good *effort*! Nice *job*! Now, though, you've got to try harder, son. Go do something that helps people instead of hurting them."

"Okay. Like what?"

"Um . . ." Christina thought. Barney had seemed to enjoy polishing the mirrors and glass the day before. "Washing windows, maybe?"

"I like washing windows." Barney's tone brightened. "I'll make you proud, Momma!"

"I hooope so, Baaaaarney . . ." Christina let her voice drift off.

All was still. Barney's footsteps had faded away in the distance. "Time to get out of here," Christina whispered. "Crawl over—okay, now get down, flat on your stomach."

"It's yucky," said Danny, sniffling.

"I know. I won't let you go. Put one leg through the opening—then the other—"

"I'm stuck!" Danny's whisper was terrified.

"No, you're not. Turn your head sideways. That's right, now you've got it—"

Danny was out. His hand, still gripping Christina's tightly, yanked her bruised shoulder down and out before she was ready. Her head banged against steel.

Christina swallowed a cry of pain. Her face felt greasy and slick. She shut her eyes, hung on to Danny's hand, and slithered out into the hopper and the fresh, free air.

They crossed the grounds hand in hand, keeping to the shadows, moving slowly. The guards were mostly there to keep the orphans working, Christina realized—they were so sure that the shock collars would keep the children on the ridge, they hardly bothered to set any kind of guard at night. But that didn't mean she could be careless. Especially when they were this close to freedom.

A thin thread of melody drifted to her ears, faint and rising in the dark. Christina paused. Was an orphan singing? Dorset should stop that at once. They couldn't afford any noise at all—

No. It was coming from behind her. Christina turned and saw the cone-shaped mound and the moon shining down from a starlit sky. It was her mother's voice.

Every night, her mother had said—every night for years, she had stood below the opening to the sky and sung this song for Christina, knowing that her daughter couldn't hear it, but singing it for her just the same.

Only tonight, she *knew* Christina was above her. Taft would have told her what had happened, and Beth Adnoid was hoping that Christina would hear and take courage from it.

Christina tightened her grip on Danny's hand and smiled. He was a mess—slimy bits hanging from his shirt, matted sticky hair, smudges on his cheeks that showed up even in moonlight. She probably looked even worse, and Christina was sure that they both smelled horrible, though after being in the garbage truck so long, she had almost lost the ability to tell.

But Danny was here, and alive, and that was what mattered. She could listen to her mother singing, and feel happy, instead of being crushed with guilt. Maybe the decision to rescue him would turn out to be a good one after all.

They crept quietly into the orphan camp and stopped next to Dorset. All around, the children lay flat, watching them with shining eyes.

"Did you remember to hang on to Bubby?" Christina whispered to Danny.

Danny reached in his pocket and squeezed. The cow gave a tiny squeak.

Christina grinned. "All right, then, we've got everybody. Come on, let's go."

CHAPTER 35

A PLACE TO HIDE

SILENTLY, quickly, the children moved down the stair-stepped terraces. The moonlight cast strong, black shadows down one half of the mine, and the small figures kept to the dark side, slipping carefully from one level to the next.

The flat terraces did not go all the way around. Perhaps there was more zoom on the near side, or maybe the far side had been kept rough to discourage thoughts of escape. Whatever the reason, Christina saw they would have to go all the way down to the bottom of the mines and then pick their way up through the rugged terrain to get over the far rim and off the ridge.

Well, at least they were outside in the fresh air. She took deep breaths—she couldn't seem to get enough—and realized, to her dismay, that her sense of smell was coming back. And she really, really stank.

She tripped over a small pile of stones in the dark: Joey's cairn. She stopped to stack them up again—at least the ones she could find by feel—and was bumped into from behind.

"Pee-ew," said a voice. "No offense, but would you mind staying downwind?"

Christina held on to Danny's sleeve as the orphans filed past. In the dark she couldn't see if they were holding their noses, but she thought they'd be crazy not to.

"I don't want to smell bad, Steena." Danny's voice was troubled. "Can I wash?"

There was a trickle of water running through the rock at their feet. Christina shrugged. How could it hurt? He could splash some water on his face and hands, and it might make him feel better.

"Sure, Danny. But be quick, all right?"

"Okay!" Danny pulled off his shirt with enthusiasm and rubbed it diligently in the water.

Christina hadn't thought he'd try to wash his *clothes*—and without soap, it wouldn't do much good anyway—but it was too late to stop him now. She wrinkled her nose. Getting the shirt damp only intensified the odor, unfortunately.

She looked back the way they had come, to the lip of rock five terraces up. No guards, no lights, no cries of alarm. They were safe so far. She turned to follow as the last orphan passed. "Okay, Danny, come on, and bring your shir—"

"Let them go! Let the orphans GO!"

The cry came from somewhere above. The children stopped dead as "GO! Go! Go!" echoed from the rocks all around.

"Shut *up*, Barney! You're waking everybody!"

The orphans melted into the shadow of the rock wall, motionless. Above them, silhouetted on the mine's high rim, was a man. He was waving his arms.

"I *want* to wake up everyone!" shouted Barney. "It's not too late! We can still be good people!"

Christina smacked herself on the forehead. This was unbelievable.

There were two silhouettes on the rim. One was shaking the other. "What is wrong with you? Have you gone nuts?"

Three silhouettes, now. No, four. Christina stared with dread and fascination, the way she might watch a train wreck that she could do absolutely nothing about.

"I started to go away," cried Barney, "but I had to come back. I don't want to hurt orphans, I want to help them! I want to make Momma *proud*!"

Oh, no, no . . . Christina grabbed her hair with both hands. All she'd had to do was tell Barney to go away and never come back, but no, she had to try to *inspire* him. She glanced up at the rocky hill they had yet to climb. If a hundred orphans moved now, they would almost certainly be seen. But if they stayed still, they would be caught for sure—

"Hey, look! The orphans! They're gone!"

Christina's heart sank as more guards massed at the edge of the rim, looking down. One had a flashlight—no, two. The beams shone down into the mine, moving back and forth, crisscrossing on the first terrace.

It wouldn't be long now. Should they run like rabbits? Or try to hide?

The guards could outrun children. But there was nowhere to hide in the open bowl of the mines, unless . . .

"Pass the word," Christina whispered to the closest orphan. "Follow me. Don't make a sound."

She turned back the way she had come, feeling her way with careful feet. There! She bent down by the cairn of stones—Joey's memorial—and patted around until she found the box with candles and matches, left for anyone the guards sent into the underground mine, the lava tube that had been blasted open by an explosion of zoom.

Shuffling, bumping, trailing roughened fingers along the stony wall, Christina led one hundred orphans into the mine. If she looked back through the crumbling entrance, she could see moonlit terraces in the distance, and the pencil-thin beams of moving flashlights.

The sound of breathing was loud in the confined space. The tunnel began to curve. The light from the entrance disappeared.

Christina stopped and fumbled in the dark with the matches, spilling the box. She bent down and found a match by feel; there was a scrape, a hiss of flame, a sudden sulfur smell. The candle's wick spurted and caught, sending a fitful glow to illuminate the frightened orphan faces that huddled close.

"Keep going," said Christina, "deeper in. They don't know we're here; we'll wait until it's safe and then we'll go out again and escape."

"But stay together," added Dorset, stepping up to light her candle from Christina's. "There might be more than one passageway."

The children who were nearest moved in to light their own candles, then turned to light the candles of those behind them. In a few moments, the line of bobbing candles stretched beyond into darkness like a string of twinkling lights. Christina followed, last of all.

The tunnel was winding; the cave was chilly and damp, with multicolored slime growing at the edges. Christina stepped around a patch of mold. The cave wasn't as bad as the garbage truck, but it wasn't good, and it smelled musty, as if bats or snakes lived there.

Christina shuddered. If she could deal with a garbage truck, she could probably deal with snakes, but she hoped she wouldn't have to.

Ahead, the line of lights slowed, bunched up, stopped.

"What is it?" Christina pressed forward, working her way up the line of orphans, passing the little boy in the undershirt, the boy with the snub nose, the girl who wanted hair ribbons, Danny, who was still shirtless and dripping and, unfortunately, smelling now of wet garbage . . .

The musty scent was stronger here, and the passageway ended in a wide room.

"What now?" said Dorset.

Christina stood still, thinking. The children crowded near. The smell of their unwashed clothes mingled with the rotten odor of cave mold, and the sound of their breathing filled the rocky cave with a soft, regular sound like the sigh of bat wings.

No, it *was* bat wings. Disturbed by the noise and light, a colony of bats came swooping out from some hidden alcove in a flutter of beating wings and shrill high-pitched squeaks. Their fur-covered bodies rushed past the children's faces and the orphans cried out in alarm, ducking low. The candles flickered; the candles snuffed out.

The children were plunged into darkness, deep and absolute.

Too late, Christina remembered the spilled matches, left on the rocky floor.

CHAPTER 36

TRAPPED

FEAR gripped Christina's chest like a claw. The tons of rock above them, which she had so far managed to ignore, hung heavy in the shadowed corners of her mind. It could cave in, like that other tunnel had done. She would be mashed by rock, instead of a garbage truck, but she would end up just as flat in the end.

An orphan began to cry. Christina was so close to doing the same thing herself, she couldn't get out a word of comfort. But then another child whimpered, and another, and in ten seconds, the whole cave was filled with the sobbing of hungry, cold, frightened children. And then, louder than the rest, came the lost wail—"*STEENA!*"

Christina made a massive effort and controlled herself. There had to be something she could do. There *was* something she could do . . . It was fluttering on the edge of her mind, she almost had it . . .

Oh. Of course. Christina lifted her chin and took in a breath.

Her voice wavered at first, but she steadied it quickly and her soft, perfectly accurate high G-sharp soared above the crying voices and echoed in the long, dark tunnel. The veins of zoom began to glimmer, faintly at first and then with greater strength. The children quieted with the coming of the light, hiccuping as their sobs ended. Christina saw Danny's head above the rest and reached for his hand.

"Sing with me, Danny," she said, as she took in more air, and Danny gulped, tucked the cow in his waistband, and opened his mouth obediently.

His clear, pure voice joined with Christina's, and the thin streaks on either side glowed, flowing sluggishly down the rock in vivid phosphorescent trails. The orphans' dirty faces shone pink and green as they excitedly started to put their tin cups to the wall, then sobered, glanced at one another, and let their hands fall.

Christina and Danny stopped to breathe.

Dorset spoke into the silence. "You know the right note? Every time?"

Christina nodded. "I have perfect pitch."

"Wow," breathed the boy with the snub nose. "If you'd been here all along, think how much more food the guards would have given us!" His thick dark hair hung in his eyes, giving him the look of an eager and hungry bear.

"They still might," piped up a girl with freckles. "We could show them all this zoom. They'd be nice to us then, I bet. They'd give us . . . lots of . . ." Her voice trailed off as she looked around the circle of orphans. Everyone was staring at her.

"Don't be stupid," said Dorset quietly.

Christina looked from face to face. The hollows in their cheeks stood out like smudges. They were starving, she realized.

Well, she didn't have any food to give them. She watched the dimming colors of pink and green, and listened with half an ear to the orphans' restless movements, to their muffled coughs, to the murmuring sound of water, somewhere, flowing over rock . . .

"I'm thirsty, Steena," said Danny.

Christina nodded. Of course he was; she should have thought of that herself. She looked around; she sang a G-sharp for more light, but she saw no running stream. Nor had they passed one on their way into the cave.

Still, the sound of water persisted, out of sight yet very near.

Christina looked at the wall of rock before her and its faint tracery of zoom. Once before, she had sung loud and long until the mountain itself had cracked open. She had had Leo Loompski's helmet then.

She had no helmet now. But could she perhaps sing enough zoom out to get to the hidden stream? If they had water, she might be able to persuade the orphans to stay in the cave for one or two more days, just until the search for them had moved on. Without water, she thought, there was no way. Water was even more important than food.

But her throat was tired. How long before her voice would grow hoarse?

Christina shook her head. She knew better than to have negative thoughts when she was working with zoom. She was *going* to find water for Danny and the rest of the orphans. She focused her thoughts on the stream she knew was there, just out of sight, and sang.

The cavern brightened. She paused for breath. The tunnel rang with echoing sound—with her pure, high note, with voices, with the tramp of feet . . .

But the children were not moving their feet at all. And the voices were coming from farther down the tunnel.

"—could have found them just by the smell—"

"Yeah, we didn't even need the shirt some moron left by the entrance!"

"Torkel signaled the orphanage—Lenny ought to be coming any minute."

"Is he ever going to be mad! He'll want us to throw 'em *all* in the masher!"

Christina watched all the orphan faces but one crumple with fear.

"Bubby's not scared," Danny said. "Steena will save us." He smiled at Christina with utter confidence.

The certainty in his voice was irresistible. Christina felt suddenly as if she could do anything, anything at all—even the very dangerous idea that had just occurred to her.

She ran back down the tunnel, singing just enough for light. She paused for breath before the last curve and listened. The guards had stopped talking; they were listening, too.

She sang the high G-sharp again, only not quite so perfectly as before. She watched the wall with narrowed eyes, and adjusted her tone a micro-step lower. The walls began to smoke.

"Get out! GET OUT!" screamed a guard. "It's going to blow!"

There was a rush of trampling feet and a confusion of voices, fading as the guards ran off. Christina raised the tone to its perfect pitch once more, and the wisps of smoke drifted harmlessly away.

She jogged back the length of the tunnel, scooping up a pocketful of matches along the way and thinking fast. The guards were out of the tunnel for now, but they were undoubtedly watching the entrance, and sooner or later, they'd be back.

She lit one of the candles again and wedged it in a crack in the wall. "Listen," she said. "We need more than water. We need to break through the rock and get out of here. I bet we can do it if we all sing together."

The orphans looked at her in disbelief.

"Just *pretend* it will work," said Christina urgently. "Make believe that you can sing so much zoom out, the rock will break. And don't stop thinking that you *can*."

The orphans' eyes were wide and doubtful in the deepening gloom. Christina gave them the note.

"But you're the one who can sing the best," said Dorset. "You don't need us."

"I *do* need you," said Christina. She looked at the faces that were becoming so familiar and felt pity and pride both. She might not have Leo Loompski's helmet to help her, but she had a hundred kids instead. Surely that would make a difference. That many voices and minds, all together, was probably strong enough to crack open the whole mountain.

Christina lifted her head and began to sing, louder and

more purely than she ever had before. She blocked thoughts of failure from her mind, and she thought of water, and breaking stone, and the free air.

Danny joined her, and then the rest of them, matching their tones to hers until the cavern rang with a powerful G-sharp and the zoom grew luminous, until the whole wall was a glowing, shimmering, flowing mass of color and light.

The streaks of zoom joined with the veins of zoom, and now, with the rock echoing and running with sound, the hidden sheets of zoom behind the rock were melting, too, pouring out of the wall like thick gleaming syrup. It covered the floor and the orphans' feet; they joined hands so they wouldn't slip and fall, and they swayed as they sang.

But there was no sudden crack, as had happened before; no rending of the stone wall. The orphan voices kept on and on, but at long last they grew weaker, and one by one they fell silent. The candle guttered out.

Exhausted, growing hoarse, Christina sang alone. The zoom poured out from the wall like a dam unblocked, glowing less and less as its level went down. And at last she realized that she couldn't go on forever. Her thin, thready tone weakened, dwindled, and finally died.

Christina sank to her knees in despair. She had failed. She had done her best, and it had not been good enough.

The voices of guards echoed in the tunnel. The shouts grew louder, came nearer.

Christina lowered her head.

And saw, in the gelling zoom at her feet, a bit of light. A dim light, a flickering light; a moving reflection of light. She looked up. There was a gap in the wall ahead, where there had been more zoom than rock and it had flowed out like a draining lake, and coming through the gap was a—

A small oil lamp. Held by a familiar hand, lighting a familiar face.

"TAFF!" cried Danny.

CHAPTER 37

BELIEVE IT OR NOT

THE orphans hurried through the gap, following Taft. It was just wide enough for two, and it took a while for everyone to move through the passage. Christina had them begin by lighting one another's candles, so at least they weren't stumbling in the dark.

But the guards were drawing closer. They were moving slowly—afraid the zoom might start to smoke again—but Christina could hear them coming all the same.

Could she pull the same trick again? She looked at the zoom, now hardened on the floor in a marbled sheet of pink and green like wildly colored linoleum. There was an awful lot of it. She wasn't sure she could control the reaction of this much zoom, all fused together like this. It would make a terrible explosion, if it blew.

The last orphan went through the gap, and Christina followed hastily. Maybe they could block off the gap somehow from inside the cavern.

But that wasn't Taft's plan at all.

Christina emerged from the gap to see a candlelit fleet of planes, children climbing into front and back seats, pilots strapping on helmets, and Taft and Leo Loompski busily moving among them all, giving instructions.

"Wow," the snub-nosed boy said reverently.

Danny had been waiting for her. "Bubby doesn't want to fly," he said.

"Christina!" Her mother came running. "I've been so worried! Thank you so much for the food and medicine, but you shouldn't have taken such a terrible risk!"

Christina was enveloped in her mother's arms. It felt wonderful.

"Darling, what's that smell?" Beth Adnoid leaned back. "Did you fall into a pile of garbage?"

"Sort of," said Christina. "Mom, this is Danny—he'll tell you all about it. I have to go . . . Okay, okay, I'm coming," she called to Taft.

"Everybody buckled?" Taft demanded. "Helmets on? Right, then go ahead, Christina—sing!"

Christina squared her shoulders. She was hoarse, she was tired, she had thought she couldn't sing another note. None of that mattered now. Through the gap behind her, the guards' voices could be heard chanting the Lenny Loompski song, but she refused to pay attention. She sang the high G-sharp to activate the zoom, and as the planes nearby bloomed into rosy light, all the orphans gasped, as if they were seeing magic.

Kid, you're Lenny's, don't forget—

Christina blocked out the taunting words that repeated, echoing in the distance, and walked among the rows of planes, singing a constant note until the rest of the planes caught the tone and began to hum. The sound spread from one plane to another in a chain reaction, and by the time the planes were glowing golden, Christina realized that she could stand in the middle of the fleet and whatever she sang would reach the outermost plane in a matter of seconds.

Love has never saved you yet . . .

"Concentrate," she called, as the planes turned from green to blue. "Think hard."

She watched with satisfaction as, one by one, bright blue zoom began to rise in the tubes, moving from the planes to the helmets like liquid through a straw. She glanced aside at her mother and Danny, and gave them a small, tight grin.

You're forgotten, lost and lone—

The jeering song heard through the gap was louder now, but Christina tossed back her ragged hair in defiance. It was too late for Lenny's guards to catch the orphans, they were almost aloft. She sang the last high, resolving E, and the planes turned an intense violet.

"Now think—GO!" cried Christina.

There was a slight bucking movement, as if the planes had hiccuped. But although the humming chord was as musical as ever, the planes didn't budge again. The orphans looked at Christina.

Any chance you had is blown . . .

The guards' voices were getting much too close. Christina

ran back to Taft. "Didn't you explain it to them? How they can make the planes fly with their thoughts?"

"Of course I did," said Taft, with a worried frown. He looked around. "Think UP!" he called.

One or two planes wiggled, that was all. The orphans slumped in their seats. Back through the gap, there was a sound of tramping feet. Beth Adnoid's face grew stern. Coughing, she pulled a metal rod from Leo's supply pile and held it up like a weapon. She moved off toward the gap. Leo, looking confused but determined, picked up a pair of pliers and followed.

Keep a-workin', harder, faster—

"They're like me," said Taft suddenly. "Listen!" he shouted. "The plane works on the vibrations of your thoughts—if you *think* you can't fly it, then you won't!"

Christina looked around anxiously. One hundred orphans looked back at her, their eyes full of impossibility.

How could she get them to believe they could do it? They hardly knew her.

Danny inched closer to Taft and Christina. He was humming under his breath, his eyes shut tight and his thumbs in his ears.

Sing for Lenny, HE'S your master!

Christina felt like plugging up her ears right along with Danny. She had never hated the Lenny Loompski song more than at this moment. How could the orphans have any confidence at all, with those mocking words filling their minds?

No wonder they couldn't fly!

Christina pulled Leo's wrench from her back pocket and pounded on the curved body of the nearest plane. She would get their attention. She would explain it all to them, and then they would understand—

But there was no time. At the gap in the rock, two guards poked their heads out and stared, openmouthed, at the glowing violet fleet.

Danny hummed more loudly, waggling his fingers.

Christina whirled. She recognized the tune, now. "Louder, Danny!"

She ran from orphan to orphan, taking up the melody of Dvořák's "Largo" from the *New World Symphony*. She didn't need to sing the words, for every orphan knew them by heart.

One by one the children sat up straight and began to hum. The tune spread out from child to child in a wave of sound that mixed with the drone of the planes. It sounded more like a battle hymn than a lullaby, Christina thought, and at a noise of clashing she turned to see her mother whacking the shoulders of the first guard coming through the gap, while Leo raised his pliers.

The guard recoiled. Beth Adnoid turned, listening. Then she opened her mouth and sang, too.

The orphans swiveled as one, their faces suffused with violet light. The voice that had sung to them, night after night, was clear and surprisingly strong. Of course it was, thought Christina—her mother had thrown it upward, as loudly as she could, for years on end.

Beth Adnoid broke off in a fit of coughing. Leo patted her

on the back, dropping his pliers. The gap was suddenly filled with guards pushing through.

No! Christina leapt on top of an empty plane and waved Leo's wrench in the air. If she was ever going to inspire the orphans, it had better be now. But there was time for her to shout just one single word:

"FLY!"

CHAPTER 38

KABOOM!

A ND they *flew*. One by one, then two by three by four, the planes glowed brighter, hovered higher, and then, like a miracle, took off in a rush of silvery violet wings.

The guards took one look and scrambled back through the fissure in the wall. Taft, who had jumped into a plane himself, cried, "Follow me!" and led the way straight for the gap.

Christina held her breath—the passageway was too narrow for the plane's wingspan—but at the last moment, Taft turned the plane sideways and it slipped through as neatly as a quarter into a slot. One after another, more planes followed, and Christina scrambled into her own craft, strapped on her helmet, and waved good-bye to her mother and Danny and Leo.

"Be careful!" cried her mother. "Don't forget to wear a seat belt!"

Christina started to laugh. "I love you, too!" she shouted back, and then to the orphans in the planes that were left, "Come on—we'll go out the other way!"

Zinging through the air, she led the rest of the orphans in the opposite direction, toward the vast cavern. Up and up they flew, spiraling for the hole that let in the sky, now the glorious pale blue and pink of breaking dawn. Humming, soaring, flying free, Christina and the orphans zoomed out of the hole like musical hornets from a nest and took to the air.

Light surrounded her, and endless sky, and for a moment Christina's eyes were dazzled. She looked down, away from the sun, and saw movement at the dark hollow that was the mine's entrance.

It was the guards, spilling from the mine, ducking and running for cover as Taft's squadron chased after them with a chord that rang in the rocks and sent the harriers scattering from their nests.

With fierce satisfaction, Christina saw the snub-nosed boy and Dorset take off after Torkel. The other children followed their example, buzzing around the guards like oversized mosquitoes.

Taft, though, headed for the pickup truck with its food supplies, swooping low. Christina saw Lenny Loompski jog heavily across the parking lot, shake his fist at the buzzing plane, and dive into the truck's cab.

Here was the man who'd kept her mother a prisoner for years. Here was the man who thought he could mash orphans and no one would stop him. Christina's plane whirled around with the force of her thoughts and sped straight for the truck with a deep and powerful hum.

Lenny Loompski revved the engine. The tires spit gravel as the truck reversed, spun, and roared back toward the road.

Taft buzzed past the driver's window and around the cab. Christina came in from the side and flew in front of his windshield. But they were too small to stop the truck.

Lenny's face grinned wildly at her through the windshield. "You're my Happy Orphans!" he cried. "Mine! All mine! I can squash you like a bug, I can mash you like potatoes, I can cream you like *spinach*—"

A shriek cut him off. It was a laughing sort of shriek, as if an inmate had gotten loose from an asylum, and as Christina turned in her seat she saw that this was pretty much the case. Leo Loompski had taken a plane himself and flown out to do battle.

His apple cheeks were bright with exertion, his white hair blew every which way around the edges of his helmet, and on his face was a grin that could have split a melon. "Lenny!" he cried, beginning a barrel roll with the finesse of a circus acrobat. "You need fixing, Lenneeeeee!"

Christina flew up and out of Leo's way and watched with horrified fascination as a small metal canister, left loose in the rear compartment of Leo's plane, slowly tipped, toppled, and rolled gently out, turning in the sun. It fell and fell, bright and glinting, until—

KABOOM!

Lenny Loompski's truck exploded. Lenny himself came flying out the window like a greased sausage and soared briefly through the air before landing with a distinct thud on the dusty ground. The food from the truck came plopping down all around him, boxes and bags bursting and spilling, grapes flying in all directions. A carton of eggs broke open in midair and dropped like small, delicate bombs on top of Lenny, and lettuce leaves floated gently down, covering the wreckage with a blanket of ruffled green.

A screech, high and piercing as a train's whistle, came from Lenny Loompski's mouth, and increased in volume.

"*OwwwoooooOOOOOOOO!* OW OW OW ow! There's egg in my *hair!*"

"You're scrambled!" cried Leo.

Lenny wiped the egg out of his eyes and struggled to his knees, his face purple with fury. "I am the *head* of Loompski Labs! I'm admired! I'm respected! I'm a honking big deal, and when I win the Karsnicky Medal, the world will know it, too!" He glared at the zooming plane. "I'll get you for this, whoever you are, you—you—"

He broke off, staring upward, shading his eyes against the sun. "Uncle *Leo?*"

"You're not the head of Loompski Labs anymore," called the wild-haired little man in the plane, swooping low, the airstream from the plane spraying chips and salsa all over Lenny's shirt. "You're nothing but a pile of garbage, and you're FIRED!"

Laughing like a child, Leo looped up and around, soared off over the ridge, and disappeared behind the circling rocks in a singing violet blur. Lenny, left below in the midst of the wreckage, screwed up his face, opened his mouth, and howled.

Christina watched him with narrowed eyes. He couldn't be too hurt if he was making all that noise. And sure enough, soon Lenny Loompski was up and limping, shedding grapes and eggshells as he went, stumbling toward the guardhouse as his best chance for shelter.

Christina had no intention of allowing *that*. She aimed her little plane straight for Lenny and zoomed at him like a wasp. She would chase him up to the giant rocks—he'd never be able to escape over the cliff. And then they could herd him back down the road, right into town. It would be an exciting way to bring a criminal into the police station, for sure.

But the other orphans had seen the explosion and what caused it. One after the other, they barrel-rolled their planes, too, and one after the other the unstrapped canisters tipped out, still filled with zoom.

BOOM. BOOM. BOOM. BOOM.

The explosions were regular, powerful, and crater-producing. Guards, stunned, huddled by the rocks at the perimeter. Harriers, screeching, flew in agitated circles above the ridge, and through it all was the steady, glorious sound of sixty-seven planes, all humming a powerful E7 chord.

Christina wondered how far the explosions could be heard—all the way to town?

KA-*BOOM*.

The cheering of a hundred voices filled the sky as the guardhouse blew up. But Christina could spare only a single glance for the wonderful sight, because she and Taft had Lenny almost cornered.

Taft zoomed at him from one side, and Lenny turned to run. Then Christina took a turn, going after him from the other side. Between the two of them, Lenny was dashing away in ever-shortening zigzags.

Just as Christina thought they almost had him, Taft missed his cue. He was staring at something over the ridge and forgot to dip down in time. Lenny pounded behind his ruined truck, across the parking lot, and was in sight of the road while Christina was still soaring in the other direction.

Dorset sped after him and began a barrel roll, followed by everyone else. But the orphans weren't exactly trained bombers. The falling canisters did a lot of damage, but the barrel rolls gave enough warning that people could run out of the way, and the damage was mostly to the ground.

Lenny scampered ahead of a falling canister and ducked behind a rock to avoid the flying debris. Christina reached back to her own canister of zoom and unscrewed the lid.

Go, she thought at her plane, *near but not too near—just overhead, if you can*—and the plane did. Stealthily, she approached Lenny from behind the rock. Gently, slowly, she reached out and poured the whole canister of zoom on his head.

He yelped in surprise and then gagged as the zoom slid down his cheeks and into the corners of his mouth. It oozed along the sides of his face, and into his hairy ears, and coated his fleshy jowls.

"Come on!" cried Christina, waving at the planes. "Don't *drop* the zoom—*pour* it! Pour it on Lenny Loompski!"

"But I'm your Happy Orphan Daddy!" cried Lenny. Still the orphans came soaring with cries of joy, canisters in hand. The little planes circled around Lenny Loompski in tight formation, and though he blustered and spun, darting at the edges of the circle, he could not escape their glowing, violet, musical cage, or the sound of their voices, joining together in all nine verses of Taft's song.

Soon it was impossible for him to even attempt to run, for

the zoom began to harden. Once he shook himself, trying to break the crust free at his joints, but drops of flying zoom hit the ground all around him, exploding like long strings of fire-crackers, and after that he just sat down in a miserable lump and let himself calcify.

Christina looped her plane up and over, making figure eights in the sky. She could hardly contain her joy. At long last, Lenny was vanquished! And she and Leo and the orphans had done it—and Taft, too, of course—

Where *was* Taft? Christina rose up, up, scanning the area. There he was, hovering just above the crooked rock teeth that lined the upper ridge, and looking out over the valley. She flew up next to him and shaded her eyes.

What looked to be half the town was driving up to the Starkian Ridge, with Leo Loompski flying ahead of the leading car. Barney was running alongside, and—was that a small woman with a fuzz of light red hair on the back of a police motorcycle?

Patrol cars with flashing lights screeched to a halt at the smoking pile of debris that had been the guardhouse. The police got out and ran after the guards, and behind them other cars parked any which way as more people emerged, milling in clots and talking loudly and pointing.

One of the people was her father. Christina smiled with relief—he didn't have handcuffs on anymore, the police must have realized they'd made a terrible mistake—and then she looked back at the shadowed opening to the mine. Her mother was walking out, leading Danny by the hand. He had a shirt on, one of Leo's, no doubt; it looked a little small.

Christina's plane began to sputter, changing from violet to blue. She had dumped all her spare zoom on Lenny Loompski's head, so she drifted downward and parked on top of the ridge next to Taft, who had been watching the procession from the town. This time, she remembered to set her brakes.

He grinned at her. "That was more fun than should be *allowed.*"

Christina looked back over her shoulder. The orphans were landing their planes one by one and descending upon the food that was strewn over the ground. Her father had just discovered her mother and was running to her, arms outstretched.

Christina let out a sigh of pure, undiluted happiness. She grinned right back at Taft. "They probably *won't* allow it anymore, now they know it's possible."

CHAPTER 39

A QUESTION
OF HOME

THE townspeople had turned out in force and, now that all had been explained, were taking the orphans back to town. It was generally felt that the children needed good hot baths and comfortable beds and a few home-cooked meals before they were brought before a judge, who would decide where they should live after that. And since the town of Dorf was small and almost everyone knew almost everyone else, this was an easy thing to manage without much fuss.

Barney, as it turned out, had run off down the road to town, determined to save the orphans and make his momma proud. But halfway down the mountain, he had met the townspeople already on their way, led by Mrs. Lisowsky.

"I may be old, but I'm not stupid," she said to Christina, as the officers corralled the cowering guards into a police van. "I knew it was you the instant you sang—I have an ear for voices, you know."

"But I was singing off-pitch," said Christina.

Mrs. Lisowsky nodded. "Of course I knew you were doing

it on purpose. And when I heard the rage in Lenny's voice and the terror in the children's voices, I thought I knew why."

"So you played dumb!"

Mrs. Lisowsky winked one bright eye. "No one can play dumb like a little old lady, my dear. A little dithering, a little fluttering, a lot of acting helpless and admiring . . . I actually quite enjoyed myself, fooling Lenny Loompski!"

Christina stood between her mother and father, watching as two familiar-looking workmen hoisted Lenny Loompski into the back of a battered brown pickup.

"Watch it, Gus!" bawled the stocky one in blue overalls. "Grab him behind his knee. That's the way—don't break nothin'—"

"Breaking might improve it some, Jake," muttered Gus through his drooping mustache, staggering under the weight. "This has got to be the ugliest lawn ornament I've ever seen."

Danny, who had been watching with fascination, stepped forward to help steady the very stiff Lenny Loompski. He took on some of the weight, allowing Gus to get a new grip under Lenny's legs.

"Thanks, kid," said Gus. "Here, grab that belt and help tie him down, will you?"

Leo Loompski was helping the men, too—actually, getting in their way more than helping—but Christina was glad to see that some of the mad light had faded from his eyes. He seemed happier, and saner somehow, as if the sunshine and air and freedom had already begun to have an effect.

"I wouldn't be surprised if he recovered completely," said

Christina's mother in a low voice. "He never stopped working, you know."

"*You* didn't lose your mind, though," said Wilfer Adnoid. He gazed at his wife in the manner of one who views a miracle.

"Well, I had the thought of you and Christina to keep me going. And I kept track of birthdays and made guesses about when she lost her baby teeth and how soon she could have learned to ride a bike and what her favorite books might be . . ." She smiled a little sadly. "But I missed the real thing."

"I drew pictures in the scrapbook you made," said Christina. "About my first roller skates and how I fell down and scraped my knee . . . and the time I made snow ice cream and the day I ate a worm—"

"You *what?*"

"I wondered how it would taste," said Christina, grinning at Taft, who was pretending to gag.

"A real spirit of scientific inquiry!" Her father smiled proudly.

"And I drew lots more. I'll show them all to you, and I'll tell you *everything*."

There was a grating sound of rock on metal as the stiffened Lenny Loompski was pushed farther back into the truck. Straps were uncoiled and tethered to eye hooks.

"Careful, now," called the chief of police. "Don't chip him. I want him intact in court tomorrow when I tell the judge how he falsified a warrant allowing officers to search Dr. Adnoid's house."

"Ah dihya ahlieye anying!"

"What?" The police chief looked around. "Who made that noise?"

"Eeeee!"

The sounds emerged from the rear of the truck, from the statue that was Lenny Loompski. Christina looked more closely at the miserable man. He had had the foresight to keep his mouth open as the zoom dried around it, but since he couldn't move his hardened jaw, his words consisted mostly of vowels.

Leo seemed to catch his drift, though. The small man appeared to grow suddenly larger as he threw back his shoulders. "You did, too. You false—you falsified—"

"Owaa?" demanded the statue.

Leo struggled to find the words. He fumbled in his pockets and patted his vest, looking lost.

All at once Christina knew what he was trying to find. She dug out his wrench from her back pocket and passed it to him.

Leo gripped it tightly, looking more confident with a tool in his hands. "You need fixing, Lenny!" he cried, waving the wrench. "You falsified *yourself*!"

The gathered townspeople murmured, surrounding the truck. As Leo's voice cracked on the final word, Beth Adnoid moved to stand beside him.

She looked up at the hardened lump on the truck bed. "He's right, Lenny. We trusted you. But you betrayed us."

"Ahh ihah eeaiy nahaaee—"

"Lenny, Lenny, Lenny." Wilfer Adnoid stepped forward, his mouth set in a stern line. "Save your breath, Lenny. Nobody understands a word you're saying. And even if we did, who'd want to listen to you?" He put an arm around his wife. "Besides, you aren't the head of Loompski Labs anymore— Leo is."

"Uhh eheeuhee uhs ee!" Lenny cried, but the scientists and townspeople had already turned away in disgust.

Danny tightened the belt that held Lenny securely in the flatbed and crawled over next to the talking statue. He looked up at Lenny's face, covered in hardened zoom, and carefully loosened bits around his mouth and jaw.

Christina watched as Danny pulled off a last large flake of dried zoom and dusted off the big man's lips. "You can talk, Lenny," he said slowly. "You can talk to me."

Lenny's eyes were wide and staring, and his lips were purple. "Why did they *do* this? I'm respected! I'm loved! Everybody thinks I'm wonderful!"

Danny shook his big head. "We don't even *like* you, Lenny." He paused, looking troubled. "And you said we were garbage."

Lenny Loompski's eyes grew suspiciously moist. "I was just kidding. I *love* you orphans. I took care of you, I gave you a home, yet you treat me like *this!*" He closed his eyes and squeezed out two tears. They made two shining, slimy lines, like the tracks of snails, down his zoom-encrusted cheeks. "All I ever wanted was for you to love me. And admire me. And praise, I love praise. But noooo . . ."

Danny sat very still for a moment. Then he reached into his waistband and pulled out the small rubber cow. He rubbed his big thumb over its ears and its purple muzzle, almost white from wear. Carefully, tenderly, he placed it in the crook of Lenny's hardened fingers. "Bubby will help," he said.

The zoom had not quite covered Lenny Loompski's whole hand. With a snort of contempt, Lenny flicked the cow from him with all the impatience it was possible to put into two fingertips.

Danny made a small, wordless sound. He hurried to pick up the little cow, and cradled it against his chest. Then he turned with slow dignity to face the man.

"I think you mean something different from me. When you say love."

He scrambled off the truck bed as Jake got in the driver's seat and started the engine. Gus clapped an arm over Danny's shoulder. "You come to us if you need a job, son. We could use a good helper."

Danny, beaming, waved an enthusiastic good-bye and wandered off after Beth Adnoid. Christina watched as the truck began to roll away and took a last look at the petrified lump that was Lenny Loompski.

He had done terrible things to get zoom, and he had finally learned to use it to make fuel, but he had never understood its greatest secret. And now he sat in the back of the truck like a large and disgruntled lawn gnome, completely coated with the very thing that would have helped him get what he wanted most of all—if only he had known how to use it.

Christina could have told him, but she doubted he would even listen. And that was just fine with her.

She went to look for Taft, but found children from the town instead, playing a game with the orphans that Christina recognized as Chase and Tap. A sturdy redheaded boy ran over to Christina and stopped in front of her, breathless and laughing.

"My name's Tommy. Are you one of the orphans?"

Christina felt a smile starting at the corner of her mouth. She had been half an orphan, without her mother. And she had been in danger of losing her father, too. But now—

She looked over her shoulder at her parents, standing hand in hand, and her smile curled up all the way. "No, I'm not an orphan. I'm Christina."

Tommy stood with his hands on his hips and looked out at the chasing children. "Would you believe none of them knew how to play Tag? I had to tell them the rules!"

So *that* was what it was called! "Maybe they never had a chance to learn."

"Yeah. I'm going to teach them every way there is to play it—Freeze Tag, Blob Tag, Kick the Can—except we don't have a can—"

Christina unhooked the tin can from her belt loop and handed it over.

Tommy grinned. "Want to play?"

"In a minute," said Christina, who had just caught sight of Taft standing alone a little ways off. She ran up to him. "Come on, let's play Tag!"

Taft shrugged. "I don't feel like it." He tried to jam his hands in his pockets, but failed. Someone had lent him a shirt that was three sizes too large, and it hung down to his knees. He crossed his arms instead and looked moodily at the grounded planes. "Why don't you activate the zoom, and we can fly for a while? I'm bored."

He didn't look bored, thought Christina. He looked worried, and one shoulder was starting to hunch again. "All right," she said, wondering what was the matter *now*.

But her singing didn't work at all. She couldn't even get the zoom to glow.

"Is the tank dry?" Taft popped off the fuel cap and peered inside. "No, there's plenty here."

Christina gazed at the plane, puzzled. She had sung directly into the speaker-funnel. There was zoom in the tank. And she had been right on pitch.

"Let me try," said Taft. "Sing that note again, will you?"

Christina sang a high G-sharp, and Taft matched it, singing along with her until he had it perfectly. Christina fell silent, but Taft kept right on singing, and suddenly the plane was glowing, rosy and pink in the bright morning sun.

She looked around her in confusion and saw her parents coming toward them. She turned back to Taft. "Why?" she demanded. "Why can't I do it anymore?"

Taft shrugged. "Who knows? Maybe you need to fall from a tree and get scared all over again."

Christina stared at him. He was right.

Every other time she had activated the zoom, she had been afraid—afraid of falling from the tree, afraid of the dark, afraid of a cave-in, afraid of Lenny Loompski. But she wasn't afraid anymore. And without fear in her voice, a high G-sharp was just another note.

But if that was true, then what was *Taft* afraid of? They were safe. Lenny was taken care of. And now they could go back home—

Oh.

Christina looked from her parents to Taft in sudden comprehension.

Taft lifted his chin and looked away. He made a short, hard sound that might have been intended for a laugh.

"Listen, you can live with us," she said in a rush. "We can do computer lessons together . . . I'm *sure* my parents will want you."

"You don't know that," said Taft, with a smile that twisted at one side. "And I'm not leaving Danny again."

"Don't know what?" said Beth Adnoid, coming up behind them and laying a hand on Christina's shoulder. "And Danny's right here."

"Oh, nothing," mumbled Taft. He ducked into the oversized collar and lifted his shoulders, looking like a turtle. "We were just talking about doing lessons." He gave Danny a half smile.

"Ah, yes," said Christina's mother. "I forgot that you would be in school together." She smiled at her daughter. "I can hardly wait to see what you drew in the scrapbook about your first day of school. And I certainly hope your father took pictures! That was one day I really regret missing."

"You haven't missed it," said Christina. "I've never gone to school yet."

Her mother stepped back, startled.

Wilfer Adnoid hung his head. "I wanted to keep her safe, Beth. After you disappeared"—he cleared his throat. "She had an excellent education through her computer, though . . ."

Christina looked up at her father's anxious face. Maybe he

hadn't chosen the best way to keep her safe, but he had tried his hardest, and he loved her. She leaned her cheek against his arm.

"I never went to school either," said Taft, breaking the silence. "Not regular school. They had a few classes at the orphanage, and we could go if we'd done our chores."

"I went to class, too," said Danny. "When they let me, I did. I learned *A* . . . *B* . . . *C*." He gave Beth Adnoid a singularly sweet smile.

"Next, you're going to learn *D*," said Taft firmly.

"*D* is for *Danny*," said Christina, hoping to see his smile again.

Beth Adnoid looked at them all for a long, thoughtful moment. Then she put her free hand on Taft's shoulder in sudden decision. "Wilfer," she said, "this young man is Peter Taft. He's John and Andrea's son, and Danny is his best friend. I think they should live with us. That is," she added quickly, "if you'd like to, boys."

"Say yes, Taff! Say yes!" cried Danny, quickly for once.

Taft looked up at Christina's mother. He seemed unable to speak. He swallowed twice.

Beth Adnoid's hand tightened on his shoulder. "That's settled then, dear. And I really think—don't you agree, Wilfer?—that the children will be much happier at the elementary school in town."

Christina felt something within her expand and expand, as if she were a balloon filling with joy instead of air. She wanted to whoop and pound Taft on the back and hug her mother all at once, but she settled instead for the biggest grin she could fit on her face.

Wilfer Adnoid took off his glasses, patted Danny on the shoulder, and peered at Taft with a kindly smile. "Why, this is a surprise, and a pleasure, too! You remind me so much of your parents! Tell me, my boy"—he polished his glasses and put them on again, looking suddenly alert and interested. "By any chance, do you like math?"

Christina was stricken with a sudden attack of coughing. She turned away, her shoulders shaking.

"Actually, yes," said Taft, glaring at Christina, who was doubled over and red-faced with laughter. "I mean, yes, sir. It's my favorite subject of all."

Dr. Adnoid beamed and pulled a notebook and pen from his pocket. "You're going to enjoy this problem, then. Say you had seven integers, three of which were divisible by two . . ."

GOFISH

LYNNE JONELL

What did you want to be when you grew up?
A writer, an artist, a singer, an actor, a brain surgeon, a pilot, and a superhero. Oh, and a missionary, during my holy periods (admittedly somewhat short).

When did you realize you wanted to be a writer?
I got the first real inklings in third grade. But I was sure one day in sixth grade, when I read the last page of *A Wrinkle in Time*. That's when I knew that what I wanted most of all was to write books like that, for kids just like me.

What's your first childhood memory?
Being tossed in a blanket by my big brother and sister. The heart-stopping swoop and drop—and laughing out loud in the middle of it, delight and terror mixed!

What's your most embarrassing childhood memory?
The day Rick Johnson caught me crawling on my stomach at the local park with a stick. Rick started to

laugh and accused me of playing army. I was too embarrassed to tell him I was a Dakota scout, about to save my tribe from the warring Apaches.

As a young person, who did you look up to most?
My dad. He was my first hero and still is.

What was your worst subject in school?
Math. It took me a long time to get over my habit of counting on my fingers. (Actually, I may not quite be over it yet.)

What was your first job?
Taking out the wastepaper baskets (when I was a kid). First job when I was a teen was working the Christmas rush at a store called LaBelle's. Two weeks of horror, as I recall, trying to look busy dusting useless objects on glass shelves, and a break room full of cigarette smoke.

How did you celebrate publishing your first book?
I can't even remember, can you believe it? I'm brain-dead, I tell you! Brain-dead! But it probably involved wine and song. And a fabulous meal with someone I loved.

But I can tell you how I celebrated when I got an offer for a second and third book together; I bought a little sailboat, and hit the water!

Where do you write your books?
Wherever I can. I start in my office at home, and when that fails, I go to the kitchen or dining room. Pretty soon, I'm out on the patio (if it's warm enough) or at a coffee

shop (if it's cold). I've written in airport terminals and at resorts and on planes and in hotels, on notebooks and computers and paper napkins. Basically, if one place doesn't work, I try another until something clicks.

Where do you find inspiration for your writing?
Also wherever I can!

Which of your characters is most like you?
I am a nice combination of both Emmy and the Rat. Part of me is Emmy, the good girl who tries very hard to do the right thing—and the other half is the Rat, who is the type to slouch in the back row and make sarcastic comments. Oh, and the Rat is also impossibly sensitive, egotistical, and dramatic. It gets a little uncomfortable in my head, sometimes, with the two of them battling it out.

When you finish a book, who reads it first?
My husband, Bill, is my first reader. He's a good one, too!

Are you a morning person or a night owl?
I am a night owl, nighthawk, nightjar, night crawler . . . my eyes don't really focus until about three in the afternoon. And then I sometimes work all night, to the dismay of my dear first reader.

What's your idea of the best meal ever?
Oh, wow. So many delicious thoughts suddenly flood my brain that it's paralyzed. Let's see. It would have to involve a green salad that absolutely sings in the mouth—let's say it has red onions, a little prosciutto,

maybe gorgonzola cheese, a light fruity vinaigrette . . . then a soup, something with clams and lobster maybe? And—oh, a lovely little pasta dish with an absolutely decadent sauce, butter and cream and wine to start, with some tantalizing spice that I can't quite name. And a very good wine, and maybe some thinly sliced marinated beef that is paired with some lovely, big, fat mushrooms and a few roasted potatoes, crispy on the outside and steaming and tender inside . . . mmmm. And then some cheese and fruit. . . . And, of course, something fabulously chocolate, with raspberries and cream and coffee. And—why not? I think a little champagne!

Which do you like better: cats or dogs?
Oh, cats, no question. They're independent, mysterious, and they have dignity. They don't drool, sniff in embarrassing places, or smell like wet dog.

What do you value most in your friends?
Loyalty, kindness, humor, and a noble heart.

Where do you go for peace and quiet?
My house is actually pretty quiet most of the time. But my favorite spot would be up high, among rocks and a few trees, with the scent of pine and a long view.

What makes you laugh out loud?
Almost everything. I am easily amused. I often laugh at what I write, especially when it's about rabbits.

What's your favorite song?
That changes constantly. But I have to say I love old jazz standards, like "God Bless the Child" and "The Nearness of You."

Who is your favorite fictional character?
David, from *North to Freedom* by Anne Holm.

What are you most afraid of?
Failing to do what I was meant to do with my life.

What time of the year do you like best?
Fall, no question. September is the loveliest month of the year, for me. Warm, glowing, golden, and fleeting.

What is your favorite TV show?
I actually don't have a regular show that I watch. But I used to love *Batman* when I was a kid. Biff! Bam!! Pow!!!

If you could travel in time, where would you go?
To the future. I'd like to see how my kids turn out in the end.

What's the best advice you have ever received about writing?
That revision is what separates the women from the girls, the men from the boys, the sheep from the goats. And to not write at all if you don't *have* to . . . but if you do have to, then don't give up until you get it right.

What do you want readers to remember about your books?
The sheer joy and delight of being swept away into another reality and out of their own. . . .

What would you do if you ever stopped writing?
I imagine at that point I really would be brain-dead. I can't really imagine it.

What do you like best about yourself?
That I'm honest.

What is your worst habit?
Checking e-mail a gazillion times a day.

What do you consider to be your greatest accomplishment?
Not quitting when things got tough—whether in writing, marriage, parenting, or any other sphere.

What do you wish you could do better?
I would really love to have a photographic memory. I hate to forget names, and I do it all the time! Plus, it would make memorizing music so much easier.

What would your readers be most surprised to learn about you?
I'm not all that funny in real life. I just think I am.

Emmy is expecting an ordinary, rodent-free visit with her elderly aunts in Schenectady. That rascal Ratty has other plans, as usual.

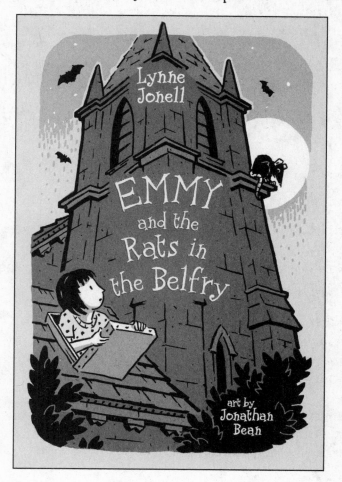

The delightful adventures of Emmy and Ratty continue in

Emmy and the Rats in the Belfry

1

THE PIEBALD RAT laid back her ears, crouched on the third-story windowsill, and looked in the bedroom. The girl on the bed was motionless except for the quiet rise and fall of breath beneath the blanket, and her eyes were closed.

The rat smiled, her sharp teeth showing, and glanced over her shoulder. "She's still sleeping, Cheswick. Get a move on."

A glossy black rodent heaved himself up a last few inches of grapevine and wriggled through the corner tear in the window screen. "Just let me—catch my breath—Jane, dear," he panted, flopping on the blue painted sill.

"Don't be such a weenie, Cheswick. You don't see *me* breathing hard, do you?"

"That's because—I carried you—most of the way," wheezed the black rat. "On my back, my precious—little cupcake."

The piebald rat narrowed her eyes. "Are you

suggesting that I'm *heavy*, Cheswick? Are you saying I need to lose *weight*?"

"No! Not at all!" the black rat cried.

"Then get busy," snapped the piebald rat, grabbing the cord that dangled from the window blind. "You can find me on the bathroom counter when you're done. I do love a nice big mirror."

"As well you should!" gasped Cheswick, but his beloved Jane had already slid down the cord and was halfway across the carpet.

Cheswick sighed. The room, in the early morning light, looked remarkably tidy for a ten-year-old girl's. Books were shelved, the floor was clear of toys, and in the half-open closet he could see clothes hung neatly on their hangers. It was really a pity to mess it up.

Still, if it would make Jane happy . . .

The girl was still sleeping when Cheswick Vole finished his work, but he hardly glanced at the pajama-clad arm outside the blanket or the straight dark hair that fell across one cheek. Through a half-open door he could see blue Italian tile and the straight, smooth side of a Jacuzzi.

The black rat leaped from the floor to the stool lid

to the tank. His hind feet scrabbled on the roll of toilet paper and sent it spinning as he clawed his way up onto the bathroom countertop, narrowly missing an open bottle of mouthwash. He pattered across polished marble to the side of the piebald rat, who stood gazing at the mirror, idly fluffing her patches of brown, tan, and white.

"All done, my little rosebud—"

"Do you think I should dye my fur?" Jane Barmy interrupted. "These patches are all too recognizable."

"But my precious pudding cup, you're beautiful just as you are! I don't want you to change one itsy-bitsy, teeny-weeny—"

"Oh, shut *up*, Cheswick. Don't you *ever* get tired of fawning?"

"Not if it's fawning on you, my little Janie-Wanie . . ." The black rat lifted his upper lip in an uncertain smile and twisted his paws together.

"And enough with the 'Janie-Wanie.'" The piebald rat sniffed twice and curled her tail elegantly around one perfectly manicured paw. "I may not be the beauty queen I once was—"

"You're prettier than ever!" Cheswick said loyally.

"And I may be just a little more furry—"

"Just a trifle! Hardly noticeable!"

"But I am still Miss Jane Barmy, and I'll thank you to remember it. The Barmy name was a proud one, once—and will be again, just as soon as I get my revenge on that nasty little Emmaline Addison!"

The last words were hissed through her long front teeth, and Cheswick Vole shivered in spite of himself, glancing through the doorway to the bed beyond. "Dearest Jane, why do you insist upon revenge? She's only a little girl."

"A little girl who turned me into a *rat!*" snarled Miss Barmy.

"But it wasn't Emmy who did that—it was Raston, that ratty friend of hers, remember? He bit you, and you shrank. He bit you again, and you turned into a rat. It wasn't the little girl at all."

"Close enough." Miss Barmy lifted her lip in a sneer. "And besides, I *hate* rich little girls. I should have been the rich one! Why didn't old William Addison leave it all to *me?*"

"Don't torture yourself, Jane! Forget the past!" Cheswick Vole clasped his paws over his heart. "We could be happy together, you and I. We could raise a family—"

Miss Barmy's whiskers stiffened. "Raise a family? Of what, Cheswick? *Rats?*"

"Well, we're rodents now, after all. It's only logical." The black rat warmed to his subject, a happy smile bunching his furry cheeks until his eyes were squeezed almost shut. "We could find a little place in the country, a nice, sandy, riverbank burrow with a view. We could get married . . ." He blushed beneath his fur. "You could have a litter. Six is a nice number, don't you think? Three boys and three girls?"

He opened his eyes, saw Miss Barmy's face, and took a sudden step backward. "Sugarplum! Don't look like that!" The black rat's nose quivered. "I didn't mean anything—of course, it's completely up to you—"

"A litter? A *litter*? Do you think I plan on remaining a rat forever?"

"Well, you don't seem able to change back into a human," said Cheswick hurriedly. "Not in the usual way, you know. Professor Capybara said it was because you needed to learn to love, but that's ridiculous. You're so dear and loving already, aren't you, my little cuddle-bunny-umpkins—"

"Stop blabbering, you old fool," snarled the piebald rat. "Professor Capybara knows how to turn us into humans again, I'm sure. We just need to make him talk."

"Well, I don't know . . ." Cheswick Vole sneaked

a glance in the mirror. He wasn't so sure he wanted to change back. When he had been a human, he'd possessed a narrow chest, beaky nose, thinning hair, and a reedy voice. But as a rat he was big, dark, and handsome, with a fine set of whiskers and a bold, bright eye. Just looking at his reflection in the mirror—such perky ears!—gave him confidence.

"Being a rat has its advantages," he pointed out. "A rat can forage for food. He can live almost anywhere, for free. And no one expects him to pay taxes."

"Yes, yes," said Miss Barmy, "but he's still a *rat*." She clicked her claws together one by one. "Even if I get my revenge on Emmaline, even if I get her parents' money and this mansion and the boats and everything, what am I going to do with it if I'm still a *rodent*?"

"You could create an indoor waterpark," suggested Cheswick eagerly. "Just the right size for rats! You could wear one of Barbie's bikinis!"

Miss Barmy gave him a withering glare. "Listen, Cheswick. I am not putting on a Barbie-doll bikini, and I am not having any litters, and I am most certainly not marrying you. Not as long as I stay a rat."

Cheswick's eyes widened. "But as a human, Jane? Would you marry me if you were a human again?"

The piebald rat smiled a long, slow smile. Then she edged closer and nuzzled the black rat under his jowls. "Chessie?"

Cheswick closed his eyes with a look of ecstasy and pressed Miss Barmy's paw. "Yes, my little pumpkin?"

"Do you *want* to marry me, my darling?"

"Oh! Oh, Jane! It would be my dream come true!"

"Then you'd better figure out how to turn me into a human again," Miss Barmy said sharply, pushing him away.

Cheswick Vole was panting heavily. "Whatever you say, precious. And is there anything else? Anything at all?"

The piebald smiled, showing all her teeth. "Well, I do have a few more ideas for making Emmy's life perfectly miserable—" She stopped, her ears alert. "What's that noise?"

A soft chittering came from the far windowsill. Cheswick sniffed deeply and froze. "It's rodents from Rodent City! A bunch of them!"

Miss Barmy stared in alarm. "Do something, Chessie! Hide me!"

Cheswick's chest swelled, and his furry shoulders squared with manly determination. He leaped for the bottle of mouthwash and tipped it over, hanging grimly on to the neck as the green liquid, smelling powerfully of mint, poured over Miss Barmy's head.

"*Eeeeheeee—urp!*" choked the piebald rat. "What do you think you're doing, you—you idiot, you *moron*—"

"Must disguise our scent," Cheswick hissed, splashing mouthwash up onto his own fur, "or they'll know we're here. Now hurry! Follow me!"

THINK YOU'RE A SUPER-SLEUTH?
HAVE WE GOT A MYSTERY FOR YOU...

The 100-Year-Old Secret
Tracy Barrett
978-0-312-60212-3
$6.99 US / $8.50 Can

Masterpiece
Elise Broach
978-0-312-60870-5
$7.99 US / $9.99 Can

Shakespeare's Secret
Elise Broach
978-0-312-37132-6
$5.99 US / $6.99 Can

Steinbeck's Ghost
Lewis Buzbee
978-0-312-60211-6
$7.99 US / $9.99 Can

The Ghost of Fossil Glen
Cynthia DeFelice
978-0-312-60213-0
$6.99 US / $8.50 Can

The Diamond of Drury Lane
Julia Golding
978-0-312-56123-9
$7.99 US

The Trolls
Polly Horvath
978-0-312-38419-7
$6.99 US / $7.99 Can

The Young Unicorns
Madeleine L'Engle
978-0-312-37933-9
$7.99 US / $8.99 Can

Danger in the Dark
Tom Lalicki
978-0-312-60214-7
$6.99 US / $8.50 Can

ALSO AVAILABLE
FROM SQUARE FISH BOOKS

Five Stories to Laugh with and Love

Candyfloss · Jacqueline Wilson
Illustrated by Nick Sharratt
ISBN: 978-0-312-38418-0 · $7.99 US

*Move to a fabulous new home half-way
around the world with Mom,
or stay home with dear old Dad?*

★ "A poignant, gently humorous, and
totally satisfying tale. Flossie is
charmingly believable."
—*Booklist*, Starred Review

Everything on a Waffle · Polly Horvath
ISBN: 978-0-312-38004-5 · $6.99 US

*Haven't you ever just known something
deep in your heart without reason?*

★ "[A] tale of a (possibly) orphaned
girl from a small Canadian
fishing village . . . A laugh-out-loud
pleasure from beginning to
triumphant end."
—*Publishers Weekly*, Starred Review

Emmy and the Incredible Shrinking Rat
Lynne Jonell
Illustrated by Jonathan Bean
ISBN: 978-0-312-38460-9
$6.99 US/$7.99 Can

*A lonely girl, a talking rat, and a nanny
whose doing VERY bad things!*

★ "A mystery is cleverly woven into this
fun and, at times, hilarious caper,
and children are likely to find
themselves laughing out loud."
—*School Library Journal*, Starred Review

The Giants and the Joneses · Julia Donaldson
Illustrated by Greg Swearingen
ISBN: 978-0-312-37961-2 · $6.99 US

*The Joneses are about to be kidnapped
by giants!*

"An exciting story with a subtle
message about respect and cooperation."
—*School Library Journal*

Penina Levine Is a Hard-Boiled Egg · Rebecca O'Connell
Illustrated by Majella Lue Sue
ISBN: 978-0-312-55026-4 · $6.99 US/$7.99 Can

*Penina has a bossy best friend, a tattletale sister,
crazy parents, and a big, fat zero at school.*

"Penina is a feisty and thoroughly
enjoyable heroine with whom readers
will easily connect."
—*School Library Journal*

SQUARE FISH
WWW.SQUAREFISHBOOKS.COM
AVAILABLE WHEREVER BOOKS ARE SOLD